I0598555

The Sinclair Seven

WILD COWBOY

GEMMA SNOW

Wild Cowboy
ISBN # 978-1-80250-998-4
©Copyright Gemma Snow 2022
Cover Art by Erin Dameron-Hill ©Copyright November 2022
Interior text design by Claire Siemaszkiewicz
Totally Bound Publishing

WILD COWBOY

Dedication

To all those working to advocate for and protect our planet. We are all in your debt.

Prologue

Istanbul, Turkey

He shouldn't have come. It didn't matter that this assignment in Istanbul would be the first time his byline appeared next to a cover article.

Reece Prescott, *One Leap Magazine* reporter.

It had seemed so important at the time, seemed like the life-changing move that would take him from fluff pieces and filler columns to the big leagues. It had seemed like that up until the minute he found himself in a busy bazaar, and every clink of a silver spoon against a teacup, every harking call of the mosaic sellers, every spliced conversation in a thousand different languages, cut through his calm and stirred a sense of panic deep in his gut.

One year. One year he had been sitting behind a desk, creating articles from images found on the computer, other people's adventures, from quotes and stories and journeys taken by men and women far braver than he was. It didn't matter that he sat on a comfortable, cushioned couch in a corner of the tea shop patio, half-hidden from the undulating movement of the marketplace. He could have been sitting on a rooftop high above the city, and he still would have felt every footfall of every mother and tourist and salesman as if they fell upon his own skin.

He tried to focus on the individual details. A year of therapy, therapy his dear old, departed daddy would have called a *'load of bullcrap'*, had taught him grounding techniques, ways of bringing himself back to the present, back to the moment, away from what his brain was making up and back to what was actually happening.

Two tents down, a family was selling spices, and every time the young girl scooped saffron or smoked paprika from the large piles into smaller paper bags, the warm summer wind would catch the scent and bring it down the road, until he was smelling reds and oranges and sweet, hot flavors, rather than the metallic scent that clung to him when the fear was closer than the rationality. His tea, which had grown cold in his hands despite their warmth and the warmth of the day, was rich and fruity and thick in the air as well, along with the rows and rows of loose leaf on display just through the open door behind him.

At some point, he was going to have to do his job.

There were a thousand reasons why he was where he was right now and the rational part of his brain repeated again and again that he was lucky for the opportunity, lucky that the scars were only scars, that the limited mobility in his left hand would one day ease, and that he hadn't been left with any lasting damage. He knew all of that rationally. And yet...

Somewhere off in the distance, a motorcycle backfired, and none of it, not the hibiscus or the saffron or the chimes or the cushions under his legs, mattered. The market was spinning, kicking into overtime, and the languages—Turkish and Arabic, English, Armenian, French, German—they blended together, a cacophony of sound that roared in his ears, the din making it impossible to hear his own rational voice in his head, making it impossible to feel the ground below his feet or the metal table he grasped with both hands.

Boom. Boom. Boom.

Pop. Pop. Pop.

If he could get one breath in, one good breath, he could focus, he could get the marketplace to stop spinning in circles around him and he could focus.

He tried to reach for the tea on the table, but gave up when his trembling hands spilled cold tea across the table and stained the white napkin beside it. He just needed to count backward. Or count forward.

He needed to get the *fuck* out of here.

Then he saw her.

It was as if the sea of tourists parted just to let him catch a glimpse of her through the movement and the bustle of the marketplace, as if time slowed, not just to its normal pace, but slower still, quieting the voices and the sounds, the clanging of pots and the haggling of customers, quieting it all until the only thing Reece heard was the breeze, as it whipped a few loose black curls that had come free from her head covering.

Her eyes were striking, blue as the lapis lazuli on the traditional Turkish bowls, and her gaze held his across the marketplace. She was the most wildly beautiful woman he had ever seen in his entire life, and when she caught his eye, that gaze piercing and overwhelming in its comfort, and smiled with full, lush pink lips, he felt the cushion below him, tasted the hibiscus on his tongue, heard the distant bustle of cash registers dinging and scales shifting. When she smiled at him, he could breathe again.

Reece was up and out of the chair before he could think, tossing a few bills on the table in a single movement. The sea of people that had parted for him to see her seemed to have filled back up again and he saw her getting further and further away, no matter how he tried to make his way through the crowd to get to her.

She turned around one last time and he savored her smile, the brilliant glow in her eyes, the knowledge of the universe trapped in a color he would never forget. Then she turned away and walked up to a man at one of the stalls, tall, broad-shouldered, clearly American. He put his arm around her and led her from the stall, disappearing them into the crowd and away from Reece forever.

Chapter One

Three years later
Blackleaf Canyon, Montana

Pain sizzled through her hand as acutely as if she had high-fived a skillet on the fire, and Morgan pulled back and shook out her palm. Montana got *hot*. She was a California girl, tried and true, and shame on her, but she'd been expecting something of a nip in the air, not the scorching hundred-degree weather that made the limestone rock face almost too hot to touch.

She glanced up, the sun partially obscured by the brim of her hat under her climbing helmet. It was midday, and her skin was coated in layers of sweat and dust and...

And she wasn't going to give up, damn it. She was on this mission not because she loved the burning ache in her shoulders, not because she could actually sleep out under the stars without the claustrophobic ceiling boxing her in overhead. She was out here for all those reasons and so many more. Because she deserved a life without fear or boundaries holding her back. Out here in the open air, she was good enough just as she was. Morgan Tempest, not afraid of anything.

Yeah, right.

That part, the not jumping at the sound of a glass tumbling off a tray in a busy restaurant, the not clenching her fists until her fingernails dug into the flesh at her palms when she heard a man yell in the park, that was going to have to come. The not being afraid didn't happen overnight, didn't happen in a year. The only thing she could do was to keep climbing, and right now that was to be taken literally.

She swung her arm up and grabbed the next hold with ease. One arm, one foot, hand, leg. All her muscles burned and sweat slid down her back, sticking her tank top to her skin, skin she knew was catching too much sun in the late afternoon.

Easy-access sunscreen.

She added it to her list—the list in her mind, at least, because she hadn't come up with easy-access notebooks just yet.

Practically speaking, this trip was a way to take the company—*her company*—to the next level. She was supposed to be making every note she could about what the modern woman wanted on her next trip around the world. How could she stay safe, engaged, and fully herself, while also tackling the tall, distant mountains?

It was a hell of a question to try to answer, and not just for the business. But if the last six months—hell, the last nine years—had taught Morgan anything, it was that staying at the bottom of the mountain wasn't necessarily safer just because it was easier.

One step. One foot. One hand. One arm.

Out of the corner of her eye, she caught sight of a flash of white, brighter than the limestone, and she realized there was another climber resting on a small ledge maybe fifty feet above her, his feet hanging off the edge like he didn't have a care in the world.

Wouldn't that be something? To be carefree again.

Soon enough, the sun still beating against her skin, her muscles burning, her hands calloused and rough against the even rougher stone, she made it to that small ledge. She found her water bottle first, downing a few large gulps of water, then leaned back against the cool, shaded rock and looked out over the edge.

Fancy that, she could just sit on a mountain's edge and watch the world around her.

So, Morgan did. She watched the clouds, watched the tips of her toes, watched the little ants climbing along the rock like they weren't nearly three hundred feet in the air.

As she was watching the ants, Morgan noticed something tucked away in the shadow of the rock. A small black notebook. She picked it up. The spine was thick and the pages had clearly gotten wet at some point. There were small stickers on the bottom, from different campsites across the country, and the familiar campfire logo she recognized as *One Leap Magazine*. Whatever was in the notebook, it was clearly loved, and she tucked it into her backpack, hoping for the chance to run into the man who had been climbing here before her. Perhaps she would even make a friend on this trip if she did.

I'm seeing things.

It must have been the glare overhead, the bright summer sun bouncing off the limestone and frying his brain. Or maybe he'd been abducted by aliens in his sleep and discarded in the wilds of Montana without his memories. Whatever it was, Reece knew it was *something* because there was no reasonable, logical, or rational explanation for why he was seeing the woman from the marketplace here, three years after his trip to Istanbul, three years and nearly six thousand miles.

He grabbed for a hold and secured his grip on the stone. At least that was real. He could always count on the sensation of stone in his hand, of dirt below his feet, of the wide-open sky high above. No matter how many cities he had lived in, no matter how many trains, planes, and automobiles he had taken over the course of his career, it always came back to him and the great wild wilderness.

All that explained why he was out climbing, this week of all weeks. But it didn't explain why he hadn't just picked up his damned phone and texted Caleb and Dante and Van when he had flown back into Bozeman or why he hadn't dropped them a line in the three days he'd been adventuring around the state. And it sure as shit didn't explain why he was seeing the woman from the marketplace here, of all goddamned places on earth.

It wasn't the first time. In the years since that first trip, she had become something of a talisman. He knew it was probably creepy as hell, but when the sight of something beautiful and safe—the sight of a woman he would never see again—kept his panic attacks at bay, then he didn't ask questions. All he knew was that when his skin got itchy and his neck got hot, as it had done so much more that first year, he could think of the stranger's smile in the market, and he could feel the ground under his feet again.

Even though he had caught sight of her in his dreams as well, weaving in and out of marketplaces in

Morocco and Santiago, showing up in the maze of places he had spent his life exploring, the sight of her had never precipitated a panic attack. She always came after, and she always grounded him before things got worse.

Back to the beginning, what the hell is she doing here?

Reece chanced a look down the mountain's edge. The climb wasn't the hardest he'd ever been on, but it pushed him enough to forget about the date on the calendar and it was sufficiently challenging to keep most other climbers away.

Not her.

It was probably some innocent brunette woman who was just trying to get her climb in for the day and he had gone ahead and projected a boatload of issues onto her. Thinking about her meant not thinking about other things and so he placed his foot in the next hold and picked up speed. Icarus, reaching for the sun.

The sun that was, unfortunately, starting to settle itself on the far end of the mountain range. He probably had another hour of good light and he wanted to get to some of the hiking trails to set up camp before it got dark.

The shadow of a cloud fell over the canyon and for a brief moment, Reece wondered if his dark mood had summoned it into existence. But when he glanced up, he realized that the near-white summer sunshine was suddenly nowhere to be found, and that dark and, admittedly, very ominous looking cloud wasn't the only one in the sky.

Stay focused.

If he knew one thing about survival, it was that it didn't do a guy any favors to be caught thinking about something else when he was six hundred feet in the air on a five-point-eight climb. Above him, a crack of lightning shot across the sky, illuminating the valley below in sharp, jagged shadows that struck like predator's teeth.

And that was his cue to very much get back on the ground. He glanced up, only to get smacked in the face with a sheet of rain, then he glanced back down. Up was only another twenty feet or so. While traveling had taken him to the edges of the world, to cities and villages he couldn't have pointed out on a map in high school, he knew the Montana weather. He'd been a ranch kid, after all, and had been caught in more than one deluge brought on by the land of Big Sky. He knew how to weather this.

More lightning, and with it, the top of the mountain came into his view, just ten feet more, just five. The holds on the rock were already growing nearly too slippery to grip and his expensive climbing shoes didn't have the same traction on the limestone surface as they had just a few minutes earlier. He was going to have to hustle his ass to get to the top without falling down the sheer cliff face and hoping someone caught him in time.

Which only served to remind him that he wasn't the only person on the mountain.

Fuck. *Fuck.* He should have just gone straight to the Sinclair Ranch and left his demons to fend for themselves, but he hadn't. He'd come out adventuring, and now he was going to have to look the woman in the face who bore too striking a resemblance to his one safehold during panic attacks. That was cool and normal and definitely not the stuff that scared women away from weird guys in the mountains.

One more hand hold. One more foot hold. Then he was pulling himself the last few slippery feet, grasping onto the permanent bolts wedged in the rock and sliding along on his belly until he was able to crawl away from the edge and finally come to a standing position. The rain was coming down harder now and the entire sky was cloaked in those rough dark clouds that looked like an encroaching dark sea tide. He reached for the flashlight at his belt and shone the light down the canyon, looking for any sign of the woman who had been climbing below him.

She wasn't there. Either she had decided it would be a safer bet to rappel down the mountain or she hadn't existed at all, and Reece was truly and officially manifesting his fear into reality and definitely not handling things as well as he had thought he was.

A few feet down the rockface, he heard a noise, and he turned the flashlight to see hands popping up over the mountain's edge. He moved as quickly and safely as he could, until he was able to kneel at the mountaintop.

"Do you need help?" he asked, shouting to be heard over the roar of the storm. When he had first caught sight of her, he'd been more than impressed by the skill and speed with which she had been traversing the mountainside, but the rules of the game changed during a Montana storm.

"Just a hand up," she called back. "It's hard to get a grip."

That was an understatement. The entire rockface where he kneeled was beginning to catch water and pour over the edge into the canyon below. He reached out and she gripped his hand, their connection slippery as they maneuvered up to the flat surface at the edge.

"I've got a quick-up tent," he called. "We can both fit." It was nearly impossible to see more than her silhouette in the storm, the rounded head of her helmet and the ridges of her backpack, but he could catch the nod.

"There's a clearing up ahead."

Thankfully, she was right. The short walk was difficult against the rain, but they were soon in a clearing of trees and dirt that would make it possible to secure the tent. The large branches took some of the brunt of the wind, as well, and made it easier to set the tent up, despite the howling sound that reverberated through the canyons like an angry echo.

And through it all, through the grabbing for the tent bag and the frenzied movements as they both grasped the edge and began to secure it down with ropes and bungees between the trees, he couldn't help but lean into the adrenaline. Sure, there'd been a fair amount of running away in his life, but he loved adventure for adventure's sake, and there was nothing more heart-pounding or invigorating than setting up an emergency camp during a breakthrough storm on a mountaintop with a stranger.

He tossed his pack into the tent to keep it from getting wetter then checked the cords securing it again. With two of them inside, it wouldn't blow away, but there was an incline to the ground, and he didn't want to risk anything pulling or tearing or tugging. The half-dozen stakes and the two extra ropes were a necessary precaution.

"It's safe," he called to this strange woman who had somehow entered his path right in the middle of the scene. "You can get inside."

She hesitated, as if only just realizing that she had no idea who he was or whether this was a good idea. Because of course she hesitated. He had more than half a foot on her and, though it was clear she was one hell of an athlete, he was a big guy. He would fucking hesitate too if he was in her shoes — natural disaster be damned.

"I promise I'm not a serial killer," he shouted.

"That's exactly what a serial killer would say," she shouted back. Above them, thunder rolled across the sky, a booming, cracking sound that truly seemed as if it would shatter the world below. That seemed to help her make up her mind. "But if you promise."

She disappeared into the tent, and with one more look to the mountain's edge beyond, Reece followed.

Chapter Two

Oh, Morgan really hoped this wasn't the worst decision of her life. She had set off on a journey to help make travel more accessible and safer for solo female explorers, and she had willingly gotten into a two-person tent the size of her closet with man she had never met in the heart of a storm so loud that no one in the world would hear her call for help.

She wasn't entirely without protection. She had been studying Brazilian Jiu-Jitsu for years and she had cans of bear spray and pepper spray conveniently attached to her belt. But self-defense was about getting away from an attacker and finding safety, and in the midst of this freak summer storm, she didn't have much hope of finding safer ground.

All she could do was hope that the man she was now sharing a tent with was not, in fact, a serial killer.

He entered the tent behind her and zipped it up, shutting out some of the cacophony of noise from the rain and wind outside. Protected as they were in the small clearing of trees, it felt almost cozy—until he started to take off his clothes.

"What the hell do you think you're doing?" There wasn't room in the tent to stand, but she was backed all the way into the corner and doing a mighty fine impersonation of it.

"Changing." He said it like it were the most obvious thing in the world. "Here, hold this up if it'll make you feel any better." He handed her a quick-dry microfiber towel similar to the one she had the bottom of her own bag, and suddenly the thought of being dry and warm was deeply enticing.

And, damn, so was he. She couldn't see much. He had tossed his flashlight into the tent and it cut sporadic light across the space, but it was enough for Morgan to catch a glimpse of tan, muscled skin and strong, powerful arms as he pulled his T-shirt off and tossed it to the side.

"Or don't hold up the towel," he said, not looking at her as he pulled a fresh shirt from his bag and yanked it over his head. "I don't care—I've changed in the wilderness enough to be past modesty."

So had she. Or so she had thought, until he reached for his pants, and she did hold up the towel that time. This was *not* the time to be thinking about what a man kept behind his climbing pants. Not that she could avoid it. The tent was big enough to sit or sleep two, but moving around, especially for a man his size, was challenging, and she heard the shuffling of his pants against the plastic tent bottom, then more shuffling as she assumed he was pulling a fresh pair on behind the screen of the towel.

"Do you have a change of clothes in your bag?" he asked. "I have some extra shirts if you need."

Even over the dull roar of the storm, Morgan couldn't help but hear the distinct, down-home accent that marked him as a Montana native. She'd heard it from several of the locals since arriving, and in the cold and dark of this random summer storm she was grateful for it, like a hot cup of tea on a chilly night. And beyond the accent, his voice was rich, a timbre of masculinity that made her forget exactly how cold it was outside and exactly how warm it was starting to feel in the tent.

When he announced that he was finished, she tossed the towel down and busied herself looking through her pack for a fresh set of clothes.

Damn it.

In her quick ascent, desperate as she had been to get up to the top of the mountain before it became entirely unclimbable, her bag must have opened. While her phone was in a waterproof case and the food was bagged, it seemed some of her clothes had gotten soaked in the sudden downpour.

"Think I can borrow one of those shirts?" she asked, "Mine got wet." She tried to focus on finding the pants she knew were at the bottom of her bag and, blissfully, dry, and not on the low, rich chuckle that came from the other side of the tent. A soft shirt landed in her lap and she muttered her thanks.

"Your turn with the towel."

He held it up obligingly and she went to remove her tank, only to realize that her helmet was still attached to her head. Funny that. She'd been so focused on getting to safety that she had been able to forget something as simple as taking off her climbing gear. She removed it slowly and placed it aside, then pulled off her tank. Her sports bra was damp and she toyed with the idea of leaving it on, until thoughts of how uncomfortable sleep would be finally won out, and she maneuvered her way out of that too. It landed on the tent floor with an audible plopping sound, and she scurried to pull his shirt on over her chilled skin.

Mistake. Big mistake. The long-sleeved cotton shirt smelled of pine and the fresh air and cool, moving water and it smelled like the man she couldn't seem to ignore, and this moment here in the tent felt big and dangerous. That, of course, was nonsense. She was doing nothing more than overreacting to the storm, feeling the side effects of adrenaline and panic. Obviously, that was it. What the hell else could it be?

The shoes and pants were tricky, stuck to her body as they were, but the challenge presented something else for her to think about instead of the man who felt too large for the tent. All too quickly, her dry leggings were on and Morgan had nothing else to busy herself with other than him.

"I'm decent," she said finally. "Guess we should introduce ourselves or something."

"Guess so."

She had heard him fidgeting with a small lantern and when he dropped the towel between them, the tent was aglow in soft yellow light.

"I'm Morgan." She stuck her hand out. "Morgan Tempest, from California."

He reached out to shake her hand. "Reece, Reece..." He looked her in the eye and his words stopped, his eyes growing round and almost panicked. Not that she knew him from Adam, but *panicked* was a little weird on a guy who had scaled a mountainside in a rainstorm and set up camp without losing his cool.

"Is everything all right?" she asked. "You look like you just saw a ghost or something. I don't know much about these mountains, but I don't think they're haunted."

"Not haunted." The confidence she had heard in his voice earlier was gone and he didn't quite meet her eyes. "The mountains...they're not haunted."

She had been going for humor in the face of his obvious reaction, but the way he said it had her sitting up straighter.

"Then what's up? We don't know each other, but maybe I can help."

That seemed to get his attention and he finally focused on her. It was then that she realized his eyes were a striking shade of green as deep as the pine trees in the mountains and full of curiosity. She wondered what the world looked like through those eyes.

Reece swallowed and looked down at his feet before returning his gaze to her.

"I have a very weird question to ask," he said quietly. "Like, I wouldn't blame you if you decided to try your luck with the storm instead, kind of question."

A rock formed in her gut and Morgan tried for a brave face. She had known it was a stupid idea to come into the tent with a stranger. She had done it anyway and now she was going to have to face the consequences.

"Okay," she said slowly. "What's the question?"

He sighed and after a beat, he nodded, as if convincing himself that this was a good idea. She was fairly certain it wasn't, and she didn't even know what *it* was.

"Three years ago," he said quietly. "Late July. Were you in a marketplace in Istanbul?" He closed his eyes. "Were you wearing a white head covering and standing with a man?"

Silence. It was as if the rain outside had stopped and even the storm was listening in on their conversation. For a moment, Morgan was completed dumbfounded, her mind rattling with the implication of the question.

"How could you possibly know that?" Her voice came out softer than she had wanted it to, fear seeping into her bones. What could this mean? That she met a man who had seen her years before?

A man she remembered.

With the sight of his face in the lantern light, a rich blond beard, his long hair wet from the storm, that trip came back in full, stark technicolor. That trip, which had been so much the beginning of the end for them, the way Aaron's hands had held her a little too tightly, the way he'd crafted the perfect schedule for their trip with no input from her, the way he had encouraged her modesty and coverage, even when they weren't visiting Holy places. It had taken her years to put those pieces together and only a few moments to remember them.

To remember Reece.

She had been waiting for Aaron in the market, wandered off from where he had told her to *stay put,* and she had seen the beautiful blond man across the square. She had wondered, in the cacophony of windchimes and tourists, what it would be like to disappear with a man like him. She had thought, in a desperate second, about what might have happened if she had merely walked right up to him and asked him, asked him to take her away, to take her somewhere. Anywhere else.

Of course, she hadn't walked up to him. She had returned to the stall where Aaron had been waiting for her and she had allowed herself one last glimpse at the troubled, beautiful man sitting in the tea shop, at the life she might have if she simply walked away from the one she was living, then she had followed her husband instead.

"I'm sorry. That question probably doesn't make any sense at all. Forget I said anything."

"I remember."

Without giving it any thought, she placed her hand on his. His skin was hot, if still a little slick from the rain, and Morgan couldn't ignore the jolt of electricity she felt at the simple touch. She looked up to meet his gaze in the glow of the lantern light and repeated her words.

"I remember."

How were they sitting so close? The tent was small, but it felt so much smaller than it had a moment before, and they were somehow wrapped in each other's space. All she could breathe in was the scent of him, and all she could see was that intense look in his beautiful eyes.

"I remember you." She had to break off the contact. She had to take a step back and get some *fucking* air. Not really an option at the moment. "You were sitting in a tea shop with a large blue sign. There was a spice seller next door and two small children walking with their mother." Now that she was there, back in that marketplace with the scent of saffron and cloves taking over her senses, Morgan couldn't leave, not until the memory was fully realized.

"You had a cup of tea on the table, but you weren't drinking it. You were watching everything going on in the square." She paused. "You were watching me."

His hand tightened into a fist below her palm, and Morgan knew that she would never have all the pieces to his puzzle, to the moment they had shared in that marketplace thousands of miles away, just as he would never have all the pieces to hers.

"You were the most beautiful woman I had ever seen," he admitted. "I couldn't look away from you."

Her breath caught, and it seemed like they were sharing that breath, like all the air had gone out of the tent and it was just the two of them alone on earth. She could have run away with him that day and her life would have been so different for it.

But she hadn't. And when man planned, fate laughed. Because here he was, the strange man from the market who had been, in that moment, a symbol of escape she hadn't been ready to take yet. And he was back on her path.

"You sure know how to make an impression, Mr. Reece," she said quietly. "A first and a second."

His expression was so intense, she wondered if he was going to lean down, going to succumb to the swirling heat that seemed to be building between them, heat that left her wondering if she would ever be cold again, and Morgan knew that if he tried to kiss her, she wasn't going to stop him.

Thunder pounded the sky outside of the tent and broke the lantern's spell between them, and Morgan moved away from him, as far as she could get in the small space. She busied herself with cleaning up the clothes she had haphazardly discarded and remembered that this was not the only sign from the universe that their paths were destined to cross again.

"I have something that belongs to you," she said quietly. "Amazingly enough."

He ached a dark blond eyebrow and the corner of his mouth tilted up. What would this man look like with a full smile? Probably devastating.

"Oh?"

"Oh." She dug through her bag and found the small notebook he had left on the ridge.

"I was going to try to catch you before you left. Seems like you caught me." *Like a fucking fly in the spider's web.* She handed over the notebook and his expression changed.

"Oh, Christ, thanks. My editor would not have loved me losing this." The talk of their real lives, the lives they lived outside this tent and this moment, seemed to shock him back to himself.

"Let's start again. Reece Prescott. Montana native. Reporter on the road." He stuck his hand out and she shook it, aware of how dangerous the contact between them was.

"Morgan Tempest," she replied. "California girl, owner and founder of Wide Open Skies Adventure."

He grinned. "No shit."

She couldn't help but return the smile. "No shit."

"Well, that's extremely fascinating, considering how much of your gear I have on me right now. How about we crack into some trail mix, and you can tell me about how that started?"

Maneuvering in the tent wasn't easy, but after a few minutes, they had a makeshift laundry line strung up with their wet clothes dripping onto the towels, two sleeping bags laid out and a small pile of camping foods that looked like the most delicious feast Morgan had ever seen. In her haste to reach the top of the mountain then to get away from the storm, then to handle whatever the hell seemed to be happening between her and the gorgeous, charismatic stranger who wasn't all that much of a stranger, she hadn't realized how hungry she was. And now she was very, very aware.

Between the two of them, there were several protein bars, string cheese, trail mix, salami, wraps and chocolate. They settled into a silence that shouldn't have been nearly as comfortable as it was, given that she had just met this man and also hadn't, and given that he was pretty much the most beautiful person she had ever seen in her life.

"While I could go for a cup of coffee and a roaring fire," he said, "I do have a little something that will help to keep us warm tonight."

It was very difficult not to think of the other ways a person kept warm on a cold and rainy night, especially since she was wearing his shirt and he was only a few feet away from her. But instead of any of that, he pulled a small flask from the bottom of his bag and handed it over.

"Tried and true cowboy tradition," he said. She took a small sip and sure enough, there was the strong and spicy taste of good whiskey. Hell, why not? She was going to need all the fortitude she could get for a night like this, so she took a real drink and handed it back to him, feeling that warming sensation as it coursed through her body.

"So, you're a real cowboy then," she asked. "You look more like a surfer-dude to me."

He grinned and the smile reached his eyes, those beautiful, captivating eyes. He took the flask from her outstretched hand and drank deeply before replying.

"Would you believe me if I said I was literally born in a barn?" he asked.

She furrowed her brow. "No way."

"Way." He handed the whiskey back. "It was in the middle of a blizzard. The snow had knocked out all the power in three counties. The roads were snowed out. One of the neighbor's boys, he was about eight years old, he hears my momma screaming into the wind and he doesn't know what to do. All he knows is that it's freezing and it's dark and my momma just won't stop screaming." He shrugged. "Liam had helped birth enough cows and pigs by then that he figured the best option was to bring her to the barn. It was, actually. With all the animals inside, it was a lot warmer than the house. So that's where I was born and that's where I spent the first three days of my life."

Morgan laughed. "I almost believe you."

"Believe or not," he replied. "It's the truth. I'll wrestle a wild steer if that'll prove it to you."

"You will not." She couldn't help the smile. Reece was charming as hell, but everything about him seemed genuine and she almost did believe the whole down-home-farm-boy thing. "Also, all that proves to me is that you were raised on a farm, not that you did the whole 'gold in them hills', Paul Newman, Robert Redford thing."

That made him laugh. "I did that too," he said. "I'm not great at sitting still."

She could believe it. Hell, she understood it all too well, herself. Her company had been born from an inherent wanderlust, a desperation to see worlds unexplored, to live her life while she was making it. Classroom and office life had never worked for her and, she assumed, had never really worked for him either.

"I feel you on that," Morgan replied, though she had to stifle a yawn to do so. Between the full day of climbing and the excitement of the storm, her adrenaline drop had pretty much worn her out.

"I think that might be a sign that it's time to turn in," Reece replied. "It's been a hell of a day."

That it had been, and they still hadn't really addressed the complete and utter weirdness of having once nearly met on the other side of the world.

Morgan zipped into her sleeping bag, grateful for the added barrier between them. He was acting every bit the gentleman and had pushed his own sleeping bag as far over as possible, but even still, they overlapped in the small space and brought Morgan a little too close to the not-such-a-stranger for her liking—not because he wasn't deeply attractive, calling to her in some carnal, visceral way, but because he was. And that *so* wasn't the point of this trip.

"Goodnight, Morgan Tempest," he said, turning off the lantern and plunging the tent into the aching darkness of the Montana storm.

"Goodnight, Reece Prescott," she replied. And though she rolled over as far as she could in the space and silence descended between them in the night, the simple, innocent statement still somehow felt so much like a beginning, instead.

Chapter Three

He noticed the scent first. Fresh and sweet, like peaches off the tree or the cherry blossoms that had lined the streets of DC in early spring. It was the kind of scent that made a person feel very much grateful to be alive and he relaxed into the soft fruity tang and the cushion of calm that surrounded him.

Next came the feel. Because something very much was surrounding him. The sleeping bag's waterproof fabric, cool against his arm, the ground under his ribs, slightly too hard for comfort, the drape of soft, smooth hair that smelled...like citrus.

And there it was.

He sat up quickly and winced in the early morning light that came amplified through the wet canvas of the tent. Even as far away from her as he could be, Reece could still smell her hair. It had dried overnight in loose curls, the kind of hair that Botticelli would have painted onto his Venus—flowing and wild, and every bit as tempting.

Not that he had any right to be tempted. They had weathered the storm together and that was all this was going to be, and if he very much enjoyed the way it had felt to wake up next to someone else, even if he was waking up on the hard ground, then he wasn't going to question it.

But then Morgan Tempest woke. She sat up slowly and rubbed her eyes, then combed a hand through her messy hair, before stretching her arms wide and...

Oh, fuck.

Tempest, indeed.

Because he had somehow forgotten that he'd lent her a shirt the night before and now she was sitting up looking like the cutest goddamned thing he'd ever seen in said shirt, and the very clear outlines of her perky, pointed nipples were showing through the fabric and he was very instantly, very painfully hard.

"Morning."

He could get used to that sleepy, sated voice far, far too easily.

"Morning." Part of him wanted to stand up and run for the hills, but it would be pretty damned obvious what he was dealing with if he did that. Cotton joggers weren't exactly designed to cover up morning wood brought on by hot adventurers.

"I have coffee packs in my bag," she said, stretching to reach her toes at the foot of the sleeping bag. "If we can get some water boiling, we can have a nice breakfast."

He should have said no. He should have thanked her for helping him pass the night and should have asked for his shirt back and should have gone on his merry way. But the idea of her taking off that shirt for any reason other than to throw it on his bedroom floor — or the forest floor, he really wasn't picky — was more than disappointing, and Reece found, against his much better judgment, that he actually wanted to share a cup of coffee with her.

I remember you.

How? In the whole *fucking* universe had she ended up back in his path? Better question, what was he going to do about it?

"I'm going to find a nice patch of trees," he said, trying to inject some humor into this entirely too domestic scene unfolding between them. "Give you some privacy to change and find some wood for a fire."

She nodded, that sleepy expression making her look vulnerable and beautiful and full of passion all at once, and the thought practically had Reece catapulting himself out of the tent to safer lands.

He actually did need to take a leak, and he relieved himself a short way away from the tent before collecting a handful of sticks and branches that looked as though they might be dry enough to light. By the time Morgan emerged from the tent, wearing her climbing clothes from the day before and a thick sweatshirt to keep away the morning chill, he already had some semblance of a fire going. The wood was starting to smoke and his starters had caught, so he considered it a good sign for the day.

"Do you have a mug in your bag?" she asked. "Or any kind of drinking receptacle that isn't filled with whiskey?"

He shot her a grin. "I told you, cowboy life," he replied. "And that also means I can start a mean fire." Thankfully, the fire gods were on his side and the fire didn't immediately go out upon his bragging.

"I am impressed," she said, sitting down on a log beside the fire. "Are those Wide Open Skies fire starters?"

He nodded. "I only use the best."

She didn't say anything to that, but he could tell the praise made her happy. She had fixed her hair in a large, messy braid, and the tip of the one visible ear turned pink at his words. He found himself wondering how the rest of her skin would look when it was pink and flushed, then found that even focusing on starting a fire with wet wood wasn't enough to keep his mind from the thought of how her plush pink lips would look parted in pleasure. Oh, he definitely didn't have a problem with wet wood right now.

"What does the rest of your day look like?" she asked. She had arranged their mugs over his fire and was watching the water for signs of boiling.

"I was going to head to the summit," he replied. "Take the long way up the mountain, maybe spend the night." Everything in him told him not to ask, told him to cut his losses and walk away from her while he had even a shred of rationality left. But she was so damned pretty, sitting there in the dissipating morning fog, and Reece couldn't have stopped himself even if he had to weather a thousand summer storms.

"Want to come with me?"

Do I want to go with him?

The visceral, very single-minded part of her brain was screaming in surround sound that *coming with Reece Prescott* would be about the most pleasurable experience of her goddamned life and she was having a very difficult time thinking around the noise it made in her brain. In the early morning light, with the soft fog spilling over the mountains, she could get a good look at him, and boy, did she ever want to look.

Even without the requisite cowboy's hat, boots and spurs, it was obvious from first glance that he was a salt-of-the-earth-type man. He might have looked the surfer-dude part to some extent, though, with the dark golden hair pulled into a knot, the beard that was slightly too long for an office and just about the perfect length to make Morgan think about how it would feel on the sensitive skin of her thighs.

He was tall. In the storm, she hadn't realized just how tall he was, and his body was clearly that of a fine, skilled athlete—hidden power, a coiled spring—and she was very much interested in what happened when he was let loose.

God damn it. She should thank him for use of his tent in the storm, give him back the shirt she had spent the night cozied up in and head off on the next adventure. Only, she didn't really have her next adventure planned. These three weeks had been marked out for Montana, for going where the wind took her and for saying yes to new opportunities. Saying yes had been so hard for so long and now it seemed like the universe was giving her a test, trying to see what she was going to do when faced with the option of following a gorgeous man to a gorgeous place or running away.

"Sure, that sounds like fun."

It was easier than she had thought it would be to say yes, apparently. At least, it was where Reece Prescott was concerned.

"Great." He had that secret smile on again, the one that made her curious and interested in things she knew she had no right to be interested in. It was only that something about this strange man clearly called to her, and given that the universe had thrown them together again, she wasn't the only one who thought so.

Prompted by thoughts of the universe, she popped back into the tent and pulled her phone out of the plastic bag. Aaron had long mocked her love of astrology, in a way that was anything but light-hearted ribbing. Reading her Twelve Houses App update of the day felt like an act of rebellion and brought with it a sense of joy and freedom. She felt further emboldened when the day's headline read *the stars are in your corner today. Trust your instincts.*

She was reading through a few non-essential emails and a couple of texts from her creative director when she came back out to join Reece by the fire.

"Peanut butter or cranberry?" he asked, holding out two protein bars.

"Dealer's choice," she replied. "Though I suppose I shouldn't say that to a cowboy."

His eyes grew heated at her teasing, and Morgan wondered, again, at the genius behind her following him into the woods, even if her sun and rising sign thought it was a good idea. It was clear that something magnetic pulled them close, and with this racing, pulsing energy between them, it was only a matter of time before her self-control would just straight-up snap.

He handed her the peanut butter bar and grinned. "Know a lot about cowboys then, do you?"

Morgan shrugged. "A surprising number of ranchers buy our products, the fleeces and wools, mostly. But I've been on a call or two."

He shook his head. "You're a pleasant surprise, Ms. Morgan Tempest." He leaned down and carefully pulled the mugs of boiling water from the fire. In doing so he got close enough to add, his voice just above a whisper, rough and hewn like the fresh dirt on a farm ready for planting, full of promise and rich anticipation, "But you have a lot to learn about cowboys."

Her lips parted and Morgan couldn't help but dart her tongue out to moisten them, aware, the whole time, of his dark green gaze watching her movements. She felt a little like a prey animal and she found she rather didn't mind it at all—as long as he was the predator.

"So, tell me then." She busied herself opening coffee packets and dumping them into the hot water, stirring with a fold-up spoon. "Tell me what there is to know about being a cowboy."

He grinned, all promise and gentle teasing. "You'll have to find that out for yourself."

Morgan shook her head and cupped her hands around the coffee mug. "Keep your secrets then. I'll get them out of you soon enough."

It was supposed to be harmless flirting. And harmless flirting should have felt good after a year of focusing on so much real, important, serious stuff. But this didn't feel harmless. This felt like the prologue to a play—and Morgan hadn't read the script. All she knew was that wild horses couldn't drag her away from watching what would happen in the next act.

They cleared away the camp quickly and easily, dried their remaining clothes around the fire as they broke down the tent and prepared for the day's adventures. In comparison to climbing several hundred feet, the hiking path felt like an easy trail, and they set off at a brisk pace, a comfortable silence descending between them like the glow of morning sun. She was doing it. She was saying yes to new adventures, she was trusting her own judgment, and she was going to climb to the top of the mountain—first this one, then the next, then the next, one foot in front of the other until she could see the whole wide world below.

"Why did you agree to come with me?" Reece asked, when they had been walking for a few hours and chatting only to point out sights or animals they saw along the way. The quiet was easy, like the kind she felt when her best friends slept over, and it was perfect for the day. After solo traveling, she had grown to enjoy the quiet of life on the mountain.

"Why did you ask?" she replied. She had seen his expression when the question had been put out, and she'd almost gotten the sense that he hadn't meant to ask it.

He didn't answer for a long moment, and by the time he responded, they had cleared a small ledge and were standing near a copse of trees overlooking the valley below.

"I suppose because I wasn't quite ready to see you walk away yet," he answered honestly, almost too honestly for her liking because that meant unpacking a lot more than she had been expecting. "Your turn."

This time, Morgan was the one who let the silence linger and she watched over the expanse of the canyon.

"I'm trying to get used to saying yes again," she said quietly. "It's been... It's been some time since I've had the choice, and now that I have it, I want to embrace it. If that makes any sense at all."

Reece smiled and it was a little sad, the kind of smile that told her it made a little too much sense to him. And she hated that it did, hated that anyone else in the world knew what she had gone through because they had gone through it too.

"It makes more sense than you know," he replied. Then they were off again, and Morgan was, yet again, left wondering about what made a man like Reece Prescott tick, and why she was so damned interested in getting to know him better.

Chapter Four

They had just paused for a late-afternoon lunch when Reece's phone rang. It was a shrill, technical sound that had no place in the Montana wilds, and it threw him for a loop until the vibration in his pocket was unmistakable.

"This is Prescott."

He didn't recognize the number, but in his line of work, picking up was usually the best bet.

"Reece Prescott, Jonathan Naylor. We met at the Fish and Game Conference in Boulder some years back."

Reece searched for the name in his memory and quickly recalled the gray-haired gentleman he had been seated next to during a keynote lunch. They had bonded over their Montana roots and Reece had given him a card in case he had ever wanted to connect again.

"Mr. Naylor, of course," he replied, though a sense of trepidation had settled in his gut. Whatever the other man was calling about years later, it probably wasn't to catch up. "What can I do for you?"

There was a long pause on the other end of the phone, and finally Mr. Naylor spoke.

"I don't know who else to go to. I think the sheriff's office is involved somehow and...we're out of options."

And that was the shoe dropping.

"All right, start from the beginning." He hadn't been at this job for nearly a decade without having come across sources desperate for help before. "What's going on?"

While Mr. Naylor spoke, Reece rifled through his bag and found the notebook Morgan had rescued from the mountaintop the day before. Thankfully, the pen was still attached.

"There's a new development," Mr. Naylor replied. "They've been here about a year, one of those companies where you can't quite figure out what they do? They've got a compound a few miles out of town and..."

He paused and Reece got the sense than he hadn't been this man's first call, and that things were probably a lot more dire than Naylor was letting on.

"It's the fish, Mr. Prescott," he said quietly. "They're dying off. Down by the river, they're washing up by the dozens and it's still early in the season."

Reece sighed. Tale as old as time. "You think the company is dumping in the water?" he asked. "That carries some heavy penalties in protected lands."

"It's not all protected," Naylor replied. "And I think they have contacts higher up. That's why I called you, and not the sheriff's department."

It was never a great situation when the bad guys were protected by the law. Out in the wild lands of states like Montana, people didn't trust too much government, and the rules and regulations that would have kept companies and organizations in line elsewhere in the country were much harder to enforce.

"What exactly are you asking me to do here, Mr. Naylor?" Reece asked. *One Leap Magazine* shared a significant number of climate-related stories, investigative pieces that had exposed companies and corporations in the past, but they usually had more information than a single worried source and witness claim.

Still, Reece couldn't shake the feeling that if a man like Jonathan Naylor—a real down-home, no-nonsense type, who fished and gamed only enough to make it through the tough winter months—was worried, that wasn't a good sign. Like too much government, journalists weren't always welcome in backcountry.

"There's a story here, Mr. Prescott." Naylor's voice was resolute on the other end of the line, no more fear or concern. It was clear he had made the decision to call a journalist for help and he was going to follow through, whatever it took. "If you can find who's behind the organization, which of the sheriffs they've paid off, maybe you can stop them before it's too late for us."

And damned, if those weren't the magic words to make Reece instantly want to agree. He'd started in this field all those years ago because once upon a time he'd been a lone cowboy out in the plains, and he'd seen exactly what the effects of too much progress could do to natural lands. In the years following, he'd seen only too many oil spills, forest fires, species moved to the endangered lists, hurricanes where there had never been hurricanes and flooding where mangrove trees had been cut down. To find out that people were dumping in his own backyard was to find out he had a new story.

"You're in luck, Mr. Naylor," he said. "I'm in town right now. Well, I'm hiking in Black Leaf, but I can be that way in a few hours. What do I need to know?"

Jonathan Naylor offered up the scant information he had, the name of the organization, a company called the Conlon Group, the local effects on the wildlife, who he was seeing going in and out of the compound. There wasn't a lot to go on, and this was going to be one hell of a project to pull off. If there was any validity to the claim, however, it would also be worth it.

"Where can we find them, Jon?" he asked.

"Thunderbolt Mountain."

Of course. Of *fucking* course, the random reporting job that had just landed in his lap was about to take him pretty much into his own backyard.

So much for an easy trip out in the wild, and all that. Then again, he'd long since learned that there really was no such thing as an easy trip out into the wild.

"I'm going to do all I can to keep the land safe, Mr. Naylor," he said. And he meant it. Damn the men who thought they could keep taking from the earth without consequences. "You did the right thing by calling me."

"I think so, son," the other man said. "I'll keep my phone close."

"And I'll be in touch." Reece signed off and for a moment he simply stared at his phone. It was ironic, really, that he was doing his damnedest to avoid the rest of the Sinclair Seven, a group moniker he and his friends had been given more than a decade ago.

It had been Beau Sinclair and the men—boys at the time—that Reece had worked alongside that summer after graduation who had given him his sense of honor and duty. He sure as hell hadn't gotten it at home. And now that same sense of honor, the need to fight for what was good and what was right, was dragging him back to the one place he'd ever thought to lay his hat, and he was sneaking around pretending he'd never been there before.

"What's upsetting you?"

Morgan had been so quiet during his call with Jonathan Naylor that Reece almost forget she was there, sitting on a small tree stump a few feet away—almost. Whether they were in a crowded bazaar or the middle of the wilderness, it seemed he would always be keenly attuned to her, always aware of her presence, comforted and warmed by it. And he found that the idea of leaving her, of walking away from the day they had shared, from whatever could be between them, made his gut ache. It went beyond wanting her, though, hell on wheels, he wanted her. But it was more than that and for all the reasons he shouldn't, he wanted her.

"Apparently someone's using Thunderbolt Mountain as their own private dumping grounds," he said. There. She didn't need to know that he was avoiding the closest thing he'd ever had to true family. "That was a guy I met a few years back. He says the fish are washing up on the banks by the dozens."

Morgan Tempest was beautiful. Hair so dark it was almost black, a built, athletic frame, plump, rich-looking lips. But right now, it was the burning anger in her blue eyes that stirred something within him. She was a woman who cared about the world as much as he did, and she looked ready to fight for it with her bare hands.

"I'm coming."

It shouldn't have taken him by surprise, but it did. He'd been expecting to have to wage war with himself about whether or not to ask her, about whether he should be taking this *thing* between them any further than it had already gone. God only knew she didn't belong anywhere near his shit storm, especially not this time of the year, but he wanted her there, nonetheless, wanted her by his side.

"I don't know if that's a great idea," he hedged. "It's not exactly going to be safe."

She raised a dark eyebrow at him.

"Did we not both scale the same mountain yesterday?" she asked. "I'm martial arts trained and AMGA Rock Guide certified. And my first-aid training is up to date." She was standing with her arms crossed now, more of that beautiful, enticing fire in her eyes that made Reece want to cross lines he had no right to cross.

"We don't know what we're going up against," he said.

"So you'll need backup," she countered.

She was right. It was smarter to at least have someone know where he was going and if her impressive CV was anything to go by, she'd be a formidable partner in—well, fighting crime. It would be so easy to say yes to her, to offer her his hand and welcome her into the world of investigative reporting.

But part of him also knew the kind of dangers that waited for them. They wouldn't have any support in the mountains and the kind of companies that dumped in forest rivers wouldn't take kindly to the coverage.

"Either you let me come," she said, "or I'll drive out there and start reporting myself."

Well, she was making the decision easy for him.

"Have you ever shot a gun?"

That seemed to throw her for a loop, but she caught up quickly.

"I've been down to the range a few times," she said, narrowing her eyes at him. "Glocks, mostly. Why?"

She looked down at his bag. "You don't have a gun in there, do you?"

"No." He shook his head. "Though I'm surprised you don't have one to protect yourself." And if there was a little snip to his voice, it had everything to do with the call from Jon Naylor and nothing to do with the weird, proprietary need to make sure that this woman was safe at all times, a need he had no right to feel. She knew martial arts, for fuck's safe. She could probably have him on his back in five seconds flat.

She'd have me on my back faster if she just asked nicely.

"Forget I said anything," he said. "We need to get back down the mountain. Where did you park?"

Thankfully, she seemed happy enough to forget his weird change in mood, given that he'd just agreed to let her come along.

"By the east gate," she replied. "Stars are in my corner, hell yes."

He didn't ask. Because at that moment, it kind of felt like the stars were in his corner too.

Chapter Five

They were by the east gate and nearing the lot less than two hours later, and still the adrenaline of this new adventure hadn't worn off. Morgan was practically giddy with it, even in the face of Reece Prescott's much less enthusiastic attitude.

She didn't care. He might have been an old hand at this, reporting and investigating and taking down bad guys, but she was on her inaugural run, and she was *ready*. Because taking down bad guys felt a hell of a lot like taking control of her own life, and even if she hadn't been able to face up to the villain in her own story for too long, maybe this would offer her some closure, some reminder that she was, as her Twelve Houses App had told her that afternoon, in charge of her own destiny.

And if the destiny calling to her included one very attractive, very much not on the table cowboy, well, Morgan wasn't going to look too much into it. The absolute madness that their paths would cross again was something she hadn't reconciled yet, and she sure as hell wasn't about to tell Reece that she had taken one look at him in a crowded marketplace and finally thought about running away — something she hadn't actually been able to do until two years later.

It was just...

Something about him drew her in, and it wasn't only the overwhelming desire to find out exactly how adventurous Reece really was. Though that had something to do with it. She hadn't wanted a man, really *ached* for one, in the kind of way that made her all hot and bothered from just thinking about him, in years.

Damned if she didn't feel that with this stranger from the mountaintop.

But it went beyond wanting him. She *trusted* him, which was honestly completely ridiculous, considering the fact that she barely trusted herself these days. But it was in the little things, the way he kept such a respectful space, listened to what she wanted and offered his opinions without immediately overruling hers. Maybe it was because she'd gotten so used to the way things had been that even the smallest hint of something better had her acting like a damned fool, but Morgan didn't think so.

"Did you rent the car at the airport?" Reece asked, as they came upon the small crossover she had picked up for this trip.

"At a place downtown," she replied. "I spent a night in the hotel and they shuttled us in." She popped the trunk and started unloading her pack, stretching the kinks out of her shoulders when she was done. Damn, it felt good not to be carrying that stuff around. "Do you think I should drop it off, so we can drive out to

Thunderbolt Mountain together?" As soon as she said the words, she regretted them. She was already butting in on his investigation, already demanding that this man she'd only met the day before take her on a dangerous trip, and she was stranding herself with him without a car if things were to take a turn.

"Do you feel comfortable doing that?" he asked her, reinforcing the thought as it went across her brain. "I know it's not always easy to travel as a woman alone."

She raised an eyebrow at that, and Reece laughed, the sound low and rich and too damn enticing for his own good.

"My best friend's little sister, she's a real powerhouse on women's rights issues. About ninety-five pounds soaking wet, but she'll take you. She traveled abroad in college and told us all about the tricks and tips for not getting murdered."

Morgan grimaced. "I'd say you're ahead of most men then," she replied, "for even considering it."

He nodded, his eyes grave, and she got the sense that he really did believe all the things this best buddy's little sister had told him. And Morgan tried to be grateful for the unknown woman, and not surprisingly jealous of any kind of intimacy she might have shared with Reece. Intimacy Morgan herself had no claim on.

"Well, you're welcome to carpool," Reece said, clearly sensing that this conversation had Morgan's mind taking a tilt-a-whirl. "These mountains can be tough to navigate, even for an experienced adventurer. But if you'd rather follow behind, that's fine too."

She'd gotten a glimpse of how difficult the roads could be on her way out here, and she had the sense that driving alone in the mountains offered its own perils. Staying close to him seemed like the safer option.

"Do you mind taking a detour to drop my car off?" she asked, instead.

The drive into town took less than an hour, and while she was dealing with the paperwork of returning the car early, Reece stopped into the diner next door and picked food up for the ride. Real food. Food that didn't come in a pouch she had to rip open.

Then they were on the road and headed out to Thunderbolt Mountain, on a mission of justice and a mission to keep her mind focused on what was coming up ahead, and not on the gorgeous man who really knew his way around a pickup truck sitting beside her. Apparently, he kept his cowboy hat in his truck because he was wearing it now, and the surfer-boy look he'd had when climbing the mountain was gone. He looked like something straight out of a *24-Hours of Christmas Romance* marathon.

"You said you were a real cowboy," she said because when the car was quiet it made it easy for her mind to wander, and when her mind wandered she started thinking about things she shouldn't be thinking about. Like the strength in his hands as he seamlessly guided the truck up the mountain, how one strand of dark-gold hair caught the breeze and had her wanting to let the rest free so she could run her hands through it, so she could pull it and make him gasp.

I wonder what he sounds like when —

"Spent a year herding cattle," he replied, thankfully derailing her wild thoughts before they could progress much further. "Started the summer after I graduated. Worked in a place called the Sinclair Ranch with six other guys."

He sighed and she got the sense there was a lot more to the story.

"They called us the Sinclair Seven, and I'll tell you, we raised all kinds of hell that summer."

She could believe it. The open air in Montana made her feel a little wild too.

"A couple of years ago, Beau Sinclair passed away. He left us that ranch, all seven of us. Said we were going to run it together. Old man was right, of course."

He spoke of the rancher with such fondness that Morgan knew their relationship had been far closer than that of a rancher and his hand.

"I stop in every now then, when I'm home from an assignment. Caleb, he mostly runs the place. Dante and Van are close to home too. A few others of us, we're on the road a lot."

"Is Caleb the buddy you mentioned before?" she asked, trying not to sound overly curious. "The one with the sister?"

Reece grinned and even from the side, she got the impression that he could see past her surface question.

"You're fishing," he said quite pointedly. "But yes, Rhylee, you'd like the hell out of her. Doesn't take shit from anyone. Well, except maybe Van, but that's a story for another day." He glanced off the road for a second to meet Morgan's eyes then returned to the task at hand. "But bravery should be rewarded, so, no, Rhylee's just a friend. Nothing more."

"I don't know what you mean by that," Morgan replied. "I wasn't fishing." Except her cheeks were burning and she had the sudden need to open the window and get some fresh air in the air-conditioned truck.

Reece made an amused, noncommittal noise.

"My turn," he said.

"For what?" Her voice sounded about as nonchalant as a kid with his hand still in the cookie jar.

"To ask a personal question."

That put her on high alert. The last thing she needed was this very hot, very enticing stranger actually trying to get to know her. That way lay much danger. Then again, Morgan had never really been all that afraid of danger.

"I can't guarantee an answer," she said. Her curiosity was mounting, and she was suddenly very interested in what he was about to ask.

"What made you start Wide Open Skies? Like, what's the story there?"

Well, she hadn't exactly been expecting that.

Apparently, it was clear she hadn't been expecting that because Reece let out a low, rich laugh.

"What did you think I was going to say?" he asked. "You'll find I don't much like it when other people pry into my life, Morgan, so I don't tend to do it to them, either." If she hadn't been curious about the sexy stranger she was now on an epic adventure with before, she sure as hell was now.

"I respect that." She was quiet a moment, consumed by the beauty of the mountains rising above them and the weight of her powerful draw to the man beside her.

"I started the company in college," she said quietly. "My parents were both professors and there was this huge pressure to succeed, you know?" She laughed. "All I wanted to do was be outside. We lived like half an hour away from the Redwoods, and from the minute I got my license, I was out in the national parks every weekend. And still, they wanted me to go to school."

She understood now, years and years later and with everything that had passed since then, that her mom and dad had been looking out for her in the best way they knew how. With the success of her business, and the wisdom of age, they'd started to see eye to eye, but in those years, Morgan had been desperate to find like-minded adventure-seekers, people who understood the call of open skies and bright blue seas. It had left her vulnerable.

"I dropped out." Even now, with a successful business and the chance to do what she loved most for her job, the words still felt like failure. "Halfway through. Made my folks furious, but it wasn't their life." A truth she had repeated to herself a thousand times. It was a truth they had eventually come to realize as well, and Morgan had to give them credit for that.

"I never went to college," Reece offered. "Wasn't in the cards for me."

That gave her pause. "Not even for journalism?"

He shook his head but didn't offer up any more information

"We're still on you. Just seemed like a sore subject, so."

It was. Even though he had his eyes on the road and was gracefully gliding the truck through the mountains, he still seemed in-tune enough with her emotions to understand when she needed rallying.

"Not prying," she replied. "But if you wanted to talk about it—"

"We're still on you," Reece repeated, before she could finish getting the words out. "You're one of the most successful business owners in the industry and you can't be more than twenty-five. I want to know the story."

It was interesting, that. She had been interviewed before, by magazines and on business panels, and

Morgan knew there was a small fame that came along with the success of the business, but she'd never really gotten used to that part.

Wide Open Skies had been about chasing the next adventure and helping others chase theirs, not about magazine features or becoming a recognizable face. Still, when Reece asked, she got the sense that he was asking about her, about what had driven her, not about the business itself.

"Twenty-nine," she said. "Thirty in a month, if it's of any interest, Mr. Now-Who's-Fishing."

The corner of his mouth tilted up and she knew she had caught him. He'd been curious about her, about the small details and the big ones, just like she was curious about him. Dangerously so.

"Long story short," she continued, "if that's still possible. I went on a trip one weekend and found these awesome iron-ons at the campgrounds where we were staying. They were like a quarter a piece and I bought them out. I didn't know what I was going to do with them, I just knew I needed to have them."

She could still feel the waxy paper on her fingertips, even now, feel the sting of the hot fabric as she touched it too quickly after the iron. It had been the sensation of jumping off a cliff into fresh, cool water, of reaching the top of a mountain, like she had known she was supposed to be creating the whole time.

"I made a couple of tank tops for friends, then a couple more, then I was buying shirts in bulk and skipping class to make merchandise," she said. "Moved to water bottles and backpacks and when the original iron-ons ran out, I tried my hand at designing my own and printing them out in my dorm room."

Those days, her life had been a flurry of activity, but even with all the late nights and early mornings, even as she had found herself saying no to camping trips or days spent climbing at the gym, she knew that she had been on an adventure of an entirely new kind — one that had taken her all over the world.

"Things kind of spiraled out of control after that. I left school, started up with a business partner, and officially developed the company into what it is today."

The business partner had been Aaron, and looking back now, Morgan could see so fully that he had chosen her, not the other way around. But the excitement of the new company, the fear of being out of her depth, even as she had never been afraid of deep waters before — it had made it all too easy for him to step in and offer his services to her, his services and so much more. It hadn't been all bad. But none of it had been real, either.

"Your turn."

Reece smiled. He had a secret smile that made her all the more curious, made her want to push and tease until he told her what was on his mind and all that she would have to do to get it. She found herself blissfully, amazingly, very interested in finding out what she would have to do to get it.

"Too bad," he said, that smile widening, no doubt at being let off the hook. "We're here."

Here turned out to be the entrance to a campground, a dirt road that Reece navigated easily, that led to a wide-open field where a handful of other cars were parked. From the parking lot, if it could be called that, Morgan could see three or four different paths, each marked in a specific color that would undoubtedly be matched by the available maps in a plastic-covered box standing at the far end.

"We go on foot?" she asked.

He nodded. "It's a good thing you pack light."

Once Wide Open Skies had taken off, she'd focused her efforts and started to purchase and plan more intentionally. That had led to the hiring of brilliant engineers and designers, who helped her to create more efficient backpacks, smaller sleeping rolls, microfiber blankets and snacks that tasted good, kept well, and gave travelers the energy they needed on the road. With the supplies in her backpack, lightly replenished with nuts and granola bars that Reece had picked up in town, she could survive in the woods for two weeks before she even started to worry. That running away was so simple and easy had always been a point of comfort to her, even on the worst days.

"Oh, and you'd strike me as the matching suitcase set type," she replied, coming out of the truck after Reece had put into park and unlocked the back doors.

"That one gets a little sticky," he said, a note of apology in his voice. "There's a trick, let me show you." By the time she had turned to the sound of his voice, Reece was behind her, and every single nerve in Morgan's body was on high alert, tuned in to his presence and the rich, dark scent of him. He smelled like their campfire from the night before, like fresh pine, and like the feeling of whiskey in her chest — warm and spicy, and filled with promises of what was to come.

"Sorry," he murmured, and God, the sound sent shivers through her whole body, shivers she had absolutely no right or desire to be feeling right now. The last thing she needed was to get herself all wrapped up in a new...*thing*. And she had the sense that with Reece, she would get very tangled, indeed. "Didn't mean to startle you."

It was just that, his low breath, so close to her ear, husky and sexy as hell, the way his hand came around the truck door to wiggle something free, accidentally pressing his forearm to her side, his tall, strong frame, only a few inches away from her, it all made Morgan wonder exactly what it was that she had been protesting again.

Chapter Six

"You didn't."

Didn't what? Reece couldn't find his own brain if it was in his hand. All he could think about was her sweet, warm scent, the impossible dangerous draw of this beautiful woman, the importance of keeping a safe distance away from her taut, firm ass because if he got too close, she would definitely know what was on his mind, and it had nothing to do with the Chinook salmon.

"Didn't?" His voice sounded very rough, and there was a good chance she was going to know about what was going through his head even without the physical evidence. He thanked *fuck* for his joggers because if he had on the jeans he usually wore at the ranch, he'd be sporting a zipper-shaped imprint on his dick without a doubt.

"You didn't startle me."

Morgan had turned around to face him, her back still against the closed truck door, and *fuck me,* she had a look in her eyes that made Reece want to beg for mercy. Or, more to the point, make *her* beg for mercy. He wouldn't give it to her. He'd keep her right on the edge of her pleasure for hours, teasing and touching until she thought she would lose her mind, and even beyond that, until she was so overwrought with pleasure that she had to give in against his orders, impossible orders, designed to push until submission, until punishment could be properly meted out.

And sweet fucking punishment it would be too.

He couldn't help himself, couldn't stop the knee-jerk desire to get closer to her if they were caught in a hurricane, and he leaned an arm on the truck, just above her head. If he noticed for a second that she didn't want to be in the cage of his arms, he'd let her out, no question. But she did. It was clear in her bright blue eyes, dancing with need she clearly didn't understand. Maybe she had never done anything like what called to him, but she'd be damned amazing at it, Reece didn't have a doubt.

"Are you sure, pet?" he asked, leaning down ever so slightly as to enter her space, while still giving her room to breathe. To his immense satisfaction, she seemed to be having trouble doing that, and Reece watched her throat work, the sight making his lips part and his own breathing go shallow. "Because you look a little out of sorts."

She looked like she was either going to give in to the obvious desire pulsing through her veins or like she was going to dart into the wilderness never to be seen again, so Reece pulled back. He shouldn't be pushing her at all. Lord above only knew that Montana was complicated enough, even without the new investigative assignments, and the last thing he needed to do was bring a woman into the mix. Even if that woman was pulling on his every last string, most of which appeared to be directly connected to his cock.

Except, not exactly. Because when she'd been telling him her stories in the car, he'd been more than interested. He'd wanted to know every last thing about her, from how she had started her business to the color of her childhood bedroom. And that was far more dangerous than a simple roll in the hay.

Pulling back couldn't have been more difficult if he had been a compass and she magnetic north, but somehow Reece managed it and he stepped away from the truck, from Morgan Tempest and her damned beautiful smile.

"We should get going," he said. "It stays light late out here, but we want to make some distance before we set up camp." More like he wanted to put some distance between the two of them because the second he got any fucking closer to her, he was going to have a damned hard time fighting this incredible pull, fighting the need to tell her what he was, what he did, and what he wanted from her.

To teach a woman like Morgan Tempest...

The thought sure as hell wasn't slowing his libido, so he went around to the other side of the truck and double-checked the pockets of his backpack before pulling it on. The heavy, comfortable weight on his shoulders was a reminder of who he was, a man on the move, a man with a job to do and a man who should be keeping his distance.

Reece resisted the urge to bang his head against the truck door, but just barely. Instead, he gave a perfunctory last call to her, locked the truck up and secured his keys in a hidden compartment at the bottom of his bag. Then he snagged one of the maps from the covered bin.

"We're headed north," he said, coming around to meet her on the other side of the truck, after he couldn't delay any longer. "So we'll want to take the green trail up to the pass, then we'll be on our own." Jon Naylor hadn't been able to give him much more information on the company, and Reece planned to play it by ear. Large industrial compounds dumping toxic waste tended to make a statement in the wilderness, especially since he'd be looking for one.

Still, he pulled his phone out one more time to check for any missed calls from Naylor, uncertain if he would have service in the mountains. Naylor hadn't reached out, but there were a handful of messages that made Reece grimace.

Call me when you're in range. There's something we need to talk about.

Reece.

Reece. Don't be an asshole.

"Is everything okay?" Morgan didn't look like she was about to be terrified off into the woods by his advances anymore. She had apparently smoothed her hair into two dark braids that hung over her shoulders, and her face was bright, likely at the prospect of this new adventure. It wasn't an adventure and he shouldn't have allowed her to come, but after two short days Reece was fairly certain that Morgan Tempest did what she wanted, regardless of permission.

"It's fine." His voice came out little frustrated and a little angry and he schooled his tone. Last thing she needed was his attitude. "Sorry, I mean it's fine. Just a well-meaning friend."

She smiled and it was like the sight of the sun coming out after a storm.

"I know the type," she said. "It's a big reason I'm on this trip solo. Well, I was."

He liked that, probably more than he should, liked that she considered them part of some kind of ragtag team. He wasn't exactly the kind of team member a woman should want for, but that didn't stop him from wanting for her.

Instead of replying, he started down the path and she followed him. They walked in companionable silence for a while, with the occasional interjection from Morgan about a bird or something beautiful they had passed. Reece envied her, in a sense. Montana was his backyard and it seemed as though he had forgotten how to find the beauty in the simple.

Maybe if you called your friends.

At least his pity party was a great way to avoid thinking about how Morgan might feel wrapped around him under the blanket of a night sky. *Nope.* He'd rather take some self-loathing than make the night ahead harder than it was already going to be. *Literally.*

As if he'd thought it, the sun began to cast its harsh, bright light, the strongest rays right before it disappeared beyond the distant horizon.

"We should start to find a place to camp," he said to her, and Morgan nodded. She was an old hand at this, more than capable of finding her way through the wilderness, and he should have been thanking his lucky stars for the education he'd probably get at her side. Instead, he was ogling her very fine ass.

A few minutes later, they came to a clearing that looked as though it had been recently used by other hikers.

"Tent or no tent?" Reece asked.

Morgan grinned. "No tent," she said. "I want to see the stars."

That had him cursing under his breath because he wanted to see the stars too, or at least the way she looked under them. But not having to share the tiny two-person tent also meant that he wasn't going to wake up pressed against her like he had that morning, so he could thank God for small victories.

They unrolled their sleeping bags, a safe distance from one another, and Reece got started on a fire while Morgan dug around in her cooler pack for dinner.

"Chili mac and cheese or spaghetti and meatballs?" She held up two packages and Reece narrowed his eyes at her.

"You had those last night?" he asked.

She made a decision and placed the other pack in her bag. "You didn't enjoy our feast of granola and jerky? Besides, we couldn't boil water in the storm."

It wasn't quite astronaut food, but he still thought of it that way. Still, it would be a welcome break from their diet of cold sandwiches and trail mix, and he had a pot of water boiling in the next few minutes on the open fire.

"If I were from Montana," Morgan said, leaning back on her small tree stump seat to look at the sky above. "I don't think I would ever leave."

Reece raised an eyebrow. "A lot of people would say the same thing about California," he said. "Especially your part of California."

Morgan's eyes crinkled when she smiled. "That's fair. I guess when it's home, it doesn't seem so exciting." She sat up and looked at him. "Have you ever ridden a bull?"

He hadn't been expecting that.

"No, ma'am," he said, affecting the accent more than was strictly necessary. It was her turn to raise an eyebrow. "I've seen too many nasty things happen to men who don't take nature seriously and I never thought to add myself to her list of conquests. But—"

That caught Morgan's attention and she leaned forward to watch him through the fire.

"I did spend time in the plains, real early cowboy stuff, herding steer for a couple local ranches, roping and riding, everything the movies tell you about." He paused. "It's how I became a journalist actually."

No summer had been able to compare to the one he had spent on the Sinclair Ranch, working with the rest of the Sinclair Seven for Beau Sinclair. So the next summer, knowing they were all scattered to the four winds, he'd hopped from farm to farm, and he'd found himself with time out in the plains. At first, he had read old newspapers and farmers' magazines, then he'd come across a call for writers in the back of *American Frontier Magazine*, and he'd figured *why the hell not*.

"You know my story," she said, her eyes wide and glowing with excitement in the light of the fire. "I want to hear yours."

No, she didn't. Even he didn't want to hear his own story, knowing how it had all turned out. A woman like Morgan, she should be safe from his past, from the bullshit that had happened then happened again. He hadn't ever been inclined to ride bulls because he already went up against the elements and forces of nature every day, and because he had seen more than his fair share of senseless violence.

"I wrote a story and I sent it in to a magazine," he said. "They sent me a check and asked me when the next piece would be coming in. So I wrote another one." It had been a secret thrill, something he hadn't shared with anyone in the first few months, but he'd gone out and bought himself a cheap laptop and a pack of notebooks and he'd written about life out west, written about the world he had come from and had never expected to leave.

"It spiraled from there. They asked me to cover a story in Colorado then a story in Wyoming, and that's when I realized I was writing more than I was ranching and that I had to make some choices about which path I was going to take next."

"Sounds to me like you made the right choice."

He smiled at her through the glow of the fire. He couldn't seem to help himself. They had only met in the real sense the day before, but it felt like he knew her, like there was something universal that pulled them together. After all, she had been the woman across the marketplace who had helped him without a word, so there was something to that.

"My friends helped," he said. "Caleb was on the road with his team, and Bastion was touring, but they reminded me why it's important to do the things you love. Up until that point, no one had ever told me it was an option."

That was more than he meant to say, and Reece wondered if he had taken this bonding with this incredible woman under the light of the summer stars too far, but then she replied,

"We're not going to get the gold watch," she said quietly. "The way our parents did it, with their forty years of excellent service, and a retirement plan and a future. We can't rely on that. So it's important to make our own way in the world, and to live our lives while they're happening."

She looked sad for a moment, and Reece had to wonder about the parts he was missing. Of course, there were parts she was missing too, parts he wasn't planning to share, but he found himself deeply curious about the rest of Morgan's story.

"Something changed for you," he said quietly. "Didn't it?" He thought back to the woman in the marketplace. She had been so beautiful that day, striking and peaceful all at one time, but there had been a sadness, a haunted look in her eyes that wasn't there now, hadn't been there in the two days he had gotten to know her, and it made him wonder. More than he had any right to do.

"The man you were with in the marketplace in Istanbul?" he asked quietly. "What happened to him?"

That earned him a long pause and he thought Morgan might just be about to call him out on overstepping his role. But then she spoke, her voice so soft he could barely hear it over the crackling of the fire.

"He wasn't very nice, in the end," she said. "And that's the reason I'm here." She stood up and walked over to her sleeping bag. "I think it's time to turn in. We have to save the world tomorrow, right?"

"Of course." He had already told her he didn't like it when people pried into his life, but here he was, pushing all the buttons Morgan clearly didn't want pushed. They were all on their own journeys, climbing to the top of the next mountain to prove that they weren't afraid of anything, and Reece knew better than anyone that sometimes those journeys needed to be taken alone. He couldn't shake the thought, however, that if Morgan was going to invite someone on her path with her, he'd rather like it if it were him.

* * * *

The sun was just breaking over the mountain's edge when Morgan woke up the following morning. It was the perfect kind of wake-up call. The birds in the pine trees around them were whistling songs, the air was sweet with dew and the sunshine was soft and warm on her skin. Even though it was early, she wasn't the first one up. A quick glance across the fire pit showed that Reece had already rolled his sleeping bag, but though it and his backpack were still there, he was nowhere to be seen.

She ran her fingers through her hair and pulled on her shoes and socks to find him, but she didn't have to go far. She caught sight of him in the clearing at the edge of the mountain and stopped in her tracks.

God above, the man is gorgeous.

He had been all power and classic masculinity while driving his truck and wearing his cowboy hat, but now, as he moved through a Vinyasa yoga flow with obvious skill, he was all coiled control, and the beauty and strength of a natural phenomenon. A natural phenomenon that looked *delightful* without a shirt. His back muscles moved and flowed, seamless as tides on the shore, and Morgan had to clench her fist to keep from reaching out to touch the smooth, golden skin of his back.

Her gaze lingered there, then followed the rigid, defined muscles of his biceps and forearms. To her surprise, he had a subtle, beautiful tattoo of a mountain range wrapping around one arm, but she couldn't keep her eyes from his movements long enough to get a good look.

He continued his flow, moving with ease through his Chaturanga, plank to upward facing dog to downward facing dog. Then he kicked off with a gentle hop to the top of his yoga mat, bowed low and rose, lifting his arms to the sky, before bringing them to heart center.

After a moment, his energy shifted.

"Did you buy your tickets?" he asked, a hint of humor in his voice even before he turned around to face her. "To the show?"

Morgan was blushing red-hot by the time he stepped off the rock and gathered his yoga mat. Only now she did she recognize it as being one from her own collection, a travel mat that folded up to the size of a water bottle and fit easily into a backpack.

"I didn't mean to pry. I just…"

The words died on her lips when he finally turned around, and she got a good look at a half-nude Reece Prescott in all his golden, muscled glory. His soft blond hair curled around his shoulders, and a matching trail led from his navel down to the waist of his shorts, shorts, that hung dangerously low on his hips. His body was a work of art. Defined muscle, tan from time spent in the sun, and strong, she knew, from climbing and hiking and running and swimming.

"You just…" Reece prompted.

"You're beautiful."

The words were out of her mouth like a shot, and Morgan actually clamped a hand over her lips like a character in a cartoon, as if that could stop him from hearing them.

"When you practice, I mean, you're beautiful when you practice." No, that really wasn't much better, and she didn't want to see the amused expression in his eyes a moment long, so she turned on her heel and headed back the short distance to their campsite.

"Coffee?" When had her voice gotten so high-pitched?

"Are you going to avoid eye contact all day?" Reece asked from behind her. "Because in that case, I'll need two cups."

"I'm not avoiding eye contact, look." When she turned around to show him that she wasn't embarrassed by this, he was so much closer than she had expected him to be, inches away, the slickness of his skin from his workout within reach, and *God*, did she want to touch.

"My eyes are here, princess," he said quietly, his voice raw and full of promise. "You can't just look at me like I'm a piece of meat." This was said with humor and amusement and the kind of confidence she had always longed for. Morgan growled.

"What is with you and these damn terms of endearment, anyway?" Not that she minded them. In fact, she knew she was supposed to hate them, knew they were supposed to bother her, but when he had boxed her in against the truck and called her *pet*, it had set off an entirely different system of passion. And now, *princess*, like he was about to swear his sword and fealty to her and worship at her throne. Oh boy, she could get used to that.

"Side effect of the lifestyle, I guess."

He said it so nonchalantly that at first she thought he meant the adventure lifestyle that they shared. But that didn't make sense. She'd been traveling and exploring for years, and she'd never felt the inclination to call someone *princess*, unless they were acting like an entitled asshole. But if he didn't mean adventure and he certainly couldn't be referring to journalism or ranching, then...

"What lifestyle would that be?" A dangerous question, to be sure of it. A question Morgan was fairly certain she already knew the answer to even before Reece's gaze shifted into something promising and demanding all wrapped in one.

Before he could answer though, giving voice to the dangerous truth behind those gorgeous burning green eyes, the sound of a phone ringing cut though the morning quiet. Reece walked over to his bag, giving her space to breathe without his masculine scent overwhelming her, but he only glanced at the caller ID and sent the call to voicemail.

"We should get going," he said, the teasing tone gone from his voice. "We don't know what we're going to find today."

He was right about that, but Morgan also had the sense that she was going to find a whole lot more than she bargained for if she let herself get too close to this enigmatic, gorgeous man whose downward facing dog had her thinking things that had nothing to do with yoga.

Apparently, it took only two days to develop a morning routine, because Morgan took a fresh set of clothes and changed behind the cover of a few trees and by the time she emerged Reece had two cups of coffee and two cups of oatmeal ready and waiting. The air between them was tense, and she hated that. She had forced her way into his adventure—though he probably wouldn't call it such—and she wasn't going to make things hard for him.

You just want that feeling again.

The feeling of comfort. The feeling of not having to parade around like some version of herself that she wasn't, that she never had been. Yeah, she wanted that feeling.

"How far away from here did you grow up?" she asked, finding herself desperate to break the tense silence between them.

Reece looked at her over his cup of coffee and even the simplest glance had her body aching for more.

"Side effect of the lifestyle."

He didn't so much look like the kind of man who would walk on the wild side when it came to intimacy, but now that she had insight into his hidden side, she could practically feel it—the control, the power and energy so firmly held in his grasp. Her idea of what men like Reece did had been gleaned from word of mouth and the occasional late-night laptop session, but just being around him gave her more insight into why women were attracted to it than any videos or books ever could.

"You can see home from here," he said, indicating with his coffee cup to the distant mountain ranges. "It's about a forty-minute drive."

"Will you stop in to visit when we're done?" she asked, and it was if she had told him she didn't believe in evolution. His entire demeanor shifted, his spine going straight and his muscles tensing, and Morgan held up her hands in surrender.

"It's not my business," she said quickly. "If you don't want to talk about it, we don't have to talk about it." But she did have a pretty good idea that whoever had been on the other end of that phone call had been someone he hadn't been ready to talk to. And though it really shouldn't, it made her far more curious about this man, and his many myriad secrets.

"It's not you," he said quietly, cleaning up from breakfast and, unfortunately, pulling a T-shirt on over his chest. She missed the sight the second it was gone. "It's not always easy for me to come home. Not all the memories are good ones."

She understood that feeling better than anyone, could see it in the darkened staircases and hallways she could maneuver by sight, ones she hadn't walked in nearly a year. Back home, there was an entire world she had packed away in a corner of her mind that she never planned to unlock again.

"We should go," Morgan said quietly instead of any of that. The last thing she needed was to share more intimacy with this man, to give over more of herself to someone she would also never see again in a few days' time. "Don't want to lose the day."

* * * *

The first hour of their journey passed without a word, and Morgan regretted the tension between them, even as she knew it was all to do with the myriad memories and thoughts that Reece was clearly managing, albeit with some difficulty. The silence and the open air gave her too much time to concentrate on her own memories and thoughts, about where she had been a year earlier, about the journey she had shared with him, from starting a business in her dorm to nearly running away to a stranger in a marketplace out of naïve, misplaced hope.

Her tangled thoughts had only grown more so, and Morgan was grateful for the distraction of rougher terrain that meant she had to focus on every step in order to avoid rolling her ankle and making the walk home very difficult. Eventually, they came to the part of the trail where they would be going off on their own and Reece pocketed the map he had been glancing at.

He paused and took a deep breath before speaking for the first time in nearly three hours.

"It's not too late to turn back," he said. "If you head back to the campsite now, you won't be liable for anything that goes on from here. The trail will lead you to the parking lot and I can call a friend." She had the sense that calling a friend was actually a lot harder for him than he was letting on, but that majorly wasn't the point.

"I'm already in this with you," she said quietly. "I've come this far." And so very much further in the year since Aaron, but that was entirely thanks to her own strength and the incredible support of her friends.

Reece grimaced. "I know. I just don't want to get you hurt or land you in jail for something you didn't need to do."

She understood it, of course she did. But journalists didn't need any kind of permit or certification. He was at just as much risk as she was walking into this story he knew so little about.

"You'd be no safer than me," she pointed out. "And you know it's better to have a partner in the wild." He couldn't deny that she knew what she was doing. They had more than kept pace with each other when climbing, camping and hiking.

"You're right," he said. "I just wanted to give you the chance."

"Chance is duly noted and appreciated," Morgan said, trying to inject some humor into her voice. "Lead the way, Mr. Prescott."

He did, taking them left off the trail they had been following and into the thicket of woods and large rocks that were likely the remnants of glacial movements millions of years earlier. The going here was even rougher than it had been on the trail, and she was thankful when Reece finally pulled them to a stop about an hour later, at the far side of a large mountain. He held up a hand and Morgan zipped her lips, before stepping closer to him. One step, two steps.

She peered over the edge and she saw it, several large trucks docked at a garage. Around the trucks, workers in white lab coats moved in an organized, seamless fashion, loading and unloading, one cargo bay at a time.

"What are they doing?" Morgan hissed under her breath. There was no doubt something sinister about the men's movements, like they had been trained and were following orders of some kind.

"Bringing in supplies," Reece replied in a low tone. He handed her a pair of binoculars and she brought them to her eyes, only to see that the boxes held an unfamiliar logo and nothing to indicate what was inside. She tilted the lenses farther away. This was just one building in a much larger compound, several of which were visible with the binoculars. From the buildings in the background, she could see plumes of smoke coughing into the air above, and her gut clenched in anger.

"We're going to need to get down there," Reece said quietly. "But not right now. There are too many people about." He pulled out his phone and snapped a picture of the boxes and the trucks, then appeared to send it to someone. "I'm going to see if anyone in my office knows anything about these guys before we get any closer. I don't want to find out we're up against a big weapons distributor or something."

He was right to be cautious. Even though she had never done anything like this in her life, Morgan's survival instincts were on high alert and her hands were clammy with sweat. She had done a lot of adventurous things in her life, but breaking into a secret mountain compound to help write an exposé on corporate pollution wasn't one of them.

As they walked, the sense of unease worsened, and her stomach churned. There were men located at the facility's edge who appeared to be armed guards, and two of them were holding very angry-looking dogs on tight leashes. The front gate where the trucks exited after dropping off their cargo was actually a series of three gates, and the trucks stopped between each one and waited before it opened again.

One by one, the trucks exited the compound and turned down a hidden road. The commotion near the back gates began to subside and they took the chance of the guards walking back to their posts to move as quietly as possible down the hill, still protected by the raised ledge of the mountainside.

"We need to get over there," Reece whispered. He had bent close to her to speak without being noticed, but despite the seriousness of the situation, Morgan couldn't help but pay close attention to his heat, to the way his warm breath felt against her skin, to the sense of sharing a secret with him. "But I don't know if we'll be able to do it from this direction."

She looked where he was indicating and had to agree. The entrance to the driveway seemed to be more heavily guarded than the other buildings in the compound, and if they were able to approach from the south side, they'd have a better line of sight into whatever was being produced in the factories.

"We'll have to go around," she replied on a whisper. "We can double back and head west at the ridge, which should give us better access."

Silently, she followed Reece down the path they had taken, through a copse of trees, until they were finally well and truly out of the line of fire — probably quite literally — of the compound.

"Is it what you signed up for?" Reece asked. There was a smile tugging at the corner of his beautiful lips, and his eyes were alight with excitement. This was his adventure. No matter how far he hiked or how high he climbed, he was always going to be chasing the next great story. Morgan understood the drive.

"It's terrifying," she admitted. "But it's kind of exhilarating too. I mean, you're going to save the environment and bring bad guys to justice."

Reece's grin widened. "*We're* going to bring bad guys to justice. Look, it's starting to rain. We should make some headway and find shelter before it gets too bad."

"I saw a shelter about two miles back," she replied. "Looked unused, maybe we could bunk there for the night." Considering it would be nothing short of walking into the fire if they had to share a tent again. Morgan was now well aware of the kind of storms

Montana offered in the summer, and the last thing she wanted was to spend the night braving the elements.

Around them, the blue sky shifted to a murky gray, and the air hung heavy with dampness, a blanket of drizzle that could easily turn into a fully blown storm at any time. Her skin prickled with the chill, and she thought about a large cup of tea, a good book and a soft couch. Maybe one day those creature comforts would be enough for her, but for now Morgan enjoyed the thrill of trying to beat the storm, even if meant things were a little more dangerous than they would be if she just stayed home.

Thankfully, the old building came into view before the rains started in earnest. It looked like it had once been a forest ranger office, but now sat closed off, two of the windows boarded up where she had to assume the glass had broken.

"Are you up on your tetanus shots?" Reece asked, giving the space a skeptical look before moving for the door.

"It's rabies I'm more worried about," Morgan admitted. "But it doesn't look too bad." Indeed, as they walked up to the front of the building, she caught sight of a sign on the door.

Weary travelers,
If you find yourself high in the mountains and need a place to stay, we welcome you to use our lodge. There is electricity and running water, and the pantry is stocked, though we ask you to leave a donation so we can keep it that way for the next hikers. Please make sure you take all trash and close and lock the door to ensure the wildlife stays in the wild. Have a wonderful trip.
- Your Rangers

"That's incredibly sweet," Morgan said with a smile. Suddenly the idea of a hot meal didn't seem so far off. And a hot shower, as well.

Reece nodded and turned the key that was attached to the chain around the front door. It opened into a one-room space. The air was musty and scented with old pine and something slightly damp, but it was dry in the cabin, and they stepped inside as the drizzle began to turn into something similar to her first night on the mountain top. Just when they had closed the door, the sky around them turned from lavender to slate gray and the clouds that had been threatening for the last two miles gave way to a deluge of rain.

"Lucky find," Reece said with a smile, as he pulled over his bag and dropped it on the couch by the wall. "And there's heat, which is nice."

It *was* nice, even if Morgan hadn't been able to stop her brain from going to the worst possible direction of *huddling together to keep warm*. Even in the large, open room, Reece took up space and make it difficult for her to concentrate. She couldn't deny it to herself. She wanted him, she wanted him like she hadn't wanted a man in a long, long time, and that was dangerous.

"I can't wait for that shower," she said, aware of the slickness of her shirt against her skin, from rain or the cold sweat that had broken out on their quick jaunt back, she couldn't be sure. What she could be sure of, however, was the raw, hot expression in Reece's eyes at the word, and she wondered if she should push it, if she should *push him*.

Part of her, the logical, rational part of her that kept the books and had started a business from the ground up, knew that engaging with a hot stranger on a mountain top wasn't a great plan. But the other part, the one that had been stuck wondering if she was making the right choices for long, dark years, the one that hadn't been able to trust men in just as long, it had her wondering what the hell could be so bad about giving in to her new-found desires.

In a short time, he had already shown her a deep-seated and clear respect for her boundaries and an understanding of the imbalance in power between strange men and women. She had little doubt that he would give her the same courtesies if things were to progress further.

And she found she very much wanted them to progress further.

"Great." He coughed and looked a little like he was trying to think of something, anything else to say, and Morgan almost laughed. He was almost always in control, almost always powerful and coiled tight, but apparently the thought of her in the shower was interesting enough to catch him off-guard. She liked that. She liked that very much, in fact. "I'll be here."

He looked longingly at the fireplace then at the lamp on a couch side table. "We probably shouldn't draw any attention to ourselves. I'm thinking no lights tonight." Right, of course, there was nothing sexier than the dim intimacy of a cabin.

"Then I better get going while I can still see all the important bits," she said, unable to keep the laugh from her voice. She snagged what she needed from her pack and headed into the bathroom, where a simple, utilitarian shower awaited her. There was a small lip and a drain into the side of the bathroom floor and a basic showerhead, but when turned it on, the pressure was good and the water was warm enough. And for a moment, she was able to focus on getting the dirt and grime from three days in the wilderness off her skin, and not the knowledge that Reece Prescott was right on the other side of the door, and how much she wanted him on her skin instead.

Chapter Seven

Morgan was naked. Morgan was naked and wet and slick with soap on the other side of the bathroom door and Reece was losing his damned mind. He had other things he needed to be focusing on, like the emails that the office had sent back with information on the seal from the compound, and the several missed calls he now had from both Caleb and Van, but all he could think about was her.

It seemed like all he would ever be able to think about was her. She was smart, intuitive, and not afraid of anything, and she had the uncanny ability to make Reece want to face down the demons he'd been running from for years. At this moment, all he wanted to do was open the door to the bathroom and catch a glimpse of her slick, wet body. Well, that wasn't *all* he wanted to do.

He heard the water shut off and his traitorous cock surged to attention at the quiet that followed. He knew he hadn't been imagining the desire in her eyes, not that morning when she'd found him during his practice on the mountainside, nor when he whispered the word *lifestyle* and left her to fill in the blanks that followed. She had, he was sure of it.

While it was smart for them to avoid turning on too many lights or starting a fire, as they didn't want to draw too much attention to themselves, it left Reece with little to do with his hands. He finally decided to inspect the pantry cabinets, and found a surprising amount of dinner options, most of which could be warmed either on the stovetop or in the antique-looking microwave above the sink.

He pulled out a box of spaghetti and a jar of marinara sauce before searching around the kitchen for a pot to boil water. This was good. He could focus on starting dinner and not the fact that she was ten feet away from him, probably smelling fresh and clean and flush with the heat from the shower. His cock throbbed.

"You're already starting dinner. You didn't have to do that." Oh, he *really* did.

"Figured you'd be hungry, and we can enjoy a hot meal. Assuming I can find a pot." He opened another cabinet on his search and his desperate attempt to avoid looking at her, and though he didn't find a pot, he did find a bottle of red wine.

"And we can toast too." She walked over and God, she did smell good, that citrus scent he'd caught on her hair, hot steam, soft, lush femininity.

"I'd say we deserve it."

He did turn then, only to ensure he didn't drop the bottle of wine, and that almost made him do it. She wore a comfy-looking pair of joggers, soft at the knees, low on her hips. But it was the tank top that made his clench the bottle more tightly in his hand. The thin straps meant he could catch sight of a lacy bra underneath, a lacy bra he found himself wanting to see so much more of. Her wet hair was piled in a loose bun on top of her hair, and dark tendrils curled around her face.

"Reece." It was his turn not to hear her and he finally snapped out of it to hand her the bottle. "Did you try that shelf?" She reached around him, pressing those small, lush breasts into his back, and opened one of the cabinets he hadn't searched yet, finding all manner of cookware inside.

"Good call." Was that his voice? It came out sounding gruff and raw and very much like a man at the edge of his control.

"I've got this," she said with a perky smile. *Perky. Of course.* "You'll want to take a shower before it gets too dark."

He took the opening she gave him and hightailed it into the bathroom. Even the coldest setting on the shower wasn't enough to turn down the heat coursing through his body. There was something about this woman that made his wish he was back at The Ranch, even though he had spent his entire time here in Montana avoiding calls from his friends. But she called to him, to those basic instincts that made him want to protect and care for her, to the sense of longing and desperation for another that had led him all around the world, to secret clubs and secret nights.

Morgan had never done anything like it, he was sure of that, but he was equally sure that she wanted him, and that she would be willing to give over to the power play between them if he so much as asked.

By the time he came out of the shower, she had finished the pasta and was plating two bowls around the coffee table in the center of the living room.

"I couldn't find any glasses for the wine," she said apologetically. "Hope you don't mind girl cooties."

"Smells good," he said, rather than exploring that particular, dangerous train of thought. "I could get used to this." She raised an eyebrow and he realized how the statement had sounded.

"Fresh hot food, I mean. Food that doesn't come in an envelope."

"Agreed." She joined him at the small table with the wine and settled down on a cushion on the floor. "Cheers to eating in the dark. Again."

He laughed and dug into the food, grateful for the distraction, for something to do with his hands that wasn't pinning her to the floor and making her scream his name.

"I will say," Morgan began, "this is one of the most unconventional friendships I've ever made on a trip."

Usually, he didn't want to strip his friends down to their flush, bare skin and have his wicked way with them, so Reece had to agree.

"I like that," he said. "Feels important." Which was admitting too much, but there was nothing like the dark and intimacy of a cabin in a storm to share secrets.

"I think it might be," she said, her voice a little wistful. "I think all of this might be very important. And I'll be honest, Reece. That terrifies me."

"What's on your mind, princess?" he asked her, the word rolling off his tongue so naturally she wasn't entirely sure that he even knew he had said it. If the term of endearment made heat race up her spine and a part of Morgan's deeper self awaken, well, she wasn't going to think too much on it.

"I like when you call me that," she said quietly. She wasn't entirely sure what she had been planning to say, but it probably wouldn't have been that. Reece moved so he was closer to her, and his nearness was a comfort and a temptation all at once. He was a big man, with wide climber's shoulders and strong, toned arms. Even his hair, piled in a messy bun on top of his head as it was now, gave him the look of being larger than life, like a powerful golden beacon directly from the sun.

"I don't know the world you come from," he said quietly, and even in a soft tone, even in a reverent state of being nearly on his knees, he still held a quiet, overwhelming command she'd seen few men master — maybe none. "But in my world, respect is foundational. I don't call you princess because I don't think you can do it, rescue yourself or whatever *it* may be. I call you princess because some of the most powerful women in history have been princesses and I think you're deserving of the same respect as them."

She thought she wanted to get that embroidered on a tapestry and hung in her castle, and she reached out almost on instinct for his hand. Reece Prescott really wasn't like anyone she had ever known before and the kind of topsy-turvy that he sent her into was as heady as any mountain-climb she had ever taken.

"I like being your princess," she replied, and it didn't feel completely insane, this giving over to him, this acknowledging all that he made her feel. Their paths had converged temporarily, and she was going to enjoy the meeting for as long as she possibly could. "It's refreshing."

He stood and took her outstretched hand, walking backward to the couch until he was seated and able to pull her onto his lap. His lap was quickly becoming one of her favorite places.

"You don't have to tell me your story, Morgan," he said. "But if you want to, I want to listen."

She didn't really consider it a story. Stories had characters, they had redemption and happily-ever-afters that wrapped things up in a neat little bow, never to be touched again. Never to be felt again. She wasn't a character. Aaron wasn't a character. They were real people, and sometimes there were no redemptive story arcs. Sometimes, just because things were over, that didn't mean things were happy. Sometimes happy was an everyday goal, a big, enormous overwhelming thing made possible by happy moments, more and more happy moments that would one day, if she had done the math correctly and lost track of time for long enough, blend together to create a happy life.

"Story makes it feel like it didn't happen," she said, more into his warm, cozy flannel shirt than to Reece himself. "Story makes it feel like it didn't really happen to *me*." Part of that was because it was a universal story. Emily and Alishia had gone with her to a few meetings, and she'd been in touch with a wonderful therapist for nearly a year and she knew how common her experiences really were. But they were still *her* experiences.

"You're right." He brushed a strand of hair from her face, and Morgan realized that she had to tell him. Her compulsion to give him her experiences, to lighten her load was suddenly front and center in her mind, and she could almost feel the relief of voicing those years aloud to someone who hadn't been there, who hadn't seen the woman she had become.

"He never hit me," she began. "When there's no bruise to see, it makes it really easy to feel like nothing is wrong. Like it's all in your head or something. People like Aaron, they depend on that. Gaslighting, you know?"

She felt more than saw his nod, and even just knowing that Reece was real was enough to fortify her to continue. Finding the real things beneath her fingertips had been so hard for so long. "The whole thing with that kind of manipulation is that you start to doubt every choice you've ever made," she continued. "I questioned who my friends were, my business decisions, what kind of food I wanted to eat for dinner. He didn't change overnight or anything, but through the years he essentially turned me into someone who couldn't made a choice without his opinion. The only choice I made in our last year of marriage was to leave. And I had help."

She had friends that had been willing to go into battle for her, and for them, Morgan would eternally place her safety, her happiness. If it hadn't been for Emily and Alishia and her mom, she would probably still be in that same place she had been a year ago, and the truth of that still haunted her.

"Ultimately, it turned out that Aaron wanted to make me so dependent on him that I gave over my owner's stock in the company so he could become the president. By that point, we were making really good money and he didn't like just sitting on the board anymore. He wanted to be in charge. So, over time, he chipped away at my sense of self and sanity until all that was left was the part that needed him."

She sighed and the air felt fresh and cool in her lungs, like she hadn't taken a deep breath in longer than she could remember. Telling Reece was more cathartic than she could have expected and though this kind of intimacy with a man she barely knew should have scared her, Morgan was just happy to take the win.

"I got out of the house first, filed a restraining order and set about divorce proceedings. We'd been together nearly a decade, and for a good part of it, he'd been turning me into a woman I never wanted to be—docile, obedient, happy with my place below another person."

She took the chance to look up at him and found that Reece was watching her very intensely. She didn't think he'd be the type to go seeking out a man who caused others harm—at least, not for physical retribution—but the very dark, very angry expression in his eyes had her reevaluating the thought.

"Anyway, I've been free of him a year and I'm trying to find the woman who's been missing the whole time."

Reece stroked her hair back from her face and tilted her chin up so their eyes met.

"You're goddamned brave, Morgan," he said quietly, but no less fiercely for it. "And not just because you climb mountains and go after bad guys, but because you were scared—and you saved yourself anyway."

It was a refrain she'd heard before. Courage wasn't the absence of fear. It was doing the thing that scared you anyway. The message held a certain personal note to it.

She wasn't entirely sure she would ever go back to being the person she had been before Aaron had turned from her business partner into the man who tore her down in pointed, calculated jabs any chance he got, but the thought was too overwhelming and too terribly sad to consider, so she went through her steps and attended her therapy and kept running so the memories would never be able to catch up with her.

"I know how hard it can be to talk about these kinds of things," Reece began, and from the tone in his voice Morgan got the sense that he really did know, probably better than anyone. "Thank you for sharing with me."

She nodded. "Thank you for listening."

They were quiet together in the cabin in the mountains for a long moment. Rain beat against the windows and sitting there on his lap, the world distant and far away from them, felt more intimate and anticipatory, like something big was on the horizon. In the span of just a few short days, Reece had found a way in, something she hadn't even been sure existed until this moment.

"It's not my business," she said, after the silence had become comfortable and lethargic, "but is that why you don't pick up your phone sometimes? Because talking is hard? You've gotten a lot of calls this week that have gone to voicemail and if you want a stranger's ear..."

She trailed off. It was none of her business and yet, Morgan found that a man like Reece might just need a little bit of a push to bare his past as she had done, if he had any intention of sharing with her.

Reece sighed, and the whole couch seemed to move with the effort he exerted merely to exist in the space. He was a large and beautiful man and Morgan admired the way his body moved below hers.

"I guess if I can't tell a beautiful stranger in a storm, then who can I tell, right?" he said, and she could practically hear the small grin in his voice. "But I warn you, it's not pretty."

She grimaced. "I know all about not pretty," she said. "And I've got you."

That seemed to do it for him, because he nodded. "I know you do, princess," he said. "I know."

How? How was it in that in four years, in travels around the world and countless hours spent on his therapist's couch, this was the way it all came out? He hadn't been able to talk to the men he considered most like brothers. Hell, he'd taken to screening their calls, as Morgan had pointed out, and all they had ever wanted to do was listen, was help him through the darkest days. But it was a stranger, a woman he'd seen only once in a previous life, who seemed to guide him through the bramble and brush of unspoken words with ease. *Fine.* It wasn't often that life gave a guy an emergency flotation device and it felt like a smart idea to grab on with both hands.

"When I first started working at *One Leap Magazine*, I had a girlfriend," he began, remembering the earliest days at the company that had taken him to heights he could never have imagined in an industry he would never have expected. "Her name was Abby and she was a photographer for the magazine. She had an eye like no one else in the business I'd ever seen, and she was only a few years into it."

Abby hadn't gone to college either, and in the great, elite world of post-graduate-degree-to-succeed-DC, they had bonded over their childhoods, over surviving and thriving despite and because.

"We got sent to a big convention in New York," Reece continued because stopping now would mean not starting again and suddenly it felt imperative to tell this story, now, to this woman. "It was a summit on sustainability as part of this weeklong event run by the U.N. International scientists, businessmen, heads of state, journalists. It was a meeting of some of the most powerful people in the world making some very important decisions about the future."

He paused and the breath he took wasn't nearly as deep as he would have liked it to be. "Unfortunately, that also made it a target."

He heard her soft intake of breath and part of him wanted to stop there, wanted to shield her from the worst of the story. But he knew from experience and from his career that not telling the end often made it so much worse.

"A white nationalist organization." Fuck, this part never got easier. "They didn't know what the summit was for. I think they would have been disappointed, actually. All they knew was that they could reach some high-profile targets. And they did. They reached the rest of us too."

He'd be able to smell the ash for the rest of his life.

"I was in an interview with an ambassador from the Finnish government," he said. "We were in a room off from the main hall, maybe twenty feet away. So, I wasn't there when the first bomb went off."

But the whole building had shaken, like an earthquake, and immediately his sense of sound had disappeared, as if the Mute button had been hit on the movie. He'd been lucky — his hearing had come back. He'd been lucky for so many other reasons too.

"Abby was photographing down at the front dais," he continued, trying to will the smell of smoke out of his memories. "She... She..."

Morgan's hand on his was like an instant balm and the rising tide of panic that had been making the edges of his vision start to get closer receded in an instant.

"It's okay," she said. "You don't have to continue if you don't want to."

He never wanted to, but for the first time in so long, he felt like he *could.*

"She didn't survive the initial blast," he said, the words nearly blurring together. "I was in and out of consciousness for three days from a head injury. The ambassador had a broken leg and cracked ribs."

For weeks, Reece had followed the stories of the explosion. He'd searched for the names of the people who had been in the building with him, for those who hadn't made it, for those who had. Some had been his friends, journalists or sources he had met along the way. Others he had been introduced to that very morning, a man whose hand he had shaken, a woman whose business card he hadn't been able to bring himself to throw away.

He had been stuck wondering, from that white bed in the white room, why he was alive and why they were not, and after days then months, then years, he still had no answers.

"You feel guilty," she said quietly. "The rational part of your brain knows that nothing that happened is your fault, but that doesn't matter, does it? You keep wondering when the other shoe is going to drop."

For four years, he'd had the creeping, anxious feeling of never quite knowing what he was afraid of, the sense of forgetting something but having no idea what it was he had forgotten.

"This week is the fourth anniversary," he said. "And I can't... So I don't."

"All the phone calls?"

"I have some pretty close friends. They like to make sure I'm okay and I should go visit them while I'm back home. But..."

"But they just don't get it."

"Right." Because Caleb had his past, the lost career, the day his wife had walked out, but he had Skylar now and the two were happier together than anyone he'd ever seen. Van would probably understand, better than Reece ever wanted anyone to understand, but Van wasn't exactly on stable ground himself, and the last thing either of them needed was a tip over the edge.

"The hardest part," he said, the part he'd really never spoken about with anyone, the part that kept him up at night, "was that everyone rewrote Abby's and my relationship. We had only been dating a few weeks, and her parents lavished me with attention like I'd been in the family for years. I know it was their way of dealing with their grief, I understand that now, but at the time it felt false, like I was cheating on top of having survived when others hadn't, and the guilt over that was something that no one understands. Abby was amazing and I would have been lucky to be with her forever. But we never got the chance."

"You have the chance to be happy now," Morgan replied. "I know it sounds cliché and I know, God, I know, it's not that easy. But for the first time in years and years, I've learned how to trust in my own emotions. And when the emotion is happy—even if only for a minute, even if only for an hour, I accept that I'm allowed to feel it and that I'm allowed to believe it's real."

He wasn't certain if it was the night or the rain outside or the new project or simply holding this woman in his arms, but in this minute, in this hour, Reece trusted his own emotions. And he was happy.

Chapter Eight

"Thanks, anyway. Let me know if you come across anything."

Reece was a different man on the phone and his full concentration in the conversation allowed Morgan to study him from where she at the small wooden table, notebook in hand and pens and notes before her on the desk.

Not long after they'd woken and had their first cups of coffee, Reece's team back in DC had sent information on the photos he had taken at the compound. It was more than they had, but not nearly enough, and he'd been calling in contacts for a few hours, asking for any information they might have had on an organization they so far knew only as the Conlon Group. At least, that had been the name on the papers that Reece's team had dug up, but that likely was just scratching the surface of what the corporation had to hide.

"Nothing from them?" she asked, when Reece hung up the phone and took a seat across from her at the table. He was in full work mode, the tight line between his eyebrows deep and worried, and she practically see the gears spinning in his head. She had little doubt that when he found a project, he went after it with everything he had, and they definitely had a project — the question was, what kind exactly?

"Eric used to be a Fish and Game warden in these parts," Reece explained. "But he's stationed in Colorado now. He said he'll follow up with a list once he finds out who's still around."

The consensus they had come to in the last few hours was that they couldn't be sure of who was involved in the local dealings, and the fewer people who knew they were poking around, the better — especially cops.

"You told him to talk to you first?" Morgan asked. She had never done anything like this before and Reece was a seasoned journalist, but it was hard not to get swept up in the excitement and adventure of the whole thing. Whatever they had seen had been *weird* and coupled with Jonathan Naylor's account of the local wildlife deaths it seemed more likely than not that the company, whatever its real name was, was up to something untoward, if not outright illegal.

"Yeah, I mentioned that we don't know who's involved," Reece replied. "He didn't seem very surprised. Out here, there isn't a lot of accountability when it comes to bad agents."

Morgan nodded. "That was the last name on your list. I'd say we should go over notes, but…"

"We don't have a lot of notes." He held up the matching empty notepad. "I know. The Conlon Group is about all we've got, and that probably won't lead us anywhere. We're going to have to go back tonight."

She raised an eyebrow at him. The storm had continued throughout the morning, and even though they were edging solidly into midday, the rain hadn't let up and the sun hadn't come out. Without trails or lights to guide them, the trip back to the compound was guaranteed to be dangerous — and that was before they took the whole 'downright illegal' element into account.

"You can stay here," he replied to her unspoken statement. "In fact, I would prefer you did."

Of course he would. Reece really didn't seem like the type of guy to allow others into dangerous situations if he could go himself. But, of course, it wasn't any safer for him to be out in the dark, in the rain, near the dangerous hidden compound on his own.

"I don't think so," she said. "If you're going, I'm going."

He seemed to accept her choice and shrugged, as if to say *you came along anyway too, so sure.* The movement was simple, but she appreciated it, nonetheless. There was a big different between wanting to protect someone and asking them to stay home and wanting to own someone and demanding it.

The rain smacked against the windows and with it came the wind, rattling the glass and blowing one of the windows open. He stood quickly and went over to shutter it and lock it into place.

"Looks like we have some time to kill until we can go back out there," he said to her. "Any thoughts on how to pass the hours?"

Oh, she had many, many thoughts on how to while away their time in this secret little cabin in the mountains.

"Tell me something about yourself," she said, instead of all she wanted to say, like *take me, kiss me, touch me...* "If you could go back to any city, where would it be?"

"Amsterdam is one of my favorites," he said, settling across the table from her. "For the weed, obviously."

"Oh no, Amsterdam was my favorite for the prostitutes," she replied, keeping her tone as level as possible. The expression on Reece's face was entirely worth it.

"Could you imagine, though?" She was out and out laughing at him and held up ten fingers with exaggeration movements. "Never have I ever visited a prostitute."

He held up ten fingers and very intentionally put one down. Her jaw dropped.

"You did *not...*"

"Of course, I didn't. I just wanted to see the expression on your face."

She growled. "We're playing for real. Never have I ever been to Australia."

He put a finger down and an eyebrow up. She shrugged. "Too much time away from work."

"Never have I ever been to college."

She pursed her lips and put a finger down. *It's not like I finished...*

"Never have I ever been published in *One Leap Magazine.* "

"Rude." He leaned back against the chair, the position so languid and relaxed that it made her stomach twist in a funny kind of a way. He looked like some kind of Greek hero, laid out in repose for a sculptor's eye.

"Never have I ever been a smoker."

She shook her head. "Never have I ever gotten a tattoo. Put two fingers down."

"Saw those, did you?" There was so denying the smugness in his voice, but she still couldn't bring herself to regret seeing his body in all its powerful beauty, even if he seemed to know it. Still,

"Those?"

"Which ones did you see?" he asked.

"Just the one around your arm," she admitted. "What else do you have?"

"Secrets," he replied. "Wouldn't be fun to show you everything at once. Why don't you have any?"

The answer must have shown on her face because Reece got quiet and his voice was low when he said, "It's your life."

"It is now," she replied. "I'm still getting used to it."

But she didn't want to think about that now, and so she was grateful when he continued on with his turn without saying another word to it.

"Never have I ever skinny dipped."

She glanced up at him. "Liar."

Amazingly enough, it was Reece's turn to blush. He did blush so pretty. "How'd you know that?"

"Because one, you're like the hottest guy ever and two, you'd never turn down an adventure. You've probably gone cliff diving naked."

"Sounds dangerous," he replied. "But yes, I have skinny dipped. And visited the infamous nude beaches of France."

She smiled and whispered a quick *thanks* quietly enough that he wouldn't have heard it if he hadn't been sitting so close to her. Rather than respond, he stroked his hand over her knuckle. It was meant to be soothing and comforting, but all it made Morgan think about was what it would feel like to have him stroking her elsewhere. *Everywhere.*

"Never have I ever sent a nudie pic," Morgan said, trying to find some kind of distraction from the heat building low in her belly.

"What makes you think I have?" Reece replied, as he put another finger down. "Are you calling me easy?"

"Ha." She lifted both eyebrows. "We both know that shaming people for their sexuality is outdated and sexist. I'm saying you're confident."

"You have a way of getting to the point. Never have I ever kissed a man."

"Cheap shot," she said, putting a finger down. "Never have I ever slept with two girls at the same time…" She paused. "No. Never have I ever slept with three *people* at the same time."

"You could have said one girl," Reece pointed out.

Morgan bit her lip and tried to keep at bay an onslaught of memories that rushed forward in a torrent of bittersweetness.

"Interesting. Very interesting. Anything you want to share with the class?"

Her face must've been bright red, given how hot it felt.

"Sometimes girls sleep together. It's not a big deal."

Reece furrowed his eyebrows. "It's not a big deal," he repeated. "But girls don't just sleep together. It's okay to be attracted to who you're attracted to, of course. It might make you feel good to say it out loud, though."

"I mean, I'm attracted to men." That was part of what had always made it so confusing. "It was just that,

Missy, she was all girl-next-door pretty, you know? It only happened a few times."

"Did you like it?"

"Of course. That's why it happened a few times." She pulled her hand out from his and released her hair from the bun atop her head to run her fingers through it, needing something to do as a distraction. "I always assumed if I liked men that was it? Missy was something else and she didn't factor in."

"It's not black and white," Reece put in. "Everyone experiences their own sexuality differently."

"I guess I was kind of nervous about what I would find if I looked too deeply," she admitted. "But yeah, I'm sure there's something there. She's not the only woman I've found enticing. And not in an I-Want-To-Be-Her way, but a I-Want-To-Be-With-Her way. It's a little harder to tell for women, I think. We're trained to see each other as competition and that muddies the waters."

"Do the waters feel muddy right now?"

She shook her head, surprised as her own honesty. "Not really. I guess all it takes is a new friendship and a storm in the woods." She paused. "Reece Prescott, I'm attracted to women." Her voice was confident and a little nervous even to her own ears, but in a new way, like she was evolving, growing, becoming the version of herself she was always meant to be. "I'm bisexual. Ooh, there it is."

He grinned. "Hell yeah. Come here." He opened his arms, and she accepted his embrace and God if the sensation of his hard body against her wasn't enough to drive her fucking out of her mind. "How do you feel?" he asked her.

"A little bit free," she admitted. "I haven't thought about Missy in years, but she's always been a part of me. I guess that's another thing I just tried to pretend away."

"Too much seriousness," she said after a moment of comfortable silence passed between them, the only noise that of the storm raging outside. "It's your turn." She tried to move away from his embrace, but he stilled her with a hand around the waist, and she accepted, moving farther into his hold.

"Never have I ever been skydiving," he said. "Would you believe I'm not a fan of heights?"

That gave her pause. "Hmm, I've been. It was fun, but I prefer to have my feet firmly on the ground." She shifted slightly, and she felt the response of his body below her, a response that her aching for something secret and hidden in the shadows of this mountain cabin.

"Okay, my turn. Never have I ever been to a strip club."

Reece looked down at her, and God, when had anyone every looked at her with such intensity, such need and veiled control?

"I've never been to a strip club," he replied. "They're predatory. It's not my scene."

"Fine," Morgan adjusted her position, only a little on purpose. "Never have I ever been to a sex club." Because she wanted to know. Because she needed to know. Because this thing growing between them felt real and important and full of possibility, and she didn't want him to hide from it anymore.

"Morgan." His voice didn't come out warning, so much as raw and husky and a little wild. God help her.

"Reece," she interrupted him. "What lifestyle?"

Chapter Nine

The cabin was quiet, the silence around them hot and loaded, and Morgan had to wonder if she had been too bold. There was no denying the heavy weight of anticipation and promise that had been building between them over the last few days and the comfort of the warm cabin made her want to move things between them from the unspoken to the very much spoken aloud. She just hoped she hadn't pushed Reece into a place he hadn't planned to go.

"Morgan." His voice was rough, more of that laced control that made her want to see how far away his edge really was. "Are you asking me because you want to know?" He paused and held her gaze, a wild tempest of greens and golds. "Or are you asking me because you want to know *more?*"

How was it that this man seemed to understand her, even as she didn't give full voice to the questions she posed? They had known each only a few days and he could already fill in the blanks, the words she wasn't yet comfortable saying.

"Tell me everything," she managed in a whisper. She knew what he had meant by the lifestyle in the academic sense, in the rational, droll, research kind of way that had never tempted her before. But with Reece, with the power he seemed to hold over her and this innate need to give over something of her own, to take things further and higher and deeper than they had ever been before, that made her want to move out of the textbooks and into the classroom.

Reece Prescott as a professor. Yes, please.

"Do you know what you're asking?" he replied. The crook of his arm had been comfortable before, but now she was acutely aware of him, surrounded by his touch and his scent and increasingly desperate for so much more than whispers. "I want you to be sure before I answer you."

"I'm asking you to tell me what it's like to dominate." Though her voice was barely there, soft and murmured into this intimate space, Morgan didn't have a doubt in her mind that Reece was always the one in charge. It was his energy, magnetic and intense, an aura that pulsed around him and made others — made *her* — sit up and take note.

"How did you know?" he asked with a sly grin. He brought one hand to the side of her face and as soft as silk stroked a finger along her jaw. "What makes you think I don't give up my control instead?"

Morgan took a deep breath, but it was shaky and, judging from the glint in Reece's piercing eyes, it just served to heighten this moment even further. He could read her like a damned book, every response, every desire, and she told him as much.

"You already know what I want," she whispered. "Before I do. I... I may not know a lot about your world, but I know it takes a certain kind of intuitive nature, someone who can look past their own desires to care for their partner's in a specific sort of way."

He smiled and there was her gut reaction to see that smile again, to seeing the pride in his eyes like she was a schoolgirl who had just answered a question correctly. Damn it, why couldn't she get this professor thing out of her head?

"That's true," he replied. "Dominants do have to be tuned in to what their subs need." He moved his finger lower now, stroking down the curve of her neck, and Morgan couldn't help the small swallow at his touch. *More like a gulp.* "We'll push you higher than you'll push yourself, we'll please you more than you please yourself, we'll protect you every step you take out of your comfort zone and we'll give you permission to give up all control, all responsibility. All you have to worry about is pleasing me."

He had been using the collective, but the final words *pleasing me* had Morgan's body reacting in a way she couldn't fully understand. Her nipples tightened to hard, pinched points, and she involuntarily moved her legs in some naïve attempt to get relief from his dangerous, loaded words.

"Stop that." The power came from the restraint in his voice. There was no raised volume, no extreme language, just two words. *Stop that.* And she did.

"Oh, princess." He looked her in the eye then, and she could see something honest, something vulnerable and raw. "You don't have to take this path. We can turn back and pretend it never happened."

She knew that. From the very first conversation they'd shared, he had made it clear that the ball was always in her court. She was, ultimately, the one in control of every step they took together. And though she hadn't known him long, she already felt like she knew him well, and knew that the second she said things were moving too fast, that she no longer wanted to experience all he had to offer, he would stop, without question.

"I don't want to stop." Since when had she sounded so petulant?

"I know," he replied. "I know what you want. But I also know you've never done anything like this before."

She pursed her lips. "Who says?"

That smile again. God, he had *dimples*. Honestly, had there ever been a man so perfectly balanced between cute and sexy?

"You do. You want to submit to me. You have this innate need to turn your body and your choices over to me. But you don't know how yet."

He was right, of course. Before him, she had never even considered anything beyond light spanking or sexy lingerie when it came to spicing things up in the bedroom. And now, now she found herself wondering what Reece would want to try first. Because all of a sudden, she wanted *everything* he was willing to offer her.

Instinct took over and she turned her gaze away from him and those knowing, all-too-discerning eyes.

"So pretty," he whispered, a note of awe in his voice. "Don't think for a moment I don't want you, Little Storm. I ache for you." God, the honesty made her ache right back, burn so hot for him her body was sure to ignite. "There's so much I want to teach you."

"Now?" It was bold of her to ask, even if the word was quietly whispered. "Will you teach me now?"

Reece stroked Morgan's cheek as gently as he could, which was amazing given how tightly his body was coiled, how much he burned with wanting for this woman. To teach someone like Morgan Tempest was a gift, and his mind swam with possibilities, of how he could make her desperate, wanting, quivering and begging for his touch.

Possibilities that were going to have to wait because his phone vibrated on the table, sending a technical, jarring sound into this quiet space. Reece took a deep breath and knocked his forehead against Morgan's because she knew as well as he did that he didn't have the option of ignoring it.

"You should probably get that," Morgan said, and it was as if her smile told him that she, too, wanted to stay in this world they had created for themselves, safe and far away from past hurts that healed but never quite all the way, hidden from vulnerability, and loss, just them against the world.

He had known her for three goddamned days and Reece was, without a shadow of a doubt, losing his fucking mind. But if Morgan stood up, then he didn't have a reason to ignore the call anymore, not with the real world tuning in.

"Caleb is pissed, man." Gabriel hadn't become one of the youngest billionaires in America by being polite. His competitors had called him brusque, rude, ambitious to a fault, but Reece knew that the teeth in his tone now were from a place of abject loyalty and protectiveness, and Reece deserved whatever attitude Gabe was throwing his way.

"I know," he said, cradling the phone to his ear and slowly standing. He worked better when he paced. "I..." He faltered and it was only when he glanced back at Morgan that he felt that long-lost strength return to his spine, like muscles long ignored and once again worked to their strongest mettle. "It's too hard for me, Gabe," he said.

It was probably the most honesty his brothers would ever get from him, and though it fell far short from what they deserved, it felt freeing all the same. Knowing that he should pick up his phone and return Caleb's call, that he could be honest about his stress disorder with Van, that he could simply be in their presence and be safe, it wasn't enough.

Long ago, the rational part of Reece had become untethered from the emotional reaction, had become something all its own, until he could watch logic float away as his brain and heart rebelled.

But here he was, saying the barest minimum as if it had taken all the effort of climbing the biggest mountain, and only one thing had changed.

Morgan.

It had been Morgan three years ago and it was Morgan now, not some vestige of a shadow that he could see across the market, but the woman herself, who was so much more than he could have ever imagined her to be, dynamic and complex, and the fit of yin to yang that had Reece feeling more at ease than a lifetime spent under the stars.

"Reece," Gabriel's voice called him back to the moment, to the phone call, to world that existed beyond his own panic and memories. "I know. They all know. He's not calling about the anniversary."

That made Reece's shoulders unclench a little and he took a deep breath before replying.

"He's not?"

"No." Gabriel was always the steadiest rock in the storm. They were down-home cowboys, at least they had been, but Gabriel was a man who played his cards close to his chest and spoke in truths, even when they were harsh. There was no sugarcoating, and for that, Reece was grateful. "They know you. They know that's not what you want." It hadn't been, but Reece also knew that he hadn't given them anything to work with.

The strange thing about being friends with a bunch of Doms was that their personalities, their needs to care for and watch the emotions and needs of people around them extended far beyond their play. His friends were intuitive, watchful, and extremely receptive to changes in mood and tone and need, and for years he had been pushing them away to weather the worst memories of his life completely alone in the wilderness. Why, all of a sudden, did that feel like a waste of the best kind of resources a man got in his life?

"Then why is he calling?" Reece asked, instead. "And Van too? Is someone else after Duchess?" Caleb Cash's fiancé Skylar had come from a family of wealthy real estate moguls, among other things, and they had spent the better part of the previous year trying to buy up the town of Duchess for the mineral rights. It had almost broken Skylar and Caleb up, but they'd come to their senses in the end, and Reece was grateful as hell to see his old friend finding love again, after his ex-wife had broken his heart.

"Nothing like that," Gabriel replied. "But you'll have to ask Caleb. It's not for me to tell."

"Is everything okay?" Reece could climb a mountain, hike a black diamond trail, scuba-dive with sharks, but the familiar anxiety haunted a part of him and weaseled through his thoughts without pause.

"Everything is fine," Gabe replied, his voice gruff, bordering on annoyed. "Which you would know if you picked up the damn phone when Caleb called. But that's not why I'm calling you. You're a big boy—you don't need a secretary."

"They should have named you most successful asshole under thirty-five," Reece replied. He could practically hear Gabriel's grin on the other end of the phone.

"Do you want to know what I've learned about the Conlon Group or not?"

"Hang on." Reece came back over to the table and put the phone on speaker. "You've got us both on. Shoot."

If Gabriel thought it strange that Reece wasn't working alone, as was his usual MO, especially this time of the year, he didn't make a comment about it. Instead, he delved right into the information he had called to share.

"I looked at the info you sent over from your editor," he said. "The Conlon Group is a pharmaceutical company, mostly specializing in meds for treating the effects of mood disorders, you know depression, bipolar disorder. They've been around since the 1970s and don't have a mark against them, not so much as a slap on the wrist."

"Is that unusual?" Morgan asked. The pen she was tapping against her lower lip had Reece's attention skittering in the wrong direction. His cock hadn't gotten the message that there had been a change in the day's programming.

"Extremely," Gabriel said. He didn't hesitate a second at the sound of a female voice on the line, and Reece was grateful for it. Whatever was happening here with Morgan was brand-new and just figuring itself out. The last thing it needed was the scrutiny of his friends. "Forty years ago, all of those companies were dumping chemical waste without consequence. Not a single one of them got out unscathed when the new EPA regulations were enacted."

"So you're thinking that they have someone on the inside to wipe their records clean?" Reece asked. "Either political or technical."

"Or both," Gabriel replied. "The other thing, not on the public record, is that the Conlon Group has an extremely large contract with the state of Montana. All I could find for the contract was "consulting". It's not even technically listed under the Conlon Group, but someone slipped up in one of the contracts, which is why I could trace it."

"How much money is the contract for?" Reece asked. "And what kind of consulting could a pharma company be doing all the way out here?"

"I can only answer one of those questions," Gabriel replied. "And say it's for a lot. Like the kind of number that turns my head." That *was* a lot, considering how early and quickly and efficiently Gabriel had made his money.

"So we're looking at money laundering, coverups, political corruption and what's almost guaranteed to be a long history of illegal chemical dumping and pollution," Morgan said. Her expression was comical, a mix of desperation and humor that hit pretty close to what Reece was feeling right at the moment.

"At the surface," Gabriel said. "Be careful if you go digging into local politics though, Reece. This is your own backyard." Unspoken was that the Sinclair Ranch and The Ranch belonged to all of them, and Reece was going to have to be very sure of what he was doing before going after the mighty and the powerful.

"That's all the more reason to make it right," he said. "Can you send me those files that you found?"

"Some of them," Gabriel replied. "Others might be harder to get my hands on. I have a few boons I can call in."

"I appreciate it," Reece replied. "As always."

Gabriel may have been intense, ambitious bordering on rude, and with enough power to take the world to its knees—even if he had never found the perfect partner to do it to, but Gabriel would always take their calls, which was more than could be said for Reece. Gabriel had been his source on far more than one assignment, and the intel he'd probably found through secret channels only open to the rich was likely to make their entire case for them.

"I know, man," Gabriel replied. "You can repay the favor by calling Caleb back."

And without another word, Gabe hung up, leaving Reece and Morgan staring at the dark surface of the phone in a bit of stunned silence.

"This is...big," Morgan said finally. "Like, government coverup big." She didn't sound nervous, exactly, but wary, as if trying to soak in the full meaning of what they were up against.

"It certainly looks that way," Reece replied after a moment. "You know it's not too late to walk away. No one would blame you if you did."

"I would," she said. "My Twelve Houses App says that I need to look at the bigger picture and stop focusing on the details."

In the months following the New York City explosion, Reece had found comfort in ways he could never have expected, the calm routine of making pour-over coffee before the sun rose, watching cooking videos for recipes he never planned to try out, searching the listings for apartments in foreign cities and redesigning them in his mind. They hadn't always worked, but they had kept at bay that prickling panicked feeling that meant he was losing control, and he understood now, with clarity he wished on no one, that every person needed their comfort, whether they had trauma in their past or not, where they battled their own rational thoughts for purchase or went through their day without jumping at shadows.

If Morgan had hers in an astrology app, who was he to make a comment on it? Hell, the sight of her face, of the woman in the market, had been a talisman to him over the worst of his fears and worries, and he owed her more nights of sleep and peace than therapy or medication had ever given him.

"I think you focus on the big picture plenty," he said. "You make safe adventuring more accessible to millions of people."

Her smile was so bold, all white teeth and bright pink lips and it spoke to who she was and how she moved through life—or perhaps how she was learning to move through life. It was a hell of a thing to see.

"I like that," she said. "Okay, so the stars aren't perfect. But I would still blame me for walking away. I want to help. I was to give back a little, you know?" He really, really did know.

"Then it's settled." It wasn't, exactly. For all that he understood her innate need to be part of the solution, he still didn't love the idea of putting others in danger or at risk. But she was here, and she wanted to go, and he knew she was more than capable of matching him step for step.

"Then it's settled," Morgan replied. "Where do we start?"

Chapter Ten

Morgan wanted to be here. She wanted to be involved in the solution, wanted to look back and say that her company walked the walk when it came to sustainability, low impact and give-back ethos, that she hadn't been one to sit on the sidelines and simply allow bad people to do bad things. Her mind, heart and soul were all screaming for her to get involved and to help Reece, but her body hadn't quite gotten on board yet. Because she was currently crouched behind a squat stone wall behind an electric fence forcing her breathing to slow and her adrenaline to chill the fuck out.

She knew adrenaline. She'd come face to face with bears and sharks and once a wild skunk that had turned its sprayer in her direction, but those had been highs, pumping her blood full of excitement until she could climb to the next summit or jump the taller cliff into the ocean. This kind of adrenaline was actually making her a little sick. Her skin felt clammy and her fingers swollen and too thick for her hands when she rested them against her thighs.

But then she caught sight of Reece beside her, his movements small and tight but effective, as if he had done this a thousand times before, crouched at hidden entrances to dangerous facilities, in search of the next great story. She had little doubt that he had and even less doubt that his next story would be a big one. After all, what the hell was a big pharmaceutical company even doing all this way, and why was this land, protected as it should be by government regulation and local infrastructure, vulnerable to abuse and misuse as it so clearly was? Something much darker than money-saving was at play.

"What's the plan?" she asked Reece, who was pocketing his binoculars and snapping a few pictures with his phone. "Are we going to try to go in?"

"Not yet," he said. "I don't know what we're looking for. The smoking gun."

The smoking gun probably wasn't even in that factory. It was probably hidden in sealed financial records lost in the waters of the Cayman Islands. But if they could find something, capture images, take videos, if there was some way to pull back that top layer of soil from whatever the operation was here, maybe that would make it a little easier to dig deeper, to find more truth about this company and the many secrets it held.

Up ahead, more of the large, nondescript trucks with that familiar logo she had come to recognize buzzed through the gates. The scent of diesel was potent, a rich, unpleasant contrast to the mountain air, and she could see plumes of exhaust puffing out as the trucks were moved through the first set of steel doors and out of sight.

"On the west side," she murmured to Reece. The closer they got to the compound entrance, the less hidden they were, and keeping quiet and unseen was of paramount importance. "Do you see the pipes?"

It was impossible *not* to see the pipes, even at their distance. There were three visible from this angle, at least as large as the tires on the Reece's truck, and they were positioned right over the river.

Up this high, the river meandered lazily through ancient glacier rocks, spilling over tiny waterfalls. It almost seemed to come to a complete stop in sections, moving only enough to swirl tiny whirlpools in bubbles and foam. But despite the calmness of the water, the glug of waste pouring from those rusted, dirty pipes mixed into the river with ease, a slush of dark sludge that disappeared below the surface of the dark blue stream, only to turn to the water to a foamy gray cloud.

There were varying levels of how bad this could be, from gray water being poured back into the river, to toxic, contaminated waste, laden with microplastics and pharmaceutical refuse, sure to poison the ecosystems around it. Based on the information they had collected from Reece's sources, it was nothing short of blindly naïve to think that the disposal was benign.

"Do you think we can get a sample of that waste?" Reece asked. His voice was calm, but his body was taut, as if ready to spring into action at any moment. "That might be very useful." An understatement, to be sure, but Morgan nodded.

"Do you have your gloves?" she asked. "Whatever that is, we don't want it touching our skin." Hell, she didn't even want the air around this toxic factory touching her skin, but there wasn't much she could do about that now. She made a mental note to check into the medical records of anyone who might have worked at the facility.

"Fish cleaning gloves should do the trick," Reece replied. There was no way he wasn't nervous, but his grin was easy, and it served to relax her, just a little. Just enough. He pulled the gloves from his pack then a small container. She recognized it as one of her own, a collapsible pouch for food or specimen storage. The challenge now was to somehow get across the broad expanse of open terrain that separated them from the pipes depositing waste on the other side. It wasn't exactly open, but the visibility was good, which was bad news for them. They'd either have to move fast or go as slow and quietly as possible.

"Follow the trees." Reece indicated toward the edge of the clearing. It was perhaps dark enough, shadowed by the large, ancient growth, to hide some of their movement as they made their way to the sludge on the far side of the compound. The movement was slow, but they soon found themselves clearing the bend, able to move down the hill and somewhat out of sight from the main entrance, a relief, since the guards were back at their posts and welcoming in a new line of white box trucks.

"How many deliveries does one factory need?" she muttered to Reece, who glanced up at the driveway.

"That's a goddamned good question," he muttered, snapping off a few more shots of the trucks on his phone. They all looked the same and the license plates were obscured, either by distance or by a cover or guard of some sort, but surely this many deliveries had to mean something.

She went to reply, went to put one foot in front of the other as they got closer to their toxic destination, when the trill of a cell phone buzzed through the mountains. Her cell phone. *Fuck. Fuck. Double fuck.*

It startled the wildlife around them, sending a flock of birds away from the trees as if the hounds of Hades were on their tails, and every second between the trilling, horrible ring and the moment she found and silenced the phone felt like agony, stretching far and long before her. Then after ages of heart-palpitating panic, the phone was quiet as a stone in her hand.

She glanced up, first at Reece then toward the gate where the strongmen stood sentinel. Their eyes were searching, and a flurry of activity could mean only one thing.

"Hey, Morgan," Reece's voice was steady, and she heard no trace of censure. "I think we're going to want to hurry up."

Chapter Eleven

Hurry up was just about the understatement of the century. Reece had known that this little sojourn into the lion's den was dangerous as all get-out, and he couldn't find it in himself to be that irritated at Morgan for the phone call. Their service had been spotty for days, and while she was adept at adventure, this was a kind of fly-below-the-radar situation she had almost no experience with. More so, he was irritated with himself for allowing her to come with him, to get all tangled up in this very messy mess from the start.

But she was here, and they were getting much closer to being discovered than they had been just a few minutes earlier, so Reece would just have to flay himself later. For now, they needed to get down to those pipes, then get the hell out of Dodge. The ground was slippery below his feet, and sharp rocks stuck out at odd angles, making the going slower than he would have liked, especially as the shouts of the men sounded around them.

Finally, as if they had been moving through molasses, they made it to the edge of the river, a bank of thick mud that caught and held his every step for a breath before release. The pipes were just up ahead, another thirty feet, twenty, ten, then they were there, at the foot of the mountain ledge where the compound rested, pulling out gear and on gloves, and looking the glugging pipes right in the eye.

He noticed the stench first, one that had grown stronger and more potent with every step closer, but it was so strong by the pipes themselves that every breath was vile and cloying. At first, it was muddy, like a thick exhaust, rich and undeniably artificial, but as he got closer, he noticed a sweetness around the edges that made him want to gag. Nothing pouring from these rusty metallic pipes could be good.

Behind them, Reece could still hear shouts and the sounds of men in motion. He had been in his fair share of emergency situations. When he had been a young kid moving steer and they'd encountered wolves or a surprise blizzard, when he'd been on assignment and shit had gone upside down. When he'd been in New York City and his entire world had shaken from the ground up. This was very quickly becoming an emergency situation.

But despite the necessity of haste, he took his time pulling on the fish scaling gloves before stepping as close as he could to the edge of the water. The bank was muddy, if it could be called that, a dark sludge that swallowed the tread of his shoe in vile sucking noises, and Reece wondered if they might get stuck here, in this hellish wasteland of muck and grime. But he was able to steady himself enough to carefully lean over the edge and capture some of the deposit from the pipes as they glugged their contents free, then he was capping the small container and nodding to Morgan.

God, he wanted this woman. He wanted to taste her and feel her and lick the sweat from her sun-soaked skin on the banks of the lake at the mountain's base. He wanted to make her beg, scream, demand satisfaction until she was so pliant and willing in his arms that she would give anything to feel his touch. He wanted to—

"Reece, come *on*." Her touch was gentle, given the likely toxic plastic container he held in his hand, but insistent. "We have to get the hell out of here."

Easier said than done, considering their entry to the compound was on the other side of the sprawling and exposed mountain. It had been devoid of guards when they'd made their way around the circle of trees at the end of the property, but now it seemed like there were guards everywhere he looked, far more than he had seen before.

"That way." He nodded in the direction across the river and Morgan gaped at him. He didn't blame her. Not only would they be taking the longest possible route back to their campground, undoubtedly requiring hiking after dark, but they were going to have to cross over the river of toxic sludge to get there.

"If my feet fall off..." she murmured, but she started down the bank, and he followed her. They would need to find some way of crossing over the widening river mouth if they had any hope of getting to safety without losing a limb in the process.

Or maybe losing a limb wasn't so bad.

The ringing of gunfire echoed around them as a spray of bullets lodged into stone and steel, and Reece's chest went tight, his abs contracting, his breath slowing, his heart pounding out an uneven beat that felt like escape.

"Down." It didn't matter that he was shouting now. It was clear they had been spotted by the guards at the top of the mountain and no amount of careful footing or quiet maneuvering was going to protect them. Now they had to get the ever-loving *fuck* out of here.

"You owe me a new pair of shoes," Morgan said, her voice stiff and taut as she stepped into the river. They were far enough away from the glug of the pipes now that Reece could no long smell their metallic rusty dust in the air, but that might have been because his nose was filled with the scent of his own sweat, and an ill-fitting awareness of the beautiful natural world around him. Pine scents and fresh air came in strong and overwhelming because panic and adrenaline were never sure and never simple.

"I will buy you whatever you want as long as we get out of here," Reece said, the words feeling a little big and a little uncomfortable in his swollen mouth. He knew this sensation too well and he had never quite grown accustomed to the feeling of fleeing, no matter how many times he'd found himself doing it in the years since New York.

Normally, when his hands felt clammy and his chest went tight, he thought of Morgan — well, he thought of the woman from the marketplace, the woman from another world and another life, who had always felt like a port in a storm. But now he didn't have to imagine her or the bright blue of her eyes or the calm steadiness of her gait. She was here now, and she was offering him her hand to follow her across the river.

He took it — Reece suspected he might always take her hands — then he plunged into the icy chill of the river. Even in the summer, the Montana mountains ran cold, and the freezing water mixed with God only knew what else shook his system back online. They were being *chased* and now wasn't the time for any sort of reflection.

"Down there!" The shouts came from above, and Morgan doubled her speed, forcing Reece to keep up. His legs were slightly longer than hers, but he wanted to stay behind her, to serve as the barrier between Morgan and the men now following them, if it ever came to that. But even though he could still hear the shouting above them, hear the sound of footsteps and movement as men followed them down the jagged cliff face, he soon touched his feet on the other side of the river and the advantage was theirs in an escape through the trees.

For now.

Morgan led the way and he was happy to let her. While Reece knew these mountains well, Morgan was a well-trained hiking expert and one mountainside trail really looked like all the rest when a person was being pursued by armed militants from a toxic waste dumpsite. She was fast and nimble, and Reece had to adjust his footing a few times to keep from spilling the container in his hand.

They ran deep into the woods, zigzagging along the mountain's edge and in and out of trees, but every time Reece thought they had lost their followers, sounds, shouts and calls came out from a distance. How far would these people follow them? What would they do if they caught up to them? The shots had been close enough that Reece couldn't imagine they'd been intended as anything other than kill shots, but how bad was the factory hidden in the mountain that they'd be willing to shoot anyone who stumbled onto their land?

Well, not exactly stumbled, but the point remained.

"There!" a man shouted, closer this time. Far, far too close for comfort, especially as Reece's lungs were beginning to burn and his muscles protested the harder push for distance. He was fit as hell, but there was only so much dodging and high-altitude running a man could manage before he felt the effects.

"Shit," Morgan muttered under her breath. "They're getting closer."

Reece stopped, pulling Morgan to a stop with him. "Go back to the cabin," he said. "And call for help. I'm going to hold them off."

"Like hell you are," she said. She took the specimen from his hand and tucked it into the front pouch of his backpack. "I can fight."

Now was so not the time to find her ability — her willingness — to fight so fucking attractive. But every mountain Morgan met, she climbed, and the more he got to know her, the more he admired that about her.

"Then let's fight," he said.

She grinned at him, then they were taking back-to-back stances as three large men emerged from the trees around them. At first glance, Reece didn't see any guns, certainly not the ones that had been spraying down bullets upon them a few minutes earlier. But the largest one, the one closest to him, moved slightly and the glint of metal caught Reece's attention. Whatever was going on here was fucking serious, and by the pounding in his heart and the clamminess of his palms, his body had figured that out a lot earlier than his head had.

"Who are you?" Morgan demanded. And if Reece hadn't gotten to know her as he had over these last few days, he would never have caught the thread of nerves in her words.

"Who are you, is the better question." The man standing closest to her was short, but wide in the shoulders, and his face looked like it would punch back any hand that touched it. "Considering you were caught trespassing our property."

"We're just hikers," she said, her tone surprisingly believable. "We got lost on our way up the mountain."

They did have some of their smaller packs with them, added some authenticity to the statement, assuming they hadn't been seen collecting water from the old, rusted pipes.

"I don't believe that's true," the man said, stepping forward toward Morgan. It was everything Reece could do not to step in front of her, but he knew she wouldn't want him to. This was not a woman who wanted other people to fight her battles for her, that much he knew.

Then the man was reaching for Morgan's wrist, and she feinted, dodging out of his way and capturing his wrist in her own, before bringing her knee up to his gut. The man doubled over, obviously surprised by her movement, but then he caught her knee and tried to spin her around.

Morgan was much smaller, but not that much shorter than him, and she kept her balance, wrapping her other hand around his and pulling the arm back until he released her knee. Instead of setting it down, she swooped under, trying to hit from the back, but this time he anticipated her move. He backed off and Morgan had to catch her balance, which gave the attacker time to recalibrate.

But then Reece wasn't watching her anymore because the other two men, large and very, very angry looking, had started to advance toward him, which sent his survival instinct rioting into high gear. He was a good fighter. But they were outmanned, definitely outgunned, and it was only a matter of time before the other guards from the compound realized where they were.

I refuse to die here.

It was a strange thought for several reasons, especially since he really should have been focusing on the way one of the men was rearing back to land what would undoubtedly be a very sound punch. Thankfully, he was big, and big men often moved slow, especially when their muscles were more for show than use, so Reece was able to move well out of range of the blow. The seconds were all moving much slower than they had been just a moment ago, as if he could see everything in a paused, distilled motion that gave him time to react, time to escape. If he learned nothing else from this, it was that he wanted to survive.

I want to live.

For so fucking long, not wanting to die had seemed like a victory. The tremors and the nightmares and the panic attacks had wrecked him for months after the explosion, and the guilt had lingered for so much longer. He'd had good days and bad, but the startling realization that he wanted to do more than just survive imbued him with what felt like superhuman strength. He was still the man he had been before New York. And he was willing to fight for it. For him. For them. For goodness and hope in the world.

He copied one of Morgan's moves and brought his knee up to the attacker's gut, nailing him hard and sending Reece's own muscles into a powerful awareness. Morgan and he had been hiking and climbing for days and had only just sprinted halfway across the compound. Still, he wasn't a trained survival expert running on adrenaline for nothing, and when the other man came around to Reece's other side, Reece struck him three quick times with his elbow in the man's chest. The man went stumbling backwards, trying to catch his breath, and the other advanced again.

But Reece was ready for him this time, and he gripped the man's arm, turning it over until the rest of the man's large body had to follow. Reece then brough his own leg over the man's shoulder and used the weight of his legs to push the man down to the ground. He pinned the arm below him to the ground with his boot then returned to the other man who had come back for more.

Beside him, he heard Morgan delivering her own kind of hell to the guard who had underestimated her, and, inappropriate as it absolutely was, he felt a smile creep over his face. This situation couldn't be more fucked up, and yet, here he was, growing aroused by the sight of a woman absolutely beating the living hell out of a man. Not just any woman. *Morgan.*

Reece punched the other guard in the face before the other man even realized what was happening, and this time, he actually fell to his knees. Whatever mercenaries or guards they had hired at the compound weren't very good at shooting and they weren't very good at fighting.

Morgan landed a hard punch, and Reece heard the man's nose crunch and crack under her hand, which sent a spray of blood into the air. It really was a day for OSHA violations. But Reece's momentary distraction allowed for one of the guards to get below him and before he could steady his base, the guard was knocking out his knees and Reece was losing his balance. He moved to land on top of the other man, then they were tussling and kicking against the ground, difficult in the muddy thickness of the riverbank.

He scrambled for purchase, but his boot slid against the mud, sticking and slipping intermittently. The good news was that the guard below him wasn't having any better luck and soon Reece had his knee on the man's chest and his fist raised above his head.

"I don't fucking think so." This from Morgan. Above him. She was holding a large stick and he looked up just in time to see her bring it down across the back of the other's guard head before he landed a blow on Reece's temple. The guard fell, and when he hit the ground this time, it looked like it might have been for good.

"We need to get out of here," Reece managed. He punched the guard below him, just enough to knock him out, and the last blow compounded all the hits from the fight. His knuckles throbbed, swollen and muddy and difficult to move, but he and Morgan had much larger problems to deal with now.

Morgan helped him to his feet, and they were running then, clearing the edge of the guards and the compound when—

The guard closest to the clearing of trees, the one whose nose Morgan had broken, got off a shot.

At first, Reece thought he had missed. They'd missed every other shot they had taken so far, but then he saw the bloom of blood on Morgan's upper arm, turning into a running stream that streaked her muddy skin and made his stomach go sour and flip as though he were falling.

"I'm fine," she said. "It's only a graze." She had no real way of knowing that, but there was absolutely nothing they could do right now, on this mountain top with armed guards chasing them, so Reece let her run ahead, let her pretend nothing was wrong, and followed Morgan Tempest out of the forest.

Chapter Twelve

Okay, so she wasn't exactly fine. Morgan was pretty certain that the gun shot had actually only grazed her. She didn't have a lot of experience with gunshots, but it seemed like a person would be aware if there was a bullet lodged somewhere in their body, right? She didn't feel anything in her arm, but that didn't mean there wasn't a hell of a lot of pain radiating through her muscles. Briefly, she wondered if she'd ever be able to climb again, but they had more pressing issues to deal with, like getting the fuck out of here. She could still move her fingers, so it couldn't be that much of an emergency, right?

"Morgan, slow down," Reece said. They'd probably only been running down the mountain for fifteen or so minutes, but it felt like so much longer, the adrenaline now wearing off making everything feel slow and dreamlike then too fast and too loud and too bright all at the same time. "Just stop, hang on."

He had to pull on her uninjured arm to get her to stop running, and Morgan didn't know if her body would ever settle back into rhythm with her head. It certainly didn't seem like it from where she was standing. *Running. Bleeding.*

"Let me see your arm, okay?"

She held it out to him, and a surprising surge of panic rushed over her at the sight of her bloody arm. Surely, she was no longer bleeding. That was blood from before, right? It probably wasn't even hers.

"Shh, calm, I've got you. I've got you. This is going to sting," he said quietly. "I'm here with you, okay?" He gently poured some water over her wound, flushing away the rivers of dried blood on her skin and exposing the small, jagged wound on her upper arm. "See, not too bad."

She would have to disagree, but if getting shot was what it took to get Reece to hold her hand like that, a little too tight, as if he knew the extra pressure would help to anchor her, then she wasn't opposed to running from armed guards with him again in the future.

"I don't think there's a bullet in there," she said, realizing only at the throbbing in her jaw that she was clenching her teeth in pain. "Still hurts."

"I imagine it does," he said, releasing her hand just to pull out the emergency first-aid kit from his pack. Another one of her products. Of course it was. "But I'm sure it's nothing compared to what those brutes back there are feeling. You are not a woman that I would want to cross."

She liked that he saw her that way, saw her as something fierce and maybe a little bit wild. After so much time under Aaron's influence, under his *control,* she'd had to fight hard to come back to the powerful version of herself that had been hiding. And it hadn't been easy.

"Squeeze my hand," Reece said. He didn't give her time to react, just applied the antiseptic pouch onto her wound. Morgan nearly screamed, catching herself at the very last second. The last thing they needed was to alert the guards as to their exact location.

"All done," Reece said quietly. He bandaged her up quicky, and to her relief, it seemed no blood stained the bright white bandage where she'd been shot.

"We need to get out of here," Reece said. "I'd like to get you to a hospital."

"That's a terrible idea," Morgan replied. They were walking again, back down the mountain's edge and hopefully in the direction of the ranger's cabin where they'd left the majority of their belongings. It hadn't made sense to carry all their gear up to the compound, and surely it would have made their narrow escape more challenging, but she wished they could just disappear into the Montana mountains without having to retrace their steps in any direction.

"You could get an infection," he pointed out.

"They could still be following us," Morgan replied. "We need somewhere to hide out where we can't be traced." It was actually kind of difficult to believe that this had become her life. Sure, she had martial arts training, had dedicated a good amount of her life to learning how to protect herself, not that it had been all that useful when she'd really needed it. But there had been only a handful of times on her many solo travels where Morgan had even come close to having to get into someone's face, and here she was, with bruised and bloody knuckles and a fucking gunshot wound.

It did hurt. A lot. But there was no purpose in letting Reece know that her skin felt like it had been scored with the burned edges of a campfire marshmallow. The best she could hope for was a few over-the-counter pain meds from the first-aid kit, and they weren't likely to help.

"Yeah." His voice was rough, and she noticed a hint of wistfulness that could have almost been shortness of breath, if she didn't know exactly how fit he was.

"Why don't you want to go home?" She hadn't meant to ask the question. For all that had happened between them in the last few days, it had only been a few days, and while they'd both openly shared some of the demons in their respective closets, Morgan knew better than most than skeletons stacked well in hidden spaces. Still, she knew he had been screening his friends' calls, knew they couldn't be more than an hour away from the Ranch where he'd said he had worked that one summer, and she had to wonder what had a man like Reece Prescott running scared.

"I do…" he said after a moment. "Want to go…back to the Ranch. It's just complicated."

She waited, allowing the quiet of the mountain behind them — blissful quiet, no armed guards or stray bullets filling the air — to give him a chance to catch up with his thoughts. "They worry, is all."

It most definitely was not all. But Morgan got it. Maybe better than most, she got it. In the months after the clouds had cleared and all that she hadn't been in her relationship became obvious, her friends and her family had hovered around her. Some days, their closeness felt like the warmest blanket on a chilly night, reassuring her that she wasn't alone. That she never had to be alone again. But some days it felt like she was sleeping in a sweatshirt, cozy when she fell asleep, then thick and sweaty and suffocating when she woke in the night.

She never quite knew which to expect, and it had put her on edge, driven her away from the people trying to care for her, made the loneliness settle into her bones in a way none of them could ever really understand.

"They love you." She said this matter-of-factly, like she believed it. Funny thing was, it was so easy to believe when it was someone else's pain, when she could look at Reece and the faceless men he cleared loved in return and see nothing short of family. Why couldn't that clarity come for her, too?

He smiled at her. God, she was *shot*, how could she possibly be thinking about sex at a time like this? But she was.

"What?" she asked, as his smile increased.

"Oh, nothing." They navigated down a root-laden path. The tread was precarious, made more so by the thick mud caked to the bottom of her shoes from the toxic river they had crossed, but it barely ranked as things she had to worry about for the day. "I'm just imagining Caleb's expression if you said that to him."

Morgan snorted, grabbing onto a small tree for balance and only belatedly realizing that it was a bad idea when a searing, shooting pain lanced her arm. She grimaced and Reece noticed.

"That's it. I'm taking you to the hospital."

"No." Her voice was firm. "That's the first place they'll look." There was no way that the closest rural hospital was big enough to get lost in. Hell, the handful of industrial parks and official buildings she'd seen while out on this trip had been surrounded by literal cow fields. She doubted they had so much as one security guard on staff. "And tell me about Caleb. Is he some weird macho cowboy type that can't tell his friends he loves them?"

"He can't tell anyone he loves them," Reece corrected. "Well, he couldn't. Skylar changed that, but he almost missed his chance." *Skylar. Pretty name.* Morgan wasn't a pretty name. Morgan was rough and tom-boyish and scraped knees. Not that Reece seemed much to mind.

"Are they…" Posing the question felt a little like pushing her tongue against the inside of her cheek after she bit it, like she was testing the waters and the waters might just hurt like a son of a bitch, if she wasn't careful. "You know…the lifestyle."

He looked at her pointedly. "For someone who just took down an armed guard *and got shot*, you seem to be losing your fearlessness."

She bumped his shoulder with her uninjured arm, intending to be playful, intending to make this whole thing a fun, ridiculous conversation between friends, talking about something they had seen in a movie or read in a book.

But she and Reece weren't friends, not if the burgeoning heat between them meant anything, not if the moment she touched him, playful as she had meant it, her body had gone red-hot with awareness and a type of desire she didn't fully understand but wanted to follow through to the ends of the earth.

And she wasn't the only one. Because in the next moment, Reece had her pressed up against a large tree, her uninjured arm pinned above her head, and his lips right at her ear, close enough for her to feel the whisper of his incoming beard against the soft skin of her lobe.

"I'm not afraid," she whispered. When had her voice gotten so breathy? "You don't scare me."

"Maybe you should be afraid," he replied, the words like soft caresses against the curve of her ear and the slope of her neck. He was so close to her, to her skin, to her throat, to her collarbones. He could lean down right now and—"Maybe you should be scared of me. Of what I want."

"Why?" She had never been one to let an adventure slip her past, terrifying as the edge of the cliff might seem beneath her feet. "What do you want?"

A dangerous question, to be sure of it. But she hadn't been lying. She wasn't afraid of him or what he might want. The thing that terrified her the most was that she might want it, too. That somewhere beneath the good girl who had played it straight—ha—who had been monogamous and far too vanilla for her otherwise adventurous lifestyle, was an entirely different version of herself.

It was a version, she was fairly certain, that was very much about to come out.

"Don't ask me that, Morgan," he said quietly. "Unless you're absolutely sure you want to know."

"I want to know." She tried to make it sound like a demand, but it somehow came out like a whimper, some version of begging she knew to be just the tip of the iceberg. "I…*need* to know."

He caught her gaze then, held it. And his eyes weren't the green of summer fields at all. They were the dark forests of the mountains in a storm, a dangerous riot that enticed her for all its shadows. For a moment, all she could do was look into those eyes, then she found herself, quite on instinct, lowing her gaze just a little. Her body was so sensitized, so aware of everything going on around her, that she could actually feel the flutter of her own eyelashes against her skin. It was nothing compared to the intense heat radiating from the man beside her.

"God, you're a natural." He didn't exactly sound as though he meant to say the words, but their rawness and honesty turned her body into a quivering nerve of need. She knew he was holding back, knew he was keeping the darker parts of himself from her, but she wasn't scared, not of this man and not of what he could offer her. Offer them both, if only he would let himself.

"I could take you right against this tree, couldn't I? Right here and right now. You'd let me do whatever I wanted. You'd let me take you to my club at The Ranch, would you? Because you've figured it, out what do we do there, and you want it."

It must have been the adrenaline pumping through her veins, her body's desperate need to distract her from the glancing blow of a bullet through the soft flesh of her upper arm. But as much as Morgan wanted to find some explanation for why Reece made her feel this way, for why she was so willing to give into him and everything he offered her — even before knowing that everything was — she knew the excuse fell short. From the very first night when they had been forced to share a tent by the rioting storm outside, the connection between them had been undeniable, the kind of heat that scored the skin and chemistry that blew roofs off buildings.

When it came to Reece, Morgan knew that she would submit. Every time.

"Yes." Her voice didn't quiver. It wasn't loud, but it was strong and firm and she felt his body tense beside her own the moment the meaning registered.

"Morgan…" *A warning.* One she had absolutely no intention of heeding.

"I would." *More honesty.* Today had been one hell of a gauntlet and she had promised herself that she would stop denying the most important parts of who she was. She deserved that much. "I don't know everything about the world you come from or what role you play in it," she said, though she was starting to get a very, very good idea, "but I've never been afraid of trying something new. Reece. I want to try."

He pulled back as if it took all his inner strength to do so and swore under his breath.

"You're hurt and we're still on the run," he said, more as if he were trying to convince himself. "I…lost myself for a moment there." Then he took off down the path, moving slowly enough for her to catch up but without looking back.

"And where exactly are we running to?" she asked. Morgan wasn't a small bit irritated. He had her on some kind of pedestal that meant every time they got close to what she wanted, to what he so clearly wanted, he pulled back, leaving her desperate and frustrated. But even with demons of her own, she wasn't going to break, and certainly not as the result of a little…colorful sex. He was hot and cold and even with her incredible stamina, she couldn't keep up with the way Reece's mind kept changing about them, about whatever he didn't want to tell her that he wanted.

"We're going home," he said finally, turning to look at her. The storm in his eyes was a full-blown tempest now, and she didn't miss the irony of that. "We're going to the Ranch."

Chapter Thirteen

Reece gripped the steering wheel on the old truck like it was the only thing tethering him to this astral plane. It had taken them well over two hours to get back to the ranger's cabin, then longer still to navigate through the mountains and toward the long-term parking where he had left the truck, but the time had flown by, each hour like a drop of water slipping through cupped fingers. Because there was only one way to go from here, and it was the path he had been avoiding.

Morgan didn't need anything spelled out. She didn't know the specifics, but she did know that going home for him wasn't easy and it wasn't simple, especially this time of year, during the anniversary. Somehow, through his haze of nerves and regret and worry and all the other damning emotions that were roiling around in his gut and his head, he'd caught on to her strange mood, as well. It was a mood he was entirely certain was related to the way he had left her, panting and wanting and ready to submit to his every whim against the rough bark of a tree.

But when she had looked at him the way she had, from under those thick, coal lashes, with the bright curiosity in her eyes undeniable, and told him that she wasn't afraid, every ounce of blood in Reece's body had gone straight from his brain to his cock. In that moment, all he had wanted to do was strip her down and bring her to pleasure so many times that her body turned to putty in his hands, that he could map the intimate curves and valleys of her form with his eyes shut. He had burned for in a way that had everything — and nothing — to do with sex, and that scared him. Almost worse than going back to the Sinclair Ranch.

"Home sweet home," he said, his tone just a touch bitter. That annoyed him. The Sinclair Ranch *was* home, more than DC or his father's place had ever been. It was the closest he'd ever had to a place where he could really hang his hat, and it was tainted by this fear of opening up to the people who cared about him.

"It's huge," Morgan said, leaning up in her seat and peering out at the land all around them. In the distance, the mountains rose, bright and slate purple, carved by moving glaciers with the powerful stance to prove it. "Montana is… *Wow*."

Despite all the other bullshit absolutely kicking up inside his head, Reece couldn't help but like that she was still amazed by things. They'd talked about their previous trips, about travels and adventure spots and what they'd loved most and where they would return if they ever got the chance. She'd been to some of the most beautiful places in the world, eaten at Michelin-star restaurants, caught sight of rare natural phenomena. And still, she was awed by the sight of a Montana sunset.

"I can't quite stay away," he admitted. "Especially this time of year." Because this place was everything New York wasn't. Quiet. Safe. Open. There was plenty of room for him to run without catching the reflection of himself in a high-rise window. Seeing the sky could set a man free.

"It hasn't been that long," Morgan replied. "Some hurts, they take a while to grow new skin. And something that skin pulls a little too tight and scars pink and silver, but it still protects the important stuff inside. And it means you've got a story to tell."

She didn't wait for him reply, simply turned back to hang her head out of the open truck window. The air was rich with summer wildflowers and tall grasses, and Reece wondered how she not only knew the right things to say, but the best moments to look away.

It had felt so fast, getting to this point, but now the drive into the ranch seemed to drag on forever, as if he needed to pay homage to every shrub and brush that he caught sight of along the entry.

"What's that big wood building?" Morgan asked, as they got closer. From here, he could just catch sight of the club from over the hill, but the front lodge loomed bright and large before them.

"Lodging," he said. "The Sinclair Ranch makes a lot of money from western weekend packages, horseback riding and roping and farming, the works."

"And you rent those little cabins out too?" she asked, indicating the small private cottages that dappled the land.

"Most," he said. "Some are for us. Caleb lived in one until he met Skylar. Van still lives in his full-time. Dante has a place in town, but like the rest of us, he crashes here a lot."

"I think if I lived in a place like this, I'd never leave," she said, a tone of wistfulness to her voice. Or maybe it was just exhaustion. Not only had their day been physically brutal — and bloody — but it had been one hell of an emotional rollercoaster, as well. "Sorry, I didn't mean to…"

"It's okay," he said. And it was, when she said it. Somehow.

"People would say the same about California," she said. "But they're usually just looking at the surface."

After all they had been through that day, that week, in the last four fucking years of his life that had tethered Reece to some shell of his former self, he found it impossible that he could be surprised, that he could let in any more complex or tangled emotions. But here he was, feeling an indescribable sense of rage that Morgan had ever felt anything close to what he had experienced in his wreck of a past. Their hurts were different colors, that much was certain, but they existed nonetheless, shades of life that had made it difficult to return to the place they had once called home, made it impossible to capture the parts of themselves on the other sides of those veils.

"And that's that building?" Morgan pointed off to the far distance horizon, where only the very tip of the Barn was visible from beyond the other outlying buildings. "Is that for the horses?"

"We do have horses on the Ranch," Reece said, "and this area gets a ton of wildlife, but no, that's not for the horses."

She looked at him and then back out of the window for a moment, and he heard that tiny hum she always made when she seemed to be thinking.

"That's it, isn't it?" Morgan asked. She said up in the seat, and despite everything that Reece knew was coming, her smile was utterly contagious. "That's the..." She faltered on the word.

"Sex club?" he offered. "Or you can just call it a club. We do promise discretion at The Ranch." He couldn't help the teasing note in his voice, especially as it came with relief, a chance to step away from his maddening thoughts and get some fresh air. Because everything about this woman seemed to be a breath of fresh air, a new adventure, a higher peak to climb.

Well, she also happened to be one of the most beautiful women he had ever met in his goddamned life, and as much as he enjoyed the lightheartedness of the car at this exact moment, the idea of taking Morgan up to the barn, of introducing her to his way of life, made his blood stir and his mind go absolutely blank of everything but the idea of how she might feel below him, atop him. He wanted to surround himself with Morgan and make her lose her mind at his touch.

And he had taken it way, way too far in the mountains earlier that day. She was injured from the fight, though she didn't seem too bothered by the pain and she was new, vulnerable, an adventurer who never turned down a dare. And he'd launched about a million her way.

"Club." She repeated the word, almost under her breath, as if she was trying it out for herself to see how she liked it. "I know you have a lot to figure out when we get inside," she said, "And we're probably in some danger from everything that happened at the compound, but maybe later..." She paused. Interesting that, his little adventurer, scared to ask him a simple question. Not his adventurer. Not a simple question.

"Could you show me around? I just—I just wanted to know."

The words were said in genuine, pure honesty about a world she had only peeped at through the keyhole, but they ran parallel to the word she had breathed to him on the mountaintop, about how she did want to know, how she wanted to know everything. And *God*, he wanted to show her.

Thankfully, Reece pulled the truck up to the front of the lodge and parked at that exact moment. Out of the frying pan and into the fire.

"We'll see," he said. As if showing Morgan that it wasn't the club he wanted more than anything else in the world.

"Caleb, Van, Dante," Reece introduced them in turn and placed her bags on the floor of the lodge main entrance. Caleb, the cowboy. He wore his Stetson as if he had been born with it tilted *just so* on his head. She'd spent plenty of time in the great outdoors, and Morgan knew all too well how to separate out the real cowboys. This guy was what all those western stars would wish they were.

Van, by contrast, was definitely military. His hair was long, not cut close, as was regulation, but he held himself with a kind of reserved stiffness that was impossible to miss, like his core was engaged at all times and it took everything in him not to fold his hands behind his back and wait for command. The dark shadows around his eyes told Morgan that Reece wasn't the only man at the Sinclair Ranch with a history he kept close to his chest.

Dante, thank goodness, broke up some of the intensity they had encountered when they'd first walked through the front doors of the main lodge. He was pretty. As if a man who easily cleared six feet and had tattoos covering both of his arms and peeking out of the collar at his neck could possibly be called pretty. But goodness, he was.

With flowing dark hair that curled just above his shoulders, a black studded cowboy hat, and a toothpick hanging from his lush lower lip, he somehow gave off vintage vampire vibes in the coolest way. And she couldn't have been more grateful for the appreciative wink he sent her way the moment she caught those beautiful eyes. Because everything felt very, very serious right now and Morgan was very much starting to feel the intensity of the day catching up with her.

"First," Reece said, "Morgan's been shot. We can't risk a hospital right now, but, Van, can you take a look?" *Van. Military, likely medic training.* Certainly, there had to be some pain killers on this vast estate that could help her manage the intense and radiating fire that scorched the muscles in her arm when she forgot about the red-hot graze and moved *just so.* Van just nodded. Morgan got the impression he didn't speak more than he needed to.

Caleb chewed his lip. "Skylar and Rhylee are in the kitchen," he said. "They deserve to be part of this conversation too."

Because undoubtedly, she and Reece were bringing danger to their door. Because whatever was happening at the compound in the mountains was so much bigger than what they had seen for themselves that morning. Caleb slipped out from behind the front desk and, God, he was a big man. Reece was an athlete, capable of scaling mountains and performing incredible feats of personal strength, but she didn't blame him for not wanting to face off against Caleb, who was now turning a sign on the front door.

"We're finished with today's check-ins," he explained. "Come on." He made for the back of the lodge's sprawling entrance and through a door marked *Employees Only* with Van and Dante close behind. Reece stepped back.

"Are you okay?" he asked. "It's been a really long day. We don't need to hash this out now."

"I'd rather get it over with," she admitted. "Then I'd like to shower and sleep for like a decade." *Then I'd like to see what you're hiding in your club, like you to finally follow through on everything you've been teasing me with for the last week.*

But Reece's tan forehead was already furrowed with concern, and she certainly didn't need to add her frustrating desires to the list of things he had on his mind. There was a time and a place for getting what she wanted, and judging by how he'd gone tight as a string when she'd asked him to show her around, the seduction wouldn't be all that challenging.

There was a chair waiting for her when they finally stepped through the door and into the kitchen and, at Caleb's insistence, she sat, grateful as hell for it. She hadn't exactly lost a lot of blood, but it had still been a hell of an exertive day. And they still had so much ahead of them.

"This should help." This from an absolutely stunning woman to Morgan's left, who handed her a bowl of hot chili and a bottle of Gatorade. "I can't imagine you've had much time to eat in the last few hours."

In the car, she'd found a few squished protein bars at the bottom of her pack that had sustained them on the short drive to the Sinclair Ranch, but the fatigue and the exhaustion were partially from dehydration and hunger, she was certain.

"Reece, eat." This had to be Skylar. She was as Reece had described, tall and beautiful, with a sort of ephemeral air about her, like she was a little too pretty to be taking up space in an industrial kitchen, surrounded by a collection of large men.

She turned to Morgan, who was trying to pace herself from chugging the Gatorade down too quickly and getting sick. Hell of a first introduction to these people.

"Hi," she said, her smile so genuine and kind that Morgan felt a little like a small child in her presence, and she found she didn't even really mind. "I'm Skylar. Rhylee's helping Van with the emergency kit, but she'll be back in a moment."

"I'm sure that's all she's helping him with," Dante muttered under his breath, but the spark in Skylar's eyes meant she absolutely heard. Hadn't Reece said something about... Not that it mattered. She'd have time to get it all straight later.

"Morgan," she said. "Thank you for this." She indicated the chili. "I haven't had a hot meal beyond spaghetti in like a week."

Skylar smiled. "So you're like our Reece, then? Always headed for the horizon."

Morgan was a few bites in and already starting to feel like herself when the back door to the kitchen opened and Van and the woman who had to be Rhylee stepped through the door. He had his medic's kit in one hand, but was raking the other hand through his hair as he looked over at Rhylee, frustration obvious on his face.

Rhylee was small, almost petite, but her expressions were a mirror to her brother, the bright eyes, the golden-brown hair that fell in a long ponytail down her back. It swished when she moved, as if she was just as annoyed by whatever Van was saying to her as he was by what she was saying to him.

"Whatever it is," Caleb said, as the two of them walked through the back door, "save it for later. We have more serious things that we need to deal with right now."

Rhylee glared at Van over the top of the backpack that she carried, and he rolled his eyes in response, but they walked through the kitchen and toward the table where Morgan and Reece were eating blissfully fresh food.

"Rhylee."

Rhylee stuck out her hand and her ponytail bobbed with the movement once more. Morgan recognized a little something of herself in this woman because, even at a glance, it was clear that Rhylee Cash had a little of the wanderlust in her blood, too, and that was a feeling Morgan understood all too well.

"Let's take a look at that arm of yours, shall we?"

Morgan gently rolled up her sleeve, the movement of her bicep sending those icy-hot shards of pain rioting up her body, and Rhylee noticed in an instant.

"I'm going to move your hair out of the way and pin it up," she said. "If at any point, I make you feel uncomfortable, you just tell me."

Morgan smiled. The kindness was so welcome, after this incredibly, incredibly long day. And the fact that she was at a *sex club* of all places, and she had to consent to have her hair touched, well everything was starting to feel a little funny. Or maybe that was just her head playing tricks on her, she wasn't sure. Hell, she hadn't even realized that her hair had come free of the braid, but she had been focused on staying alive, so she couldn't really fault herself for that.

"That's fine," she said. "Are you a doctor?"

"Hydrogeologist," Rhylee said.

Morgan almost spat out her Gatorade. "What?"

"I work at the lab in town," Rhylee explained, gently pulling Morgan's hair off her sweaty skin and untangling it the best she could with her fingers. The pinch was nothing compared to the pain in her arm from the position. "But I'm also a volunteer EMT down at the fire department, so you have nothing to worry about."

"But the rest of us do," Van muttered, settling into a chair beside them. "It's too dangerous."

"And it's not your decision," Rhylee said. "Donavan's a medic. He's going to look you over. We just don't want you to feel overwhelmed. This group can be—" She looked them over. "A lot."

Morgan could swear she heard Van growl, but then Caleb stepped in.

"Morgan, are you okay to talk?" he asked. His voice was gruff, but kind, and she could kind of appreciate his frustration. She nodded.

"Good," he said. "Then you two need to talk. What the fuck is going on?"

Reece took a deep breath and adjusted the ice pack he currently held on his knuckles.

"Morgan and I met over in the Blackleaf Canyon," he began.

He gave them the run-down of everything that had happened since the call had first come in from his source, how Reece had been communicating with his office back in DC and how they'd learned that the compound was doing a lot more than it seemed. He explained the events of the day that had led to them getting shot out and, in Reece's words, "kicking the shit out of some busted up guns for hire."

Caleb had gone an interesting shade of red to find out that Gabriel had been helping them on this particular mission, if it could be called such, and she figured he would probably be making a very specific phone call as soon as this conversation was over.

Morgan filled in the gaps where she could, but it was difficult to concentrate when Van started inspecting her wound for signs of internal damage. He finally declared her free and clear and started to stitch up the wound, at which point Morgan finally caved and asked for something stronger than an Advil.

"What now?" Caleb asked. "Are these people coming after you guys?" She must have been really, really woozy to like the idea of *you guys* including her and Reece. Rhylee had finally given up the good meds and it was only a matter of time before Morgan was out of the conversation for good.

"I have no idea," Reece said honestly. "We needed to get somewhere safe, get Morgan patched up. But I don't know. We needed help. I...I needed help."

The edges of Morgan's vision started to go a little gray, but she heard one last thing before she felt into the sweet, painless sleep of the drugs, Caleb's voice floating over the kitchen.

"You have help here, Reece. You're not alone."

Chapter Fourteen

Reece hadn't wanted to put her down. Not only did he have a hell of a conversation he'd eventually need to have with his brothers, but Morgan felt like the most wonderful weight in his arms. She was soft, pliant as he shifted her, and she still smelled sweet, even though they'd been shot at, drenched in sweat after running down a mountain peak, and spent the last several days camping in general roughness in the great outdoors. She had an inherent sweetness, floral and lovely, and he knew he could get a little too used to the scent of her, to the feel of Morgan in his arms.

Of course, it would be ideal if she was in his arms because she wanted to be there, not because she had passed out from strong medication after getting shot.

He was starting to feel a little shot himself, and it had nothing to do with the pain in his knuckles or the growing bruises where he'd taken a few hits to the stomach and the hips. The conversation, sharing everything that had gotten them to this point, had felt more like an interrogation, and Reece absolutely hadn't wanted to go over those harrowing events again, even as he knew that the others deserved to know if he had brought danger right to their door.

Even Van and Rhylee's bickering, which he normally found incredibly amusing, had grated on his, a little too loud and a little too rough at the edges, and it felt like he might have had the beginnings of a migraine, until Morgan had slumped forward in her chair, caught only at the last minute by Van, and Reece had finally called it a day.

But he couldn't hold her in his arms forever, especially since there was nothing Morgan needed more than a good night's sleep, so he finally settled her down on the bed in the small cabin he called home when he was back on the Sinclair Ranch. The space wasn't much. The most it had to delineate it as his was a handful of *One Leap Magazine* issues and some photography equipment, but seeing her there in his room, in his bed, her curls escaping the half braid Rhylee had attempted, her pose soft and languid, peaceful…it stirred something positively virile in Reece.

He meant to lay her down on the bed, to place her into his space and walk away. But Morgan clung to him, wrapping her arms around his neck in her drug-addled stupor, and Reece let himself be pulled down to the wide-open canvas of the bed. He was beyond exhausted, terrified of the day's events and everything to come. He could only imagine how she felt. Of course she would want a friend by her side, someone to comfort her. Right. This was comfort. And Morgan Tempest was just a friend.

The last thought Reece had, as his head hit the pillow and he followed Morgan into sleep, was that he didn't want to be *friends* with Morgan at all.

Morgan was having a wonderful dream. It was warm, and it wrapped around her like a cloud, keeping her safe, keeping her anchored, but still allowing her to fly free, to be the version of herself she was always meant to be. A port in a storm, not a shackle, a quiet place to call home. She snuggled into the warm feeling, and it felt as though she were dipping her toes into the sun-warmed sand of a far-off beach, the water nearly as warm as the air, the sun not too hot, gently caressing in the sky.

She never wanted to lose this feeling.

But then she heard slow, murmuring words, so quiet at first, she though them to be the call of those distant waves touching the shore. But no, they were words. Not words. Her name, whispered against the curve of her ear in a delightful burst of warm air that turned her skin to fire. This was hotter than any sun, and it warmed her in an entirely new way, from the inside out, intense and wild and terrifying.

"Morgan…princess…please stop moving…"

She knew that voice, was coming to know the morning-roughened tone all too well, knew the scent that washed over her as she drifted away from that far-off beach and found purchase this side of sleep. *Reece Prescott.* Fresh mountain air, hot coffee, adventure, wildness. And he was whispering in her ear because…

Because they were entirely tangled together, legs wrapped around one another, his arm tucked under her, the other below her head. His chest was solid and warm against her back, even through the fabric of her tank top, and she felt consumed and overwhelmed, and entirely welcoming to his touch, everywhere. And it was everywhere because...

She shifted and he let out a long, low growl that went straight to her own hot spots, and her nipples tightened in an instant, her pussy pulsed and her skin turned sensitive.

"Morgan." If he wanted her to stop moving, maybe he shouldn't use that tone, the one that made her want to buck all his commands, only to see what he would do about it.

If he wanted her to stop, maybe he should stop. Because she knew how the body worked, knew how *his* body worked, knew how every tendon and lean muscle stretched and strained when a man was trying so very hard to hold himself still and wasn't quite succeeding. All at once, Morgan's mind was flooded with images, of yoga on the beach, on the peak of a mountain top, only it wasn't yoga, not exactly. It was them, supporting each other, connecting, wrapping around and....and...

Reece gripped her hip and the tightness of his fingers on her skin had the exact opposite effect of what she knew he wanted. Because even though he kept walking away, even though he seemed so fucking terrified to give in to this obvious heat between them, she wanted a look into his world more and more with every glimpse she got. She like the touch of pain, liked the way his fingers felt digging into the soft, sensitive flesh at her hip, and she wanted more, wanted him to push harder, to mark her skin as proof that he had been there. As if she wasn't already indelibly marked by him.

She knew she was playing with fire, knew that once she took the plunge, there was no going back. Of course, Reece would stop the moment she asked. But Morgan was, without a shadow of a doubt, going to be a changed woman.

"Make me."

She didn't see him move, barely felt it, the motion so fluid and so quick, a natural instinct built from the inside out. Then she was on her back, her uninjured arm pinned over her head, and the weight of Reece's body hovering just above her, as if he knew exactly how much she wanted to feel him against her skin, and he wasn't quite ready to give it to her.

"Do you know what you do to me?" he asked.

He was still in the same clothes they had arrived in, and Morgan could only surmise that he'd carried her down to this cabin after she'd taken the pain medication and fallen asleep himself. Part of her wished she could shower, get the sweat and grime off her body before they touched for the very first time, but it was too late for the bedsheets, and honestly, she didn't give a fuck. Her body was on absolute fire for this man, and a little bit of dirt wasn't going to be the thing that stopped her when she was this close to having him.

"Tell me," she teased, because she couldn't get enough of the glow in his eyes when she pushed him, because it was a little like an adrenaline rush, seeing just how far she could get away with pushing this wild man before he cracked. She bucked her hips for good measure, and Reece brough his free hand down to her hip this time.

Only this time, he didn't apply any pressure at all. He merely stroked the contour of her hip bone through the fabric of her hiking pants, the gentlest, softest touch she could have possibly felt, and she let out a soft, desperate mewl that made his eyes spark with that golden green of sunshine on the sea.

"Tell you that I can't stop thinking about touching you?" he demanded, more than asked. "Tell you that I've been fantasizing about making you come on my tongue since that very first night we shared a tent? Tell you that once I get you into my bed, Morgan, I'm never going to let you out, that I want to push you so hard and so high you forget everything but the taste of my name on your lips and the way I make you come?"

He leaned down, somehow hovering just over her body, so she felt consumed by him but left empty all at once. She wanted to feel his full weight, the weight of everything he had to offer pressing against her, and he knew it. *Fucking tease.* But then he was whispering in her ear, and the scrape of his beard against her skin had her bucking up, her heart skittering, her nipples tightening to painful points and her pussy throbbing in anticipation of so, so, so much more.

"I'm not going to go easy on you, pet," he said.

That word. That fucking word. It practically made her lose her goddamned mind right here and now. "I'm going to hold you right at the edge until you're sure you can't take another second of pleasure."

She whimpered.

"Then I'm going to leave you, tied up and begging and waiting and desperate."

His hot breath ticked the curve of her throat and she squirmed. He shifted, so their bodies still didn't touch, not nearly the way she wanted them to.

"And you're going to like it. You're going to like waiting, waiting to see how long I'll hold you at your edge, tied up and exposed, where anyone could come and find you."

He licked the outside shell of her ear and Morgan shuddered. Wet heat flooded her pussy and she realized she was whimpering.

"You like to being held at the edge, don't you?" he asked, trailing one strong finger down the slope of her neck.

She nodded. She couldn't help it. He had this uncanny way of pulling the truth from her. Even as she wanted to goad him, she found she wanted to do as he asked, wanted to answer to his call as if she were the tides on the shore and he was the moon. Only Reece was the sun, blazing hot and melting her with barely the touch of his finger to her skin.

"Say it." His words were quiet. But he knew they would be enough.

"I like…" Oh God, how had they gotten to this point, where she was here, admitting to things she'd never even admitted to herself. "I like…"

"Morgan." He tilted her chin up and held her eye. "Tell me." And she wanted to. She wanted him to know exactly what it was that stirred her body to life and made her pussy wet and her nipples tight and —

There was a knock at the door and Morgan was fairly sure that the combined weight of their glares would set the damn thing ablaze. Reece went to move off her, but she locked her legs around him and held his gaze, their foreheads almost touching. Not that it was enough. Almost would never be enough with this man.

"I want this," she said. "All of it. Everything you have to offer. Don't run from this, Reece. Promise me. Please."

He stared into her eyes, and God, when was the last time she felt so *seen*? She wanted to dive in right here and now, her body still thrumming and so fucking aware of him atop her, but the knock came again.

"Just a minute," Reece called, and Morgan took perverse satisfaction in the tightness of his voice, that he was as ready to burst as she.

"Are you sure?" he asked.

"I've never been more sure of anything in my life." And damn if that wasn't the truth.

"Then I promise," he said. "Tonight. All of it. I'll show you everything you want to know."

The door opened just as Reece climbed off her and out of bed. Was it normal to want someone this badly? Even though her body still ached and shards of pain laced her arm when she wasn't paying attention? Even though she was covered in the muck and grime of a week in the wilderness, and they were distracted and overwhelmed by whatever they had stumbled upon up in the mountains? Was it normal to still want to walk over to the door and shut it in the face of whoever had pulled Reece away from her?

"I wanted to check in on Morgan this morning." Rhylee was standing there, looking pretty as a picture in the morning sunshine, and Morgan couldn't be that upset, not when she'd shown such kindness the night before. "And Gabriel is up at the lodge." There was a strange note to her voice, like this wasn't usual circumstances, and Morgan had to wonder…

"That can't be good." And worry confirmed. Reece had told her enough about the men that he ran The Ranch with that she knew who she could expect to see, and Gabriel hadn't been on the list. He was some wealthy hedge funder, real estate mogul, world traveler businessman type, and he rarely got away from work for long enough to stop back in Duchess. That he had arrived twelve hours after they did couldn't be an auspicious sign.

"No." Rhylee bit her lip as if in thought. "Anyway, let Morgan know I'm here to help, if she needs anything."

"Actually, I need something," Reece said, stepping back into the room to allow Rhylee to follow him. Rhylee caught sight of her and smiled.

"How's the arm?" she asked. "Any signs of infection or bleeding?"

Morgan glanced down. In the heat of moment with Reece, she'd completely forgotten to even look at her arm, and had barely realized it was hurting at all. But a quick glance showed that the white gauze Rhylee had wrapped it in the night before was still pristine, except for the dirt Morgan was still wearing, and she didn't feel feverish.

"I think we're okay," she said, aware that her voice was tired and not nearly as grateful as she felt. "Thank you. Really. I... This has been a lot."

Rhylee smiled back. "Don't I know it? But I'm here if you need help washing your hair or anything. Just let me know."

Reece came back in from the bathroom where he had disappeared, the small jar of river runoff in his hand.

"This is what we got at the compound," he said. "Whatever's in this water, I think it warranted them shooting at us. Can you test it?"

Rhylee nodded. "No problem. I'm headed back to the lab this afternoon." They were going to find out what was so secret that the compound in the mountains had to be protected by armed guards who were willing to shoot at trespassers, and Morgan had the sense that none of them would like it.

Reece looked back over at Morgan, and the heat was still there in his eyes, as if he wanted nothing more than to take her back to bed. Bad guys with guns, dirt and grime, some possible conspiracy, none of it as important as having her. Morgan couldn't blame him. She wanted him just the same.

Though now that she was up, and the haze of lust surrounding their early morning flirtation was gone, she also really wanted a shower.

"I should go see what Gabriel has to say," Reece said, his voice apologetic and tinged at the edge with something flint-rough, as if he was trying to will himself away from everything they could have had, too. "Do you want to come?"

"I'd really like to wash up," Morgan admitted. "And maybe change the sheets. There's a lot of dirt." All three of them glanced to the rumpled sheets on the bed and Rhylee let out a delicate cough. Morgan laughed.

"Whatever you gave me last night knocked me out. Sleep took precedence over shower." If Rhylee didn't look convinced, Morgan couldn't exactly blame her. There was a large, comfortable-looking couch sitting right there, and it was clear that both sides of the bed had been slept in.

"I can come by in a few and show you up to the lodge," Rhylee offered. "Unless you could use a hand with the bandages."

In the end, Reece splashed his face with cold water and Rhylee stuck around. Morgan couldn't have been more grateful for it, since she was stuck in a sweaty, dirty sports bra which would have been difficult to get out of even without a fresh bullet wound in her shoulder.

"Must be kind of amazing, living here," Morgan said, as Rhylee helped her out of the tank top that felt absolutely glued to her skin. "I mean, I've been a lot of places, but this…"

It was possible that the sense of euphoria and freedom she had come to associate with Montana had a lot less to do with the natural beauty and a lot more to do with the man who had been her tour guide, but she and Rhylee had only just met, and though Morgan already felt incredibly close to the other woman, there were some things she wanted to work out for herself first.

"I left for a bit," Rhylee admitted, turning slightly to give Morgan the privacy she needed to maneuver as much out of the bra as was possible in her current circumstance. "For school. Then I came back. Guess I just couldn't stay away."

"That seems to be a theme." She hadn't really meant to say the words aloud, but Rhylee didn't seem all that surprised.

"This place has a way of bringing you back," she agreed. "Caleb left. He was going to the majors for baseball. Van joined the army. Reece, well, Reece has always been destined to travel the world."

"Me too." Morgan was quiet for a moment. "You know, we saw each in Turkey. Three years ago. I never thought I would see him again, and certainly not in the middle of a storm on a mountain top in Montana."

"You saw him." Rhylee stopped what she was doing with the first-aid kit. "That feels kind of like fate."

Morgan looked down and it was her turn to fidget, rolling over the shirt in her hand until puffs of dried dirt burst out into the air.

"It does, doesn't it?" She smiled. "I know a lot of people don't believe in that stuff, but I love my astrology. I can't help but think that there's something, some net or thread pulling us all in different directions. Butterflies flapping their wings and all that."

Rhylee smiled. "The scientist in me is absolutely opposed to astrology, but I'm Sagittarius through and through." She caught Morgan's eye in the mirror.

"Did you talk to him? In Turkey? Did he tell you anything about...?" She paused, as if realizing she might have been overstepping.

"Not then," Morgan said. "But he told me about New York one of our first nights together. A little." It had been more than a little, but she had felt to the bottom of her hiking boots that Reece had told her more than he'd told anyone else about what he had been through in the years since the explosion. "And no, we didn't talk in Turkey. We just caught eyes in a crowd. Very Old Hollywood style."

Rhylee grinned. "I think the universe might be trying to send you a message."

If Morgan had listened to that message three years ago, if she had left Aaron waiting for her and walked toward the handsome, blond-haired man in the bazaar, she would have saved herself a world of hurt and heartache.

Walking away from Reece wasn't a mistake she had any intention of making twice.

Chapter Fifteen

Gabriel North didn't have a hair out of place. Reece had been all over the world, London and Monaco and Istanbul, and not once had he arrived to any of his destinations looking as polished and clean and put together as Gabriel did now. And according to Caleb, who had caught up with him at the far fence, Gabe had come in on a helicopter after midnight, which was not a form of travel known for keeping one fresh.

Suddenly, Reece was very, very aware of how long it had been since he'd showered or even changed his clothes. Not that Gabriel would mind. Wealth had made him many things, but with his upbringing, he would never be a snob.

"I can't say I'm glad to see you," he said, stepping into the kitchen and shaking Gabriel's hand. At least Reece's hands were clean. Sort of. "You don't typically make house calls for pleasure."

"And you don't typically come home this time of the year," Gabriel pointed out. "So, I guess you could say we're both in unfamiliar territory."

Reece could appreciate that. Sometimes the others tried to step around the anniversary, to give him space or pester him into talking with euphemisms and innuendos. But Gabriel didn't have time in his schedule of — oh — running the world's economy to bother with niceties.

"You're in trouble," he said, to double down on his point. "Word of what happened up in the mountains is already causing chatter on some of my channels. And I can't imagine that's a place where you want to be."

"We should wait for Morgan," Reece said, settling down at the table and accepting a cup of coffee from Caleb, who poured himself one and sat beside them. "She's as much part of this now as I am."

"How's her injury?" Gabriel asked and Reece had to wonder if the guy was fucking psychic. Or, more likely, his friends were as bad as a bunch of clucking, gossiping housewives.

"Seemed better this morning," he said. "Rhylee is helping her redress the bandages and take a shower."

"I would have thought that would be more up your alley," Dante said, walking through the back door with a muffin the size of a softball in his hand. And his mouth. "Unless our dear little Rhylee has decided to sample softer pastures."

"Don't," Van growled, the first words he'd said since Reece had walked through the door. *Well. Word.*

"Morgan and I are..." *Taking things slow. Complicated. Desperate for each other. Struggling like hell to keep our hands to ourselves.*

"So, you want to." Dante pointed out. And pointed with the muffin. "But you're holding back out of some misplaced sense of honor and righteousness, correct?"

Reece let out a low sound that wasn't quite not a growl either.

"We have nothing else to discuss until she gets here," Gabriel pointed out. "Not like you to be hesitant."

It wasn't. Reece had always been a man that dove into adventure with both feet. Even after the explosion, he'd still craved new curiosities and histories and cultures the way he craved his next breath. But Morgan. Morgan felt like something special and the idea of scaring her away—

"I like this one," he admitted. Because of all the things he could admit to his friends, about the anniversary of the explosion, about the survivor's guilt and the claustrophobia and the nightmares, talking about Morgan felt like the easiest thing in the world. And it wasn't only by comparison. "She's kind of amazing."

"And you're terrified you're going to scare her off because you own a little bit of leather," Gabriel inferred. Actually, it was Gabriel who owned more than a little bit of leather, but the point could be made with any of the tools in Reece's personal box. "Isn't she some adrenaline junkie too? Like swimming with sharks and jumping out of planes and all that?"

"Yup."

The silence in the room was enough to put all of Reece's concerns on full display, and they didn't look nearly as terrifying in the morning light. And he had promised her that he wouldn't run. Not tonight. Not this time. He had every intention of showing her all the things he had been dreaming of for days and he had quite the active imagination. He was saved from having to answer by the opening of the back door and the arrival of the very person they had been discussing.

She looked fresh and clean and absolutely beautiful in a pair of light pink leggings with a matching pink bra peeking out from a fresh white tank top. Her hair was still damp, and piled on top of her head in a messy bun, with a few loose tendrils falling free, and he wanted to chase with his tongue the lone drop of water that spilled down her neck. The only thing that brought him back to the present situation was the sight of the white bandage wrapped around her upper arm. They were in trouble. If Gabriel was here, they had work to do.

"You must be Gabriel." She was confident in her stride as she walked into the kitchen like she hadn't just been introduced to the space yesterday and stuck out her hand for him to shake. "Nice to finally meet you in person."

"And you."

Reece was going to kill him. Before he got another word out, before he so much as looked at Morgan, he was absolutely going to murder one of his oldest friends in cold blood. Except that would do nothing more than prove exactly what Gabriel was trying to prove, which was that Reece wanted Morgan and it was time he did something about it.

Morgan, for her part, only looked the tiniest bit flustered at the lingering caress of Gabriel's fingers on her own, or the extra touch of eye contact that lasted a breath too long to be misread. But Reece wanted to be the one to make her cheeks turn that very special shade of pink, and he didn't want to stop with the cheeks on her face.

"Gabe!" Rhylee darted across the kitchen and half jumped into Gabriel's open arms after he released Morgan's hand. Gabriel wrapped her in a bear hug, all pretense forgotten, just two old friends catching up. "I know there's shit hitting the fan right now, but it's so good to see you."

Gabriel kissed Rhylee's hair, no more or less than the way Caleb might have, but there was no denying the glint in Van's eyes from across the room. God, this place felt more like a high school locker room every time he came back. And speaking of coming back.

"I'm sure you're busy," he said to Gabriel, "so fill us in on what brought you out this way." While he spoke, Reece stood and filled a cup of coffee, which he handed to Morgan, along with one of the enormous chocolate chip muffins Rhylee had left in a basket on the counter earlier that morning.

She accepted them without a word, as if their morning routine had become so predictable that they didn't need to speak or communicate in any way, and he liked very much the idea of having a morning routine with her.

"Remember how I told you the factory is just a shell company?" Gabe asked. "Well, they're a pharma company, that much is real. But they're not producing the drug they say they are. Hepacelium or something like that. At least, not exclusively."

"It's a cover." Morgan stated it as fact and Gabriel nodded.

"And a big one," he replied. "This goes up to the state level. So far. Reece, you said that your source didn't have any luck when he went to the local sheriff." Reece nodded, and Gabriel continued. "There's a reason for that. Sheriff Messing is on the take, and he's just one of many."

"How high?" Reece asked. "And how much trouble are we actually in?" Because if he brought Morgan into the line of fire—well, again—or if he dragged danger and trouble back to the Sinclair Ranch, he would never forgive himself if something bad happened to one of the people he considered family. Which was quickly starting to include her.

"Congress." Oh. That was bad. Because out here, even the politicians still practiced a type of wild west justice that meant a lot of backdoor deals and loaded negotiations, and Reece couldn't help but wonder just how much more was hidden, if a mountain compound employed armed guards.

"Malvern."

It had to be. The only thing bigger than Dick Malvern's mustache was his ego. He was a ninth or tenth generation rancher, and he believed in God, Guns, and Country with a vehemence that would have rivaled the Almighty's himself. Reece had no issue with that, save that Malvern had shown his true colors more than once when running the state, destroying natural land protections to make way for new business, running shady practices to enhance his own wealth and generally bulldozing through any laws that might actually help Montana, until they were barely recognizable versions of their former selves.

Reece had lived in DC for years and had worked as a reporter for longer, and the day that business took over was the day that the little guy lost, every single time.

"Looks that way." Gabriel's voice was very, very serious. "I know the man seems like some old western fool, but he's more powerful than you know. The money he's got stashed away is formidable, and with those kinds of resources and no scruples, you could do a lot of damage. As you've already seen. He's going to come after you, Reece." He looked across the table. "And you too, Morgan. You guys have to protect yourselves."

"Morgan did break a guy's nose," Reece said, his tone off-hand because he had dragged her into this, had brought this danger right to her doorstep, and he had just let her come along.

Gabriel smiled, but a touch of worry shone through, and it was that worry that made Reece's gut clench.

"Nothing is going to happen to you guys here," Caleb said. "They don't even know who you are and it's not like they can just show up on the property." But from what Gabriel had told him, from what Reece had seen for himself in the mountains, from everything he had learned about the way the world worked, they weren't going to be safe anywhere until Dick Malvern was brought to justice.

Chapter Sixteen

Reece was quiet as they walked down the mountain path and back toward his small cabin on the far side of the lodge, and Morgan didn't know how to break the tension in the air between them. Because there was tension in the air, and it had everything to do with the fact that he blamed himself for putting her into danger. Finally, as they neared the door to the cabin, she just came out and said it.

"It was my choice to come with you." She stopped before him on the path, so he had to look her in the eye. Or, at very least, the shoulder. "I practically forced you to let me tag along this grand adventure. There was no possible way you could have known that some greedy congressman was scheming to make money by any means necessary or that we might end up in actual danger."

He caught her eye and she knew that her words weren't getting through.

"How many times have you been shot, Reece?" she asked.

"I've been shot at a few times," he said finally, stepping past her to open the door to the cabin. "But I've only had to get medical service for an injury from a bullet once."

"And of all the jobs and assignments you've gone on," she said, "would you agree that the odds were very much in our favor of *not* getting shot?"

She stepped through the door behind him, coming up short when she saw he was stripping out of his shirt. Because even angry—and growing angrier by the moment—Reece really was a sight to be behold when he took his clothes off.

"They were," he agreed.

"So how are you going to throw yourself in front of this guilt train when you couldn't possibly have known how dangerous this assignment was going to be?" she asked. "Reece, I've eaten poison pufferfish and gone swimming with sharks and traveled solo across half of the United States, and I wanted to go with you. That's the end of it."

"It's not." His voice was very, very tight.

"Why not?"

In the next second, Reece was halfway across the room and boxing her in against the far wall of the cabin. His bare chest pressed against her own skin, and God, she wanted to taste him, to pull him down and kiss the anger off his lips and—

"Because it's my job to protect you," he said, not giving her a second to counter that ridiculous statement, "because you're different, Morgan. To me, you're different."

Then it was Reece who claimed her mouth. The kiss wasn't sweet and it wasn't soft. It was a brutal demand, as if they each had to prove to themselves that the other was there, right there with them and alive and whole, and she didn't want to waste a second of touching him, not when he spoke such claiming, dangerous words, not when he made her want to commit to him in the same way he seemed so hellbent on committing to her. His tongue pressed against the seam of her lips, and she opened to him, the way she knew she would always open to him, and Morgan gave over, gave everything of herself over to this man and simply kissed him. Because she wanted to.

She brought her good hand up to his hair, running her fingers through the soft, thick strands that she'd been wanting to touch since the moment she had first met him on that mountain top in the middle of the storm. And because her instincts always seemed to take over where Reece was concerned, she tugged, just a little. He growled into her mouth then moved his lips lower, so he was licking at the pulse point of her neck and Morgan lost her grip on his hair, lost her grip on everything that wasn't the way Reece felt in her arms.

"I have wanted you since the moment I saw you," he said. "And I swear to God, Morgan, the next time I have you in my bed, I'm not going to let you out." Then, as if it cost him everything, he stepped back.

She let out a low, keening moan from the back of her throat because he had to stop doing this to her, had to stop pushing her so close to the edge of her control, only to pull back just when she was ready to take the final leap.

"I want you to be ready," he said. "Before I take you to the barn tonight."

Through the haze of lust, Morgan could see the benefit in that. Her limited understanding of what lay up the hill was that it centered around communication and trust, but the rest of her body wasn't in full agreement that they should stop what they were doing.

"What do I need to know?" she asked.

"Morgan." Her name was so sweet and so severe on his lips all at one time and how was her body already responding to him? "I'm going to get clean." Because of course, this little erotic sojourn hadn't included much actual washing. "If you want this to go further, I want you waiting for me on the bed when I get out. If you want to walk away, to go slow, I understand. But if you want to know how it feels, be there when I get out."

As if there was any question at all.

She pushed to her feet, feeling just a little wobbly, then she slipped out of the bathroom and into the cabin at large.

In the time they had been at the lodge, a service must have come in and turned down the sheets, because the bed sat fresh and clean. And her. Because she didn't want to wait until tonight and she sure as hell didn't want to go slow.

Did he want her naked? He hadn't said a word except that he wanted her waiting on the bed for him. Sitting? Kneeling. She was beginning to get into her own head about this and her complete lack of experience when the water shut off in the bathroom, which meant she was running out of time.

Finally, Morgan kicked off her shoes and climbed onto the bed. She knelt at the foot, spine straight, head down, heart thundering in her chest. This felt crazy, like the most insane adventure she had ever taken in her entire life. People didn't just run off to sex ranches in Montana. But it turned out they kind of did, and if it wasn't right, if it wasn't right for her, then why did she feel so perfect sitting her like this, nerves turning her body to heat and desire as she waited for Reece to come out of the bathroom and what? Inspect her, praise her, give her so much pleasure she lost her goddamned mind? All of the above.

Across the room, she heard the door to the bathroom open, but she kept her head down, following her instinct to satisfy him, because it seemed like every time she went about pleasing Reece, he returned the favor tenfold.

"We're going to go slow." She practically felt his words more than heard them, because when Reece took up the mantle of this dominant man, his voice became a low timbre that caressed the skin, even at a distance. "We're going to go slow and you're going to promise me, Morgan, that you'll be honest with me about your needs."

She didn't lift her head, but she did nod. "I promise."

His bare feet made soft padding sounds as he stepped slowly toward her. Were men supposed to have pretty feet? Or maybe it was just Reece and this incredible effect he had on her whenever he was near.

"We have safe words here," he said. "Green is for keep going. Yellow is for slow down. Red is for stop. Say them back to me."

"Green for go," she said. "Yellow for slow down. Red for stop."

"Red for stop *right now*," he reiterated. "If it's too much, if you're overwhelmed or feeling out of control and you don't like it, use your safe words." He was standing right in front of her now, and his presence was like the very mountains they had scaled that week, foreboding and intense and dangerous. She was drawn to him as much as she was drawn to the Blackleaf.

"This is important, Morgan," he said. "Because there may be moments when you tell me to stop, when you tell me it's too much, that you can't possibly…and you're not going to want me to stop at all."

God, those words. They were laced with innuendo and brought to mind a thousand ways he could push her so close to the edge without ever letting her fall over. Or maybe Reece was the kind of man who liked to torture his partners with pleasure, giving it again and again until they lost their minds.

"I understand," she said. She took a risk, the familiar feeling of adrenaline catching her low in the gut, the way it did when she scaled mountains or jumped off cliffs. Only this time it was accompanied a warm heat between her legs, by the clenching muscles of her pussy, desperate for satisfaction. "Sir."

He placed two fingers below her chin and slowly tilted her head up to catch her eye. The movement was so simple, so easy to shrug off if she wanted to, but she didn't want to, she didn't want to do anything that might make him pull away, that might make him feel any cause for disappointment or displeasure.

"Do you know what it does to me when you call me that?" he asked. She shook her head and Reece's smile was almost gentle. Would have been gentle, if his eyes didn't burn with lust and demands she had every intention of meeting. "It makes me ache, Morgan. It makes my cock so hard I can't remember my own name. Seeing you on your knees, spread out and ready and waiting for me… It makes me want."

Another risk. "And what do you want, Sir?"

He slid his thumb over the seam of her lip, so gentle, so light that she almost didn't feel any pressure against her skin at all, only it was impossible not to feel when it was Reece touching her.

"So many things," he said. "I want you tied up and bent over my lap. I want you bound to the bed and waiting for me. I want you touching yourself so slowly you think you're losing your mind. But for now...."

He dipped his thumb between her parted her lips and she took him, accepted his touch, his finger without question, sucking him in and wrapping her tongue around the fresh, clean skin. She glanced back up to meet his gaze and more of that hot green fire burned there. For her.

"For now," he said, and she didn't think she was imagining the choked sound of his voice, as if he didn't have as good a grip on his control as he wanted her think he did. "We're going to take things very, very slow."

It should have been disappointing. Reece seemed hellbent on introducing her to the world with every training wheel and harness—okay, bad example—that he could find. But Morgan had no doubt in her mind that the slowness of this particular lesson would only add it to the pleasure that came with it.

"Let's start with a game," he said. "It's simple. I ask you a question. You answer honestly, I reward you. You lie to me...you remove a piece of that pretty little workout set."

Morgan had to fight to keep the moan from escaping.

He slid his thumb free and swiped it across her lower lip. "Did you see how they looked at you in the kitchen?" he asked. "Gabriel and Dante and Van? Did you see how they ate you up with their eyes?" She hadn't noticed much of anything but him. "But it's me who gets to have you. And I will have you, Morgan. Make no mistake of that." As if she possibly could.

"Question one." He stroked one hand down her throat and the sensation made her shiver. "How are you feeling right now?"

Morgan swallowed. Hard. "Green," she said, the word not as unfamiliar on her lips as she might have expected.

"Good," he said. "Now tell me how you *feel*."

This was a little harder. Because even though her nipples were peaked to hard, tight points and her pussy ached with need, this was new territory and saying her dirtiest thoughts aloud—

"It's just me," he said, his voice reassuring and demanding enough that it did feel as though telling him what he wanted to know would actually make him proud. And God she wanted to make him proud.

"I'm aroused," she tried. "My pussy is wet and achy and…and my nipples are hard…and…"

"And?"

"And I want to be filled."

The growl that emanated from the back of Reece's throat was a sound that she would hear in her dreams, and more wetness slicked the insides of her thighs. Removing her workout set wouldn't be any kind of punishment at all.

"So sweet," he said. "I love it when you use this pretty mouth to tell me all your most filthy thoughts."

This time, it was Morgan who let out a low sound and Reece raised one eyebrow.

"You have more?" he asked.

She hesitated only a moment before nodding. His grin, dark and promising, was more than worth the honesty, worth whatever he planned to make her say or do next.

"Save them," he said. "I want to give you everything you need and, Morgan, I am already so close to losing myself to you."

He stroked her nipple through the fabric of her workout gear, so gently that she wasn't even sure he really touched her, except that her body couldn't handle being near Reece without being incredibly overwhelmed by everything he had to offer, the scents and touches and dangerous, filthy words.

Then, before she could prepare herself, he leaned in and wrapped his lips around the fabric covering her swollen nipple. Pleasure coursed through her entire body, especially when he scraped his teeth ever so gently across the tip, and she fell back, losing her balance to the power of his body pressing against hers, to his touch and his caresses and all those promises.

Reece was large and strong and though they had spent their fair share of days in tight quarters, though she was aware of just how big he really was, nothing had felt like this, like the way his body draped over her, muscle fitting to curve, his smooth skin still damp from the shower, and the scents of soap and freshness feeling like an intimate caress all their own.

Finally, he pulled back, hovering over her as if holding up his body weight was no struggle at all, which, of course, it wasn't. Reece was too strong and too powerful and too capable, and he wanted her.

"I want to take this slow," he whispered into her ear. "But God, I want you."

"Please…" Her voice barely sounded like her own, desperate and wanton and already bordering on full release. "I want you, Reece…Sir." Because even though she was still brand-new to this world, so much of it felt instinctive and natural. "I want everything."

He didn't answer, simply leaned down and kissed her hard and rough, telling her everything she wanted to know about how good things would be between them. Then he was sliding her pants down her hips ever so slowly, gently following the curve of her breast with his lips. His beard tickled and the light drops of water that fell from his hair sizzled against her hot skin and made her extremely aware of every sensation, each one threatening to overwhelm her in all the best possible ways.

"Question two." His mouth was just there, hovering just a breath away from where her panties were so soaked and her pussy ached with need. "Do you want to visit The Ranch tonight?"

"Yes." The word came out long and languid, a desperate breath that meant Morgan couldn't hide a thing from him. Not that she would want to. Reece didn't respond, at least, not with words. Instead, he leaned down and licked a long, slow line down the curve of her panties, and Morgan screamed and clenched at the sheets below her.

"Fuck, please, more…"

He glanced up from between her legs and one tiny piece of her brain turned back on. "Please, Sir,"

"Say the words and I'll do it," he said. "I love hearing filthy words come out of your pretty little mouth."

"Please eat my cunt." Because there was no shame left, only pleasure and need and desperation. "Please make me come."

"With pleasure." Then he leaned back down, eating and stroking and consuming her. The soft fabric of her cotton panties was thin, but too much separated them. Still, Morgan couldn't deny the way the fabric added a new sensation to his touch. Or maybe, far more likely, it was just Reece and his fingers and his tongue and the way he always seemed to know exactly what it was she needed in order to be pushed to the very highest heights.

And, in true form, he slid her panties to the side and pressed one thick, strong finger into her ready opening, brushed across her swollen clit as he stroked in and out. Pleasure laced through her body, and her nipples ached and her pussy throbbed, but still Reece moved slowly, torturously slowly, as if he loved nothing more than dragging her right to the edge of pleasure and keeping her there.

"Such a good girl," he murmured. "Do you want more?"

"Yes." It was barely a word, more like a desperate whimpered. "Please, I'm so close."

"But not close enough." He teased her clit again. "Tonight, Morgan, I'm going to own your orgasms. Your pleasure will be because I offer it, because I grace you with it. I promise, you'll think of nothing except my touch and my touch alone."

"Yes, Sir. Only you."

He slid in another finger then, slowly stretching her, slowly opening her to him. What would it feel like when Reece was buried deep inside her, filling her up, making her come again and again on his cock?

"It makes me so hard to hear you say that," he said, and the pride in his voice did something funny to her too, like all her pleasure and lust was wrapped up in making him proud, in pleasing him and taking it in return.

"Question three," he said, as if there was any way she could think straight with what he was doing to her body right now. "Would you come when I told you to? Find your pleasure at my command? Would you do me proud?"

She wanted to, that innate sense of submission and need to please coursing through her body with honesty and a streak of pleasure.

"I would, Sir," she managed. "I would do whatever you told me."

"Then come for me, pet," he said. In the same swift movement, he leaned down and suckled at her clit and it was all too much, the words, the sensations of his fingers against her most sensitive skin, his tongue lapping at her clit and Morgan gave up the fight, released herself to the insane sensations coursing through her. The orgasm caught her around the middle, her abs clenching and her skin prickling with awareness as she fell deep into the endless abyss of hot, wet, intense sensations, overwhelming and wild, and so incredibly free. And all that she remembered was the beautiful expression of Reece looking up at her from between her wet, spread thighs, before her vision grayed and she passed out.

Chapter Seventeen

"I owe you guys an apology." He wasn't quite making eye contact with his friends, and if that made him a coward, Reece wouldn't deny it. But this was hard enough without seeing the truth of his deepest fears reflected in the faces of the men he respected most. That he wasn't quite the man he had been before, that he might never be that man again.

"You don't owe us shit," Van said. Van knew, better than the rest of them, what it was to have closed and locked doors with contents that got shaken around, so you were terrified to ever open them for fear of what might spill out. Even now, years back from the Middle East and, to Reece's best knowledge, in control of the vices that might have once led him astray, they knew little of what had happened to him during his service. They might never know more.

And in realizing that it made him a little sad, a little regretful that he couldn't help his friend the way Van might need him to, Reece realized he *could* say the things he had been avoiding, he could tell his friends the truth, the worries that plagued him, the nightmares, the guilt, and they would understand. They wouldn't see him as anything less than.

"The anniversary," he started. "I made a promise to myself that I wouldn't hide, you know?"

It seemed his little revelation had opened up new avenues, because he found it that much easier to meet their eyes, now. First Van's, dark and quiet, but stronger than Reece had ever thought his own would be. Dante's, open and full of unbridled love, because for all that Dante was covered in tattoos and piercings, he loved with an openness that Reece could only marvel at. Gabriel's, knowing, kind, intelligent in their understanding, and Caleb's. Somehow, Caleb was the hardest, the man who Reece had seen survive so much of his own hardship, the big brother he'd wished for a thousand times, the closest to home Reece had ever had. And all he saw in Caleb's eyes was strength, strength to borrow when he needed, a place to hang his hat when the big wide world got too lonely.

And with that borrowed strength, and the vision of Morgan in his bed still fresh in his mind, he told them everything he had so easily told her in those first few days on the mountain top. Told them how he didn't really have the nightmares anymore, how this time of the year, as the week rolled around, he still got flashes of panic and fear, told them about Abby, and the guilt he felt at the treatment he'd received in losing his partner, the survivor's guilt and so much more.

And his friends merely listened, didn't offer advice or condolences, didn't try to tell him his feelings were too much or lasting too long. They simply sat around the kitchen that they had all worked so hard to make a home for lost souls, and they listened to him unburden all that had weighed so heavily on his soul. Then, when his eyes were wet with tears and the weight of the world felt as though it had been so easily lifted from his shoulders, they loved him, held him, gave him those rough, manly touches that told Reece they would never think differently of him, that he was still the same man he had been all those years ago, and that they would love him all the same, even if he weren't.

And, as he stepped out into the fresh Montana air, which somehow felt all the sweeter, all the softer on his skin, Reece knew that this, the closeness he felt with his brothers, the ease with which he took his next breath, was thanks to Morgan.

"Reece."

Reece turned from the sight of the sun splashing gold on the far distant mountains to see Caleb stepping out through the back door.

"I'm good," Reece told him. And he meant it. He was good. The ground was steady below his feet. The Sinclair Ranch like coming home.

"I know," Caleb replied, coming to stand beside him. They'd taken a place of this great outdoors and made it their own, and for that chance, Reece would always been grateful. "That's not why I'm here. And it's not the reason I've been calling this week."

Reece turned to face him. "You mean I didn't have to spill my heart and soul out to you guys?" he asked. "You could have told me earlier."

Caleb grinned. "You didn't have to," he said. "But we're all glad you did."

Reece just nodded. The emotions felt clean, but the rawness was still there, and he needed some distance from all he'd just shared. "So, what do you want to talk about?" he asked.

"This." Caleb handed him an ivory-colored card, and it took Reece a moment to realize what he was looking at.

You are cordially invited to the wedding of Skylar Wedgeworth and Caleb Cash.

"You've set a date." Reece couldn't help the grin that was spreading across his face now. He had been there the day that Caleb had proposed, and there no doubt that the two meant to be together. It had been inspiring and joyful to watch them fall in love.

"We did," Caleb said. He kicked the dry ground with one booted foot. "And Skylar asked me to plan my side of the wedding party."

"The Sinclair Seven strikes again?" Reece asked. "Assuming Rafe and Bastion can make it."

"They both said they're going to try," Caleb replied. "But I'm more interested in your reply."

"To what?"

"To being my best man?"

"Seriously?" The wind whipped pine needles and wildflowers heads around them, and it felt like the wild mountain air was just for them, a special moment caught in warm air and sunshine.

"Seriously," Caleb replied. "I wanted to ask you in person, but..."

"But I've been as ass," Reece finished for him. "I'm fucking honored, man. Of course. Thank you."

He embraced Caleb in a manly hug with a lot of backslapping.

"I think I might have been more nervous to ask you that than to ask Skylar to marry me," Caleb said on a laugh. "I'm glad you're on board."

"We're family, Caleb," Reece replied, feeling the truth of that deep in his bones. "I'm on board one hundred percent."

And for the first time in a very long time, it felt like the truth.

Chapter Eighteen

Morgan woke to a soft tapping sound, and it took a few seconds of blinking her eyes to remember where she was, that she was in Montana, in Reece's bed, recovering from the sensation of coming all over his mouth and hands. God, they hadn't even fucked yet, and he had still made her pass out with pleasure.

"Come in," she called, before peeking under the blanket to see if Reece had readjusted her pants before leaving. He had. Of course. As she climbed out bed, she spied a note on the bedside table.

I can't wait to see you tonight. I hope you're well-rested, pet.

Her face flushed hot, just as Rhylee stepped into the room with Skylar, who held a garment bag folded over her arm.

"We're here for the montage," Rhylee said, "you know in movies where there's a makeover montage?"

She laughed and Skylar just shook her head. "Anyway, we figured you might need a new look for the night, since camping."

Morgan groaned. She hadn't even thought about what she might wear. Rhylee was right, of course. The only things in her pack were workout clothes, gear and rations.

"Thought so," Rhylee said with a laugh. "But first, exams." She handed Morgan a thick folder. "Read up and sign. Protocol, ya know?"

Rhylee hadn't necessarily seemed like the type to frequent a sex ranch, but it made sense that if she was part of the group here who so clearly treated each other likely family—hell, she was Caleb's sister—that she would at least know what was going on on the other side of the mountain. Perhaps she more than knew what was going on.

"This is a lot of information," she said, sitting on the edge of the bed. "You guys are serious."

"As a heart attack," Skylar said, sitting in the comfortable-looking chair just across the room. "The guys don't fuck around when it comes to keeping their patrons safe."

"Well, they do some fucking around," Rhylee pointed out. "But definitely not when it comes to safety or comfort." She pointed to the packet in Morgan's hand. "Some of that info is for tourists. It's the last few pages you want to read through. Skylar and I will set up the Sinclair Boutique."

Morgan settled in with a smile and turned to the packet in her hand. She set the tourist and lodge information aside, and began to read about the club. The pages were clinical, more contract than erotic promising, and it felt a little ridiculous to mark off her limits like it was some allergy test at the doctor's office, but the straightforward, no-nonsense tone put her a little at ease. She trusted Reece. Hell, he had literally saved her on more than one occasion, but this was still uncharted territory, and Morgan knew all too well how important it was to be careful when taking leaps into the unknown.

Despite its clinical tone, she read through the packet with relative ease, scanning certain parts twice, just to be sure she entirely understood all that was expected of her. She marked her limits, of which she was surprised to find she had relatively few hard limits, then she was signing her name on the dotted line.

"I'll take it up to the lodge in a few," Skylar offered. "Tonight is about blowing your man's ever-loving mind."

Morgan laughed. "He's not my man."

Rhylee turned from where she was unpacking dresses and furrowed her eyebrows. "Better tell him that," she said. "He sure was looking at you like he wanted to mark you right there in the kitchen for everyone to see."

Morgan's stomach tightened and her skin went hot at the thought. To be fair, it went hot at the thought of Reece doing just about anything.

"Ooh, she likes that," Skylar teased good-naturedly. Despite being the quieter of the two women, Morgan wasn't surprised to see she had a bit of a wicked streak. She would have to, to keep a man like Caleb in check.

"Spill," Rhylee said. "What excites you?" She waggled her eyebrows. "What's that thing you always wanted to try but didn't want to scare away your boyfriend?"

And there was the ice-cold water dumping itself onto Morgan's joy and arousal. These women were kind and open and supportive, even after barely a day of knowing her, and she absolutely didn't need to burden them with the sour nature of her one and only real relationship.

"Hey." It was Skylar who spoke this time, and her eyes were soft and kind when Morgan looked up. "I got pregnant at sixteen and got kicked out of my family. I raised my daughter Callie on my own and it was the hardest and most wonderful thing I've ever had to do. These guys have totally accepted her and me. Don't feel obligated to tell us anything, but know that you're safe here. Truly."

Morgan's smile was sad, but it was a smile. Amazing to think that Skylar, this model-like beauty who seemed so confident and self-assured when she stepped into the room, had struggled with her own self-worth and place in the world. But then again, didn't they all?

"My ex-husband," Morgan said quietly, almost too quietly to hear in the now near-silent room, "wasn't a very nice man." A fucking understatement, if ever there was, but certainly a place to start. "He kept a very close watch on me."

Toward the end, he had made her feel unwanted by her friends and family, had made her feel so completely alone and disconnected from anyone who might have seen what he was doing, might have been able to rescue Morgan earlier.

In the end, she had saved herself, but sometimes she wondered if she had saved all of herself, or if maybe there were a few pieces she hadn't been able to grab in her rush out of the door.

"I happen to have a very large collection of rifles," Rhylee said, and there wasn't a hint of humor in her tone. "And I never miss."

Morgan reached out and her new friend was just there, taking her hand, grounding her, giving her a place to lean when those memories she'd been so good at compartmentalizing escaped their boxes.

"Mixed martial arts," Morgan said, managing a smile. "I gave him a broken nose as a parting gift." It had been more satisfying than the day the judge had declared Wide Open Skies her business and given Aaron nothing more than lawyer bills.

"I knew I liked you for a reason," Skylar said with a small smile. "Does Reece know?"

"Some," Morgan said. "My ex, he was never violent. He never raised a hand to me. He didn't need to."

Because she had been so young and naïve and easy to manipulate and that ease with which he was able to isolate her from friends and family was still the thing that hurt the most.

"You got out," Skylar said. "You're a goddamned fighter, Morgan. No wonder you didn't seem fazed by that bullet wound."

A wound she had actually forgotten in the pleasure and unfolding events of the day. She peeked at the wrappings now, but they seemed to be holding up nicely.

"Some scars heal easier than others," she said finally.

"Isn't that the truth," Rhylee replied. "But Sky's right. You're kind of amazing, for a lot of reasons."

"You're one to talk."

"As much as I love a love fest," Rhylee said with a grin, "We came here to do a job, didn't we?" She pulled a dress free from the pile tossed over the back of one chair. "Now, what do we think about blue?"

Chapter Nineteen

"You need a drink." Dante was leaning against the dark wood of the bar top in the Barn and watching Reece a little too intently. "You look like you're about to snap, and not in a good way."

The talk with his friends and the exciting exchange with Caleb had put Reece at ease, made him feel like he was part of a family, capable of taking on whatever the world might throw at him. But here he was, sitting at the bar, bouncing his legs and feeling a sudden and overwhelming sense of panic that Morgan might just walk away.

He didn't want her to go anywhere, except into his private room of the club, and the idea that he was nervous to see her wasn't something he had any plans of analyzing. He'd never been nervous with a submissive before, even a brand-new one, but Morgan felt different in ways he just couldn't quite understand.

"Whiskey, please," Reece managed. Because cowboy courage most certainly had its place.

Dante poured him a generous glass and slid it in his direction. "This one's got you tangled in knots," he said. "And that's more of Bastion's area of expertise."

Ironic, that they had met climbing. Reece had done plenty of research on the areas of kink and erotic play that had interested him over the years, and Shibari, the rope play that Bastion was known for around the club, was actually a big no-no for climbers and athletes who relied on complex dexterity and strength in their hands. Even an experienced practitioner could still get something wrong, and that could mean loss of essential strength or feeling needed to climb or play. No, there were plenty of other things that called to Reece's baser self.

Not the least of which being the woman now walking through the door.

It was all he could do not to run over to her, which didn't exactly prove Dante wrong. But God, she had been gorgeous covered in mud and sweater from hiking uphill all day. Now. Now she was a vision.

She wore a tight pink skirt, leather maybe, and a sheer black long-sleeve top that showed over the plain black bra below. The shoes were high black boots that went over the knee. It was the perfect touch of feminine, but it was still Morgan. Even the makeup was light, though it still stood out as a stark change from the clean-faced look he'd become so accustomed to in the mountains. And her hair. It was pulled back into a high, tight ponytail that made his fingers clench. He wanted to pull her hair and kiss her neck like he wanted his next breath.

Rhylee was walking in beside her, but even as Dante greeted her at the bar with a kiss on the cheek, Reece only had eyes for Morgan, and one thought kept racing through his useless mind. *Mine. Mine. Mine.*

"Hey there, cowboy," she said, striding over to the bar like this wasn't her first time in a club, like she wasn't currently making him as hard as the wooden bar top with her vision, alone. "Want to share a drink?"

"I'd like to share a lot more than a drink," he murmured, and maybe it came out as a growl. Reece wasn't paying much attention. "But let me get you started." He dipped his index and middle fingers into the whiskey, then held them out to her. Morgan didn't hesitate, didn't pause to look around the room to see who was watching them. She simple leaned down and wrapped her glossy pink lips around his dripping fingers and sucked them deep into her mouth.

The thoughts disappeared from Reece's brain completely. His cock was painfully hard now, throbbing against his dark jeans, and it was all he could do to keep from guiding her down to the floor to take a whole lot more than just her fingers into his mouth. But this was her first time, and while she took to the teasing and submission like an absolute natural, he had a responsibility to keep her safe, to give her the control that would allow her to call this to a stop at any point.

"More?" he asked because he was pretty sure he could watch her suck his fingers between her pretty glossy lips all night.

"If that would please you," she said, a touch of attitude coloring her tone, as if she knew exactly what this confidence and power was doing to him and she had every plan to push as far as he would allow. And he would allow. To a point.

He dragged his thumb over her pretty lips, smearing the gloss she'd applied and loving how she parted so instinctively to him. He couldn't wait to see what else was wet and ready and waiting for him when it came to Morgan Tempest.

"You know it would," he said. "But thank you for asking, pet." He turned to Dante.

"We'll take that whiskey to go," he said. He took the bottle in one hand and wrapped his other arm around Morgan's waist. Because here, in his domain, the urge to claim her was too strong to resist, and the soft heat of her skin through the mesh of that black top was a tease that had Reece hurrying faster than he might have down the hall and away from the watching eyes of the guests in the Barn.

"I think you deserve a proper welcome to the Barn," he said, when they were in the relative privacy of the dark hallway. He placed the bottle on the floor then pressed her up against the wall, pinning her hands above her head with a single one of his own. "What do you think of our little kingdom."

"There's nothing little about it," she said, as his obvious erection brushed against her thigh. "Sir."

Reece moved slightly, enjoying all too much the way her lips parted at the feeling of his cock.

"Not when I'm around you," he said. "When you walked through that door, there wasn't a single person not watching you. But I'm the one who gets to have you." He leaned down and nipped at the soft flesh below her ear, which made her gasp. "Did Rhylee help you pick this out?"

"And Skylar, Sir."

"That was nice of them." His words were almost a growl now. "Remind me to thank them tomorrow."

"Yes, Sir."

"I wonder…" He was sliding his hand up her leg, slowly and gently, but even the brush of her warm skin against his own was enough to make him ache with need. "If Rhylee followed all of my requests."

His fingers brushed the tight curve of her ass and Morgan moaned, low and rough.

"Looks like she did." Her skin was so smooth and warm, muscled from time spent outdoors, adventuring, trying new things. He could only hope she enjoyed this new thing as much as she liked taking on mountains and oceans as her playgrounds. He couldn't help himself. He swiped his fingers forward, through her folds, and fuck, she was already so fucking wet, hot and slick against the inside of her thighs.

"Come," he said, sliding his hand down her arm to wrap between her fingers. "There's so much more to show you."

It was difficult to pay that much attention to his words when his touch was hot and possessive and his fingers tangled with hers in a caress more intimate than anything they had shared so far, but Morgan couldn't deny that her interest and desire were piqued with every new room he introduced her to.

Some were private, a bed or couch, a subtle, well-designed theme to the space, like the dark leathers of a study or a library, or a relaxed, lounge-like space adorned with white linens and statues and large, overflowing plants that brought to mind Greek gods and goddesses indulging in the summer sunshine. There were rooms currently occupied, with couples on display for an audience of onlookers to enjoy. Some held groups, kissing and sucking and pleasuring each other in kind, others had female dominatrixes, dressed in flowing black dresses that weren't nearly what Morgan might have expected from a club like this one. She watched as submissives followed the directives of their masters and felt her pussy heat and ache.

"What interests you, pet?" he asked, when they came to a room with a window for looking inside. There was a small stage, and a woman sat on a lounger, her hair falling over the edge in golden ringlets. Above her, the man who was clearly her Dom teased and coaxed her to orgasm with a vibrating wand, pinning her to the lounger when she finally submitted to her pleasure. Only he didn't release her. Instead, he pressed the wand to her clit again, forcing her back to the edge, even as she still rioted from her first release. Morgan's breath caught at the sight, her body overcome with need and a potent desperation to be in that position, spread wide for the whole room to see as she gave over to her release again and again.

"I wonder," Master Reece said, and she felt his intense gaze on her as she watched the show through the small window. Still, she couldn't quite look away. "If you're turned on by the idea of being watched, or the idea of being forced to come again and again."

"Both," she whispered. "Please, Sir, I…" She didn't know how to articulate what she wanted, but she didn't have to, because he knew, always seemed to know exactly what it was she needed, and he took her hand, guiding her away from the window.

"I have one more room to show you," he said. "My private space. Only for my partners and I."

His room was at the far end of the hallway and when she stepped through the door, she knew exactly why Reece had chosen it for himself.

The room was glass on three walls, opening to the mountain view all around. In Montana in the summer, the sun set late, and the sky remained vibrant and bright for hours past dinner, and now was no exception. Golden light framed the mountains, making the lavender blue of the distant rock appear to shimmer, and in the distance, the early turning of the leaves made for a blanket of soft reds and golds.

And it wasn't only the walls that laid the room exposed and intense. Above the enormous, four-poster bed was a skylight nearly the size of the entire room, through which she knew she could watch the stars for hours. Reece was a man used to sleeping out under the open skies, and it was clear he had designed a space for himself that would give him that, even when indoors.

When Morgan could finally tear her eyes away from the shimmery indigo sky above, she was able to take in the rest of the room more clearly. It was modern, with a Pacific Northwest feel of dark woods, greens and grays, and the style was minimalist while still fully expressing Reece's personality. The floor was wood, but slightly warm to the touch below her boots, and when she spied the enormous tub beside the far wall, she understood why. She was surprised to find that there were few signs of kink or erotic play around the space, but she was beginning to understand exactly how deep Reece went, and she knew he likely used this space as an escape as much for his mind as his body.

"What do you think, pet?" he asked.

"It's you," she said on a breath. "It's your way of adventuring at home. She turned, taking it all in, the bed swing in the corner, the wall of running water, the rainforest shower tucked against the far wall. "It's stunning."

"It's much better with you standing here," he said. "Don't go anywhere. Just stay right where you are."

He stepped away, to where she presumed he kept some kind of closet space, and when he returned, he held a large camera. "Can I photograph you?" he asked. "Just for me. Just to capture this moment?"

She knew it was probably a terrible idea, to let him memorialize this moment of vulnerability and eroticism. But she wanted it all the same, wanted Master Reece to have memories of her after they went their separate ways. She didn't want him to forget her. She knew she would never forget him.

"Tell me what to do," she said quietly.

The pride in his eyes was enough to set her skin on fire and Morgan couldn't help the grin that spread across her face. This was unlike any adventure she had ever taken before, and she knew, without a shadow of a doubt, that she would be an entirely different woman when she left The Ranch.

"Against the window," he said. "Hands up, press into the glass."

She followed his directives with ease, the cool glass a unique and sensational contrast to her heated skin, and Morgan almost moaned at the touch, and only a little because she knew he was watching. He took his photos with the skill of a lifelong artist, and she felt more and more at ease with every direction he issued.

"Touch yourself for me," he said, "just a little, tease yourself."

She knew that if she wanted to, she could call this whole scene to a stop in a second, but instead, she moved one hand to her nipple and allowed her head to fall back against the glass as she circled the tight, peaked point.

"So beautiful," Master Reece said, "How far will you go with the camera on you? How much will you let me see?"

All of it. All of me.

She slid down the glass wall until she was sitting on the wooden floor. It was warm, just as she expected, and that made it all the easier to spread her legs as wide as she could in the tight leather skirt, to open to him, to display herself for Master Reece's inspection. As if on instinct, she parted her lips and slipped three fingers into her mouth, moving them in and out slowly, a promise of the way she would take Master Reece's cock in her mouth.

"You're so fucking perfect." His words were practically a growl, and the next thing she knew, he was stalking toward her, no longer the professional photographer, with artistry and eroticism on the mind. Now he was all Master. All *her* master. Temporarily, at least.

She whimpered. Fucking *whimpered,* but Reece just laughed. "You'll have your pleasure," he promised. "Don't you worry."

Morgan didn't say anything, but she did shoot him a glare that she hoped implied just how frustrated she was.

"There are rules in this world," he explained, and she was pretty damned sure she could get off on nothing more than the sound of his voice like it was right now, pure masculine heat, rough beauty, promise. "Listening to me, even when I tell you something you don't want to hear, is one of those rules. Spread your legs for me, pet."

He added the last so nonchalantly that she almost missed it, but she was attuned to him now and she wanted to do as he told her, wanted to experience this in its full beauty, whatever that meant. "We also have rules about what we call each other. For instance, I can call you whatever I please." He looked her over. "Princess, pet, little storm, kitten, queen. And you'll listen. Because you'll want to."

Damned, if he wasn't right about that.

"I like titles," he said. "Some of my friends, they don't mind. But I follow those rules, and you will too. Unless otherwise requested, I am Sir. Understand?"

Morgan nodded, caught sight of the glint in his eyes, and opened her mouth to say the words aloud.

"Yes, Sir." Oh, that shouldn't have sent a rush of pleasure flooding between her legs, but damned if it didn't. Her pussy clenched, hot and needy with the way those words had felt on her tongue.

"Did you like that?" he asked her, though damned if he didn't already know the answer. "Tell me how it felt."

"Right." She stumbled with the truth of that. "It felt right, Sir." He raised an eyebrow as if urging her to continue. "It made me feel good."

"More," he replied. "How did you it make you *feel?*"

Involuntarily, Morgan arched at the words, her body giving over to the rush of pleasure he demanded from her, the pleasure she wanted so desperately to give.

"It made me wet," she whispered, unable to look at him now, her head bent and her eyes lowered with embarrassment at the words. Or maybe something else. Definitely something else.

"You can call me Sir as much as you like," he replied. "Or Master Reece. Master alone is reserved for those who play monogamously. Does this make sense so far?"

She nodded and adjusted. "Yes, Sir," she replied. It would take some getting used to, but not nearly as much as she had expected.

"Look at me, Morgan," he replied. She did, moving so quickly it was nearly without conscious volition. "The most important thing for you to know is that the power is in your hands. Always. No matter what happens, you have control. You give consent. We play because you play. Do you understand?" His words were vehement, the very foundation for the game they were about to embark upon.

"Yes, Master Reece."

"Good. Now, we'll explore your limits over time. But for now..." He reached over and spread her legs wider, so there was nowhere for her to hide from his inspection. To be on display like this felt overwhelming and intense, but not shameful. On the contrary, she loved the way he looked at her, like he wanted to *devour* her.

"Oh, you are so pretty." His voice was rich and raw, like fresh honey, sticky and to be savored in the heat of a setting summer sun. "It's going to be hard to resist you, Little Storm."

Morgan bit her lip to keep the moan from escaping, but judging by the expression in his eyes, he knew about it anyway.

"You don't have to resist," she whispered. God, she didn't want him to resist. He grinned, wolfish and predatory and if her panties hadn't been wet before then they sure as hell were wet now.

"Of course I don't," he replied. "I could have you right now, on the floor, on the stage, out on the Montana mountain top, and you'd beg me for more."

Damn it, yes, she would.

"But I don't want you just to want it," he continued. "I want you to crave my touch so desperately it's like there's nothing else in the world. I want you to be consumed with pleasure and desire and need for release until all you can think about is doing exactly what I tell you. It's not just wanting, Morgan. It's needing."

She was pretty damn needy right now, if she were being honest.

"One finger," he said. "Brush one finger along your wetness. Slowly."

Her finger was shaking as she ran it between her folds, never breaking eye contact, not daring to allow herself to give over to the pleasure of it, for fear that she wouldn't be able to stop, and the tiny rational part of her brain that was still functioning knew that Reece was going to make her stop.

"How do you touch yourself at home?" he asked. "Do you stroke that sweet pink pussy when you're alone in bed until you're clutching the pillows and writhing against the sheets? Tell me."

She nodded and took a deep breath. Any shame or embarrassment she might have felt was gone, lost to the pleasure he promised her with those deep green eyes and quirked, wolfish smile.

"I read the books," she replied. "The erotic romance novels. Then I slip my hand into my panties."

"Do it."

She had never touched herself in front of anyone before him. Hell, she'd never even touched herself in front of the mirror, but all of a sudden being on display and for such an eager and responsive audience was just about hottest, most arousing thing Morgan had ever experienced.

"What happens in the books?" Reece asked. "The ones you read. What turns you on, pet?"

"Being told what to do," she admitted aloud for the first time in her entire life. Being bent over the desk and told to wait my turn."

The grin that spread across his handsome face was positively lascivious and in it she saw one hell of a night.

"So perfect." He paused and leaned forward to watch her, his arms resting on his legs in a position of controlled power and extreme masculine strength. "Because I'm very good at giving direction and" — another pause, weighted and thick in the air — "making my partners wait."

She didn't have time to ask him what he meant by that because he leaned back.

"Show me how you do it at home, Morgan. I want to see what pleases you."

She fell back against the cool glass and slid her hand lower to play with her swollen clit. Her pussy was soaked and clenching on nothing, desperate to be filled and slick and wet when she swiped her fingers through her folds. Her release was close, so *fucking* close, made closer by the weight of his gaze upon her, by the sheer eroticism of being watched and being told what to do. Her back was arching now, her nipples painfully hard and her legs throbbing with the onslaught on pleasure and just as she was there…so close, almost —

"Stop."

She almost screamed her frustration, but she stilled her hands, quivering with the exertion of pausing before that one final stroke.

"Fucking beautiful," Reece murmured. "And so good for me. Are you angry right now, pet?"

Morgan growled and he just grinned. "Good. You're not ready yet."

She wanted to argue that she was absolutely, definitely, one hundred percent ready, that her body was vibrating with her unreached pleasure, but she had the distinct sense that he already knew that and it pleased him immensely.

"Touch your nipples for me, Morgan. But don't give in."

She sighed and slowly pulled her hand free. Fine, if he wanted to torment her, she could torment him right back. Before doing as she was told, she slipped her two wet fingers between her lips and sucked. It was arousing to taste herself, but even more arousing to be the cause behind the dark and broody expression in Reece eyes, and she slowly pulled her fingers free to trail them down her chest to the top of her loose tank and down further, lower.

Only then did she follow his direction, moving to cup one swollen breast in her hand and circling the painfully tight nipple between her finger and her thumb. The movement was a series of mini lightning bolts that beat a hot, rich pleasure though her bloodstream with every movement and holding onto the edge of the cliff was nearly impossible. She was just about to give over to it, to finally take the pleasure he been denying her, his direction be damned when...

"Stop."

This time, Morgan couldn't stop the curse that escaped her lips and she had to grit her teeth until her jaw ached just to pull back that escaping pleasure. There was no doubt in her mind that she was pouting, which only seemed to please him more.

"See," Reece explained, his voice too fucking calm for all he seemed happy to put her through, "when you chase your pleasure all the way, you never know how desperate you can actually get, how much better it can be. I'm going to show you how much better it can be, Little Storm. But you have to trust me."

Amazingly, she did trust him. She had to trust him. In all the books and popular culture references she had come across from a lifestyle like this one, trust and communication were absolutely the key. She trusted him, but that didn't mean she had to like him very much right now, given how tightly strung her body was and how he refused to allow her to uncoil.

"Pinch them," he continued. "Hard. And tell me how it feels."

It felt like she wasn't going to be able to do as she was told. Her nipples had always been sensitive, especially when it came to the fine line between pain and pleasure, and even the simple scraping of her nails across the swollen flesh was nearly enough to send her flying. But he was sitting right there, watching her with that damned potent expression in his eyes and making the choice between chasing her pleasure and doing exactly as he told her not a choice at all.

"It feels good," she managed on a breath. "I like the pain. It makes me wet and achy."

"Good," he said. "I have something for you. Since you've been doing so well tonight." He stood and moved over to a cabinet and even in the dim light, she could easily make out the bulge of his arousal behind his jeans, and damned if that wasn't the hottest part of this whole night, pleasing him, making him want her as much as she wanted him.

He was back a moment later with a small leather pouch that at first sight could have held toiletries, but she'd gotten very wise in a very short amount of time and Morgan had a decent sense that she wasn't about to be presented with a toothbrush. Her instinct was validated when he unzipped the bag and held it up for her.

"Pick, pet."

Inside was a small assortment of toys, some of which she had seen before and some of which were entirely new territory, territory she would no doubt enjoy exploring with Reece when the time came. Since this was all still new and she had no doubt that he was planning to torture her regardless of her choice, she selected a familiar purple vibrator and pulled it from the bag.

"Pinch your nipple again," he direct, closer this time. She wanted him so much closer. "I like the expression you made when you're so close to coming."

Her hand was already there and she followed his direction until the pinch of pain became a fully blooming riot of pleasure and desire.

"Now the toy."

The setting was low, but she still practically jumped out off the floor when she placed it to her swollen pussy. Even through the fabric of her panties, it turned her body into a pulsing, aching, writhing thing, desperate to find release by any means.

"You're going to ride it," Reece instructed. "The orgasm is going to come and you're not going to give over and you're not going to stop. Use your control to keep from coming, Morgan. Make me proud."

She shook her head. Her body was already way too tightly wound and if he wanted her to ride through the pleasure without giving over to it, then he was going to be disappointed. She'd been high on desire and anticipation since the first moment they met and now she had a vibrator pressed to her clit and her fingers pinching her swollen nipple and there was no way, no *way* she was going to survive this.

"Morgan."

Well, when he said her name like that.

"It's too hard....Master Reece." And damn it, calling him by his formal title sure as shit wasn't helping.

"Would I make you do something I didn't think you could?" he asked. "Or am I giving you the direction because I know you're capable of following it?"

She certainly wasn't capable of following this conversation right now, giving the sparks of pleasure burning her skin and making her buck against the cool glass, but she imagined that somewhere, off in the foggy distance, he probably made a good point.

"It feels too good," she whimpered. "I can't... "

"You can," he said it with such truth that she almost believed it herself. Almost. "You can, Morgan, and you will. For me. Hold it back."

It being the monumental tidal wave of pleasure that was mounting ever higher, the wracking, wild, totally out of control heat that was destined to burn her up.

"Hold it back." This command was muttered low and rough and brought her aching need to please him to the fore. The pleasure would be temporary. The pride in his eyes if she just did as she was told was sure to last so much longer.

Despite how close she was, despite the intense pressure of the vibrator on her clit and the powerful, painful eroticism of pinching her swollen nipples, she held it back. She didn't stop, didn't break eye contact with him, just kept the totally insane, overwhelming pleasure from bursting through with sheer grit and determination. It was just like climbing to the top of a mountain, one hand in front of the other until she was nearly, so very, very nearly at the top.

"Come for me, pet."

She shattered. Like the storm that had driven them inside, she gave over to the wildness of her desire and she came and came hard. For a moment, her body wracked with the aftershock, pulsing sensations that sent heat and desire rioting through her until she finally, *finally* began to calm.

Reece was at her side in an instant. He settled beside her on the couch and moved one arm around her shoulder to embrace her gently, all the while stroking her still-damp hair and lulling her into a state of absolute relaxation.

"You did so well, Morgan. I'm so proud of you."

Her brain was a little foggy with the aftereffects of her orgasm, but even from a distance, she could tell that his voice had changed. He was no longer Master Reece, the potent, powerful man pushing her to new heights she could never had reached alone. He was Reece, the man who had helped her on the top of the mountain, the man who started his day with yoga, who had dedicated his life to helping the disenfranchised and the vulnerable.

She cuddled into his embrace, her eyes already starting to close, and he made room for her until she was practically in his lap.

"How do you feel right now?" he asked her. "Was that too much?"

She shook her head, sleepy and sated. "It was perfect. You're perfect." And with her head on his shoulder, she drifted off into a blissful sleep.

Chapter Twenty

He was going to get mighty used to cuddling in the arms of a soft, lush woman. Morgan's scent was familiar now, and so fucking enticing that Reece wondered if he could sprain his cock just from denying it for too long. Watching her come before passing out in his bed had been agony of the most pleasurable, desperate kind, but watching her follow his orders, do whatever it took to please him, to make him proud—it was unlike anything he had ever experienced before. He knew Morgan had never done anything like it, and yet she had settled into the role as if they had been practicing together for years, and that was...a lot.

She let out a soft whimper and shifted in her sleep, pressing more of that delicious, toned ass against his already painfully erect cock. She had wanted him, he knew that. He could have had her. But even though she had taken to their play like a seasoned professional, he had wanted to move slowly. Already, he was afraid of overwhelming her, giving too much, too soon. He couldn't deny the attraction he had felt for her from the very start, and in play where control was the name of the game, distance was key.

Except he didn't have much distance right now and his balls ached with need, his cock surging against her ass. He dug his nails into the flesh of his palm, but he had always been partial to a bite of pain with his denied pleasures and the movement only served to heighten his senses and make him more aware, more desperate to touch her. Hell, they hadn't even kissed the night before and here she was, cradled in his arms like they were long-time lovers.

It had felt like that. She had trusted him so implicitly and so beautifully, and when she had crawled into his arms and fallen asleep, Reece had known he was in serious trouble. But he'd never been the kind of guy to walk away from danger, not difficult stories for work or tall mountains for play, and Morgan Tempest was exactly the kind of dangerous adventure he enjoyed most.

She moved again and this time he brought his hands to her hips and stilled the motion.

"You're doing that on purpose," he murmured into the curve at the base of her jaw. "I know you're trying to tease me."

Her breathing steadied and he knew he had hit his mark. She was a little bit bratty in their play, and he found himself deeply aroused by the challenge of it.

"No." Her voice was husky and soft with morning sleepiness. "No, Sir."

He gave that delicious ass a light swat. "I prefer it when you say *yes, Sir*," he replied. "And I prefer when you tell me the truth."

She tried to roll over to face him, but he held her in place. So, she just wiggled more, which his cock really fucking appreciated.

"I want you to touch me," she murmured, not a small amount of whimper to her voice. "I wanted you to touch me last night." That had made two of them, then.

"You'll get it when you behave," he said instead. "Are you behaving right now?"

He could practically hear the smirk in her voice when she replied, "I'm behaving badly, Sir."

Reece couldn't help the low chuckle that escaped at her words. Wasn't that the damned truth?

"Badly behaved girls don't get to touch themselves," he replied. He stroked one finger alone the curve of her exposed waist, her skin hot and soft and so damned tempting. "And they don't get touched either."

Her breathing shallowed and Reece knew that the chance of him getting out of here with his pants on was disappearing by the second.

"Please, Sir. I'll do anything."

"Anything?"

"Anything."

"Tell me what you want. Something you've never told anyone before. I want to know what stirs you, Little Storm."

She was quiet a long moment. "You know how I mentioned the desk thing last night?"

He nodded into her hair, and she continued. "Well, I don't just want to be bent over a desk. I want to be bent over and filled, you know?"

Images sprang to mind of her, leaning over the desk in his room at The Ranch, her pert ass raised high in the air, slightly red from spankings he had administered, and firm and hot in his hands. She had a hell of an ass, something he hadn't been able to ignore in their days of hiking. It was clear she pushed her body to the limits, and he was more than happy to reap the benefits, even if that required more self-control than he'd ever practiced in his entire life.

"Tell me more." His cocked surged, as if in agreement. "I want to know every sordid detail of this little fantasy, pet."

She wanted to tell him. It was clear that her desperate need to give over to this wild pleasure now warred with the shame and embarrassment she had likely been exposed to her whole life. The things they did were natural, an extension of human nature, of basic, carnal need with a dash of creative thinking and willingness to be bold. And Morgan was most definitely bold.

"I want something in my mouth," she whispered, so quietly he wouldn't have been able to hear her if she hadn't been wrapped in his arms.

"What do you want?" he replied. "A gag? A toy?"

"A toy." She was already nearly whimpering, and he had plans to push her so much further, so much higher. Teasing Morgan was a challenge that offered a world of possibility. "I..." Hell on earth, she was fucking cute when she was embarrassed. "I like sucking."

Of course she did. Because God and the Devil had sent him a woman who would break him of his hard-won control in under a day.

Reece shifted and slid his hand up the column of her throat until he was able to stroke her jaw and bring his hand to her lips. She was still pressed up against him and turned away, but he knew she had taken the initiative and opened for him when he felt the hot slide of her tongue along his thumb. She sucked him into her mouth, and he swore under his breath, the sound of her slickness and the undeniable eroticism of her taking his finger deep was almost too much and, with great regret, he slowly pulled back.

"You like sucking." He repeated her earlier words. "That does work out rather perfectly." His image of her on the desk shifted to include a thick rubber toy sliding in and out of her lips as he bent her over. Or, better yet, her hands tied behind her back and the toy on the desk for her to drool over.

"Are your hands tied?" he murmured, giving life to the fantasy. "Clasped behind her back so you're vulnerable to whomever comes along?" Her gasp was audible, and Reece knew that however far he had pushed her the night before, it was nothing yet compared to the depths of what she wanted, what she had never been given the opportunity to explore.

"My hands are tied," she replied. "And my legs are spread." He very much looked forward to introducing her to the beauty of the spreader bar. "And…"

He fucking loved *and.*

"And what, pet?" He couldn't stop from stroking her lush lower lip with his slick thumb. He'd have her there sooner than later. He'd have her everywhere. "If you tell me, you might just get what you want."

"I cheated on a test," she replied. "And I got sent to the office and the headmaster doesn't abide cheaters."

"No, he doesn't." Reece slid his other hand down the curve of her side, across that fine, toned ass, gently, slowly, not nearly as much contact as he needed with her body, and yet, already he was at the end of his tether. "Girls who cheat get disciplined."

She wiggled and he didn't think it was on purpose this time, so much as an instinctive movement to get more pleasure, more pressure, more *something*. He could relate.

"I'm sorry, Sir," she whimpered. "I won't do it again, I promise."

"I want to believe you." He stilled her movements, partially for the game they played and partially because she just felt too damned good writhing against him and he wanted this to last beyond the first act. "But you have a history of taking things too far, don't you, Ms. Tempest?"

"I'm sorry." This time it came out on a gasp because he moved his hand lower and squeezed her ass at the same time. "Please."

"Please, what?" he asked. "Please let you go with a warning and detention? That's not how it works in my school." He could feel her breathing shallowing, close as they were to each other, and he noted her fantasies and her begging for future use. "At my school, we discipline." He stroked her exposed skin. "Then what, Little Storm? This is your fantasy." Though it was quickly becoming one of his as well.

"I'm bent over the desk and my skirt is flipped up and you take a wooden ruler and you tell me to count each stroke of the ruler against my skin." She swallowed but Reece didn't dare interrupt this particular story. "And when you've gotten to ten, you put the ruler down and you rub my sore ass and that's when you realize that my panties are wet…"

"It was supposed to be punishment," he replied. "And you enjoyed yourself. That won't do."

She nodded. "And you tell me to stay still because you're going to make sure I learn my lesson and when you come back, you have all these toys. You tell me to open up my smart mouth and you push one inside and tell me not to drop it, no matter what. Then, then…"

After all this, she was getting shy and he had a fairly good sense of what was going to come next, beside Morgan, herself.

"Then you tell me that since I can't even be punished properly, you're going to take it to the next level, and you press a plug against my ass…"

He couldn't see her face, but he was certain it would be red with flush and heat and embarrassment.

"And that's when I struggle, only I've got the toy in my mouth and my hands are tied and I can't tell you no and you wouldn't stop even if I did, right?"

He moved his hand lower to the curve of her ass where it hit the upper thigh and where a causal stroke could accidentally brush her quivering hole. If she wanted to play at loss of control and non-consensual scenes, he would be honored to be her safe place and safe partner to do so with.

"It burns so good when I push it in, though, doesn't it?" he practically growled. "You didn't realize it could feel so good to have a toy in your tight little ass, but it does."

"Yes." Her sob was pulled from her chest, and she was clenching the pillows like she was about to come from nothing more than this unfolding story. Good. "I fight it because I know I'm supposed to, but it feels *good*. Then you're unzipping your pants and sliding your cock into me in a single movement and it's too much…"

"Is it too much?" Reece asked, stroking her hair away from her face. "Or are you not putting enough effort in for me? Are you giving up too easily? Pleasure is better when it's hard-won. You know that."

"Yes, Sir." She arched and he couldn't help himself. He slid his hand between her parted thighs to her soaked panties and stroked. Morgan shuddered and Reece was pretty sure he had died diving with the sharks or something because this was a bone-deep kind of pleasure that he couldn't understand but craved with his whole being. "I'll be good this time, I swear."

"Yes, you will, pet," Reece murmured, bringing his other hand up to her hair and tugging gently on the loose braid. She gave over to the sensation and followed his unspoken movement with ease. "You'll do anything I tell you, won't you?"

"Yes Sir. *Fuck*, yes. Anything."

"Good. Don't come. I know you want to. I know you want to so bad it hurts in all the best places, but you're going to listen to me, aren't you?" Her whimper was a thing of beauty, and he pushed her panties to the side to tease her swollen clit until she was bucking and shaking in his arms.

"If you're good for me, Morgan, I'll bend you over that desk and fill every one of your holes and spank your pretty ass pink. But if you're not…"

"Sir?"

"I'll leave you here like this all day without permission to come."

That got her attention, and she made a clear effort to slow her body's desperate movements until it appeared that she had some control over herself.

"Good girl," he whispered in her ear, at the same time he sank a finger deep into her tight pussy. She clenched around him, hot and slick with need, and

Reece wanted to fucking howl at the moon. Another finger, more clenching and desperate whimpers.

"Hold on, baby," he murmured in her ear. "I promise I'm going to make you feel so good. You just have to trust me." The third finger was a tighter fit and he moved his thumb to circle her clit at the same time, reveling in the delicious sounds she made when she was so on her edge, silently begging her to hold on just a little bit longer. "You're doing so well, princess. Ride the pleasure. Own the pleasure."

She was remarkable good at denying herself and God if it wasn't the fucking hottest thing he'd ever seen, this beautiful woman right on the edge of her orgasm, holding off because he told her to. He shifted slightly and slid his fingers back into her mouth at the same time his other hand toyed with her pussy and teased her clit.

"Beg me, pet," he half-growled, like the wild animal he was turning out to be. "Beg me for that sweet release." He wanted her choking on his fingers while she did, which she seemed to enjoy immensely if the erotic gasps escaping her lips were any indication.

"Please." Her words were slightly muffled, but unmistakable. "Please can I come, Master Reece? I need... I need it."

He pumped lazily into her body, stroking, sliding, pushing her higher and closer to the edge until she lingered right at the precipice, then he leaned down and growled in her ear.

"Come all over my fingers. Give it to me." And he pinched her clit.

Morgan screamed into the moment of pleasure and rode his fingers hard and fast, coating them in her sweet release and wracking hard against his body and it was all the sensations Reece was coming to love most in the world.

Finally, her pleasure became calm and he slowly withdrew, gently pulling her against his body. She shifted and looked up at him, her eyes laden with lust and spent pleasure, her lips swollen, her hair mussed. Morgan Tempest, the perfect picture of erotic desire and all his. For now. Instead of resting her head on his shoulder, as she had done the night before, Morgan moved to sit up, her gaze full of heat and promise.

"Now it's your turn."

The man's restraint was unrivaled. Even though the fog of unadulterated pleasure Reece had given her, Morgan had been able to feel the thick heat of his cock pressed against her ass and surging with every moan and whimper. He wanted her and, judging by the size of the erection in his pants, he wanted her as much as she wanted him, which was to say in a sort of out of control, off-the-rails, at the mercy of her baser natural instincts kind of way. And still, he hadn't ordered her to touch him. Hell, he hadn't even touched himself.

She knew there were rules to this sort of thing. Of course, there were rules about pleasure and consent, and she was all too happy to follow those, to respect and embrace them. But when it came to giving pleasure to others, was she not allowed to touch him unless he gave her explicit permission?

She decided she was rather interested in finding out how he responded to insubordination. When she lifted her eyes to meet his, Reece's expression held heat and intensity like she had only ever seen on storms out at sea. But there was curiosity there too, like he was just waiting to see what she was going to do next and how far she was going to take this heat between them. Morgan had never been called a coward and Reece Prescott was one mountain she very much looked forward to climbing.

Disentangling their legs, she moved to straddle him and God, the strength and muscle of his athletic body was nearly enough to make her come all over again. She had seen him shirtless on the mountain top, in his smooth, dancer-like movement of yoga flow, but there was something different about feeling it and even though he still wore a cotton sleep shirt, there was no denying the intense power that it concealed below, power she very much wanted to explore with her own two hands.

"Little Storm," he said quietly but firmly, never taking his eyes off her. "What do you think you're doing?"

Morgan rocked slightly, sliding the inside of her slick thighs along the ridge of his cock, clear and straining against his pants. Reece brought a strong hand up to her waist and steadied her movements.

"Besides not listening to me, that is."

She smiled and she was fairly certain it came across as coy and probably a little bratty. Something about this man has her wanting to act out of character, to push him just as far as his rules would bend and to see what he did to her in retaliation.

"I'm making you feel good," she replied, a little more whimper in her voice than she had ever heard before. "Isn't that okay?"

He raised a dark blond eyebrow. "What do you think?"

She sat back, reveling in the small groan that escaped his lips when she accidentally — honest — slid across the ridge of his cock.

"I think I *want* to make you feel good," she replied. "And that I'm not allowed to. Isn't that right?"

He grinned that wolfish, dangerous grin. "You're allowed," he replied. "I just wanted to hear the magic words first."

It was her turn to grin. "Please, Sir?" she asked, the words more natural on her tongue than she would have ever expected.

"Please what, pet?" he slid his thumb across her bottom lip. "Ask me for what you really want, and you might just get it."

"Please can I suck your cock?"

That seemed to take him by surprise. If Morgan were being entirely honest, it took her by surprise a bit too. She had been planning to tease him, to push things a little at a time until he was just as desperate for her as she was for him, but it turned out there wasn't nearly as much patience or self-control in her reserve as she had thought. Reece, apparently, agreed.

"So needy," he replied, continuing that fucking stroking motion along her bottom lip. "Why don't we slow down?" He loved the slow ascent, the edging movement that brought her so close and kept her there until she just about thought she would die, and apparently his own pleasure was not exempt from the burn either.

Slowly, as was his style, he pressed his thumb between her lips and Morgan's instinct to please him, to give him everything she could and everything he deserved, took over. She leaned forward and swallowed his thumb, sucking deep and long and teasing the tip with her tongue until Reece was groaning and cursing low from the back of his throat.

"So sweet with something between your lips," he murmured, though satisfyingly, the sound was rough with pleasure and need. "You can't be smart with me when your mouth is full, can you?"

It was a rhetorical question, but Morgan hummed a response around his thumb from the back of her throat, which appeared to reverberate through him. She wanted more, she wanted his hard, thick flesh in her mouth, and she wanted it now — which almost definitely meant she wasn't going to get it.

"Want more, pet?" he asked.

She nodded and he slowly pulled his finger from her mouth and brought it down to her breast. She hadn't even realized how aroused she was, focused as she had been on doing as he told her, but a quick glance and the cool touch of his slick finger against her nipple, showed that her breasts were swollen and her nipples were tight and clearly visible through the fabric of her tank top.

"Yes, Sir," she managed, even as he circled the achingly tight tip with agonizingly slow movements. "So much more."

"Tell me," he replied. "Hearing your fantasies makes me hard." As if on cue, his cock surged against her ass, begging for attention. "If you please me, I'll let you have what you want."

There was some twisted logic here that she had to beg him for the chance to give him pleasure. Of the men she had been with, none of them would have turned down a blowjob for a day off work, and here she was, desperately begging for the opportunity. And yet, logic or no, it really fucking worked for her, made her pussy clench and ache, made her feel relaxed and desperate enough to share the things she hadn't even told Emily or Alisha, not even in wine-fueled sleepover hazes that only best friends would understand. But in just a few short days, Reece had reached in and touched something she hadn't even known she had, an instinct, a want that had been dormant and was now on full display, wild and ready and needy.

"I like being scolded," she admitted, rocking against his cock now, since he had released his hand from her waist and was apparently allowing it. If Reece didn't want something to happen, Morgan was quickly learning, it didn't happen. Still, every pulse of movement against the hardness between her thighs sent desperate pleasure racing through her body, making it hard to concentrate on what she was supposed to be doing, which was making Reece desperate enough for her touch that he gave up his control and allowed her to take it.

"Scolded," he replied. "Like for cheating on tests?"

She nodded. "And for…shoplifting, throwing a party, whatever it is. I've always been good and sometimes I don't want to be good. I want to be bad, and I want to be punished for it."

His cock surged at the words and Morgan's own body responded in kind. It was true, all of it, even if she had never acknowledged it in such simple words before. She was a good girl. Even though she had dropped out of school, she had been successful and capable her whole life. Being good, being obedient and understanding, there was definitive proof that there was definitely too much of a good thing when it came to pleasing everyone in her very recent past, and she didn't want to please everyone anymore. She just wanted to please Reece—and herself in the process.

Now, it wasn't an expectation. Now it was a choice and that made all the difference.

"You'll get it," he half-murmured, half-growled. God, she wanted to see him completely lose his control and give over to her more than anything. "Tell me, how bad can you be?"

Considering this was about the naughtiest thing Morgan had ever done, there wasn't a lot of truth to go off of. Instead, she focused on the things she wanted, the instinctive desperate things she had never let herself search for when she was online because she had been afraid of what she would find out about herself.

"When you have a big meeting with a new client," she replied. "I want to be under your desk with my hands on your legs, inching higher and distracting you from your big job." He growled and she took it as encouragement to continue. "Then I'll slide your zipper down and slowly tease your cock until you can't pay attention to anything other than the way my skin feels against yours, then the way my tongue feels around your swollen head." For a moment, all Morgan could focus on was the way he felt sliding against her needy hole, but she wanted so much more, so she brought her attention back to the story.

"Then your client figures out something's going on and he comes around to the other side of the desk and sees me on my hands and knees with your cock in my mouth. But he doesn't get angry."

"No?" Reece asked. "What does he do then, Morgan?"

"He says the deal is yours," she replied. "As long as he can watch me finish you off." *Fuck.* There really was something to say for being honest.

"Do you let him?" he asked.

She nodded. "We move away from the desk so you can lean against it and I'm on my knees and he's sitting across from us with his hand fisted around his fat cock watching me choke on yours and...and..."

Reece seemed to sense that she was losing her grip on the story and shifted their bodies. In a moment, he was standing with his back against the arm of the chair, and she was kneeling at his feet, just like the version of herself from the story.

"Give me everything, pet," he whispered to her, his voice rich with need and emotion and everything she would have to evaluate later and not right now. Right now, she had a lot of other things on her mind. "Take whatever you want. I'm right here with you."

Embolden by his words, she tugged at his pants. The elastic stretched easily, and they were down at his ankles in a second. But all Morgan could focus on was his thick, throbbing cock, hard and hot and just an inch away from her lips.

"Sir?"

"God, yes."

She didn't waste another moment, didn't deny herself anymore, just leaned forward and took him into her mouth. He was hot and hard, but the skin was soft to the touch, like velvet coating steel and she sucked him like she had been aching for it. Hell, she had been burning to touch him for two days, to enjoy his beautiful, magnificent body, to give over to the submissive side of herself she could no longer deny. Reece ran a hand through her hand and tugged just enough to send a wave of heat and pleasure coursing through her and Morgan doubled her efforts, feeling her own pleasure heighten as he grew closer to his edge. She'd never come from giving head before, but this was turning out to be a week of firsts.

"*Fuck.*" Even through the string of muttered swear words and groans, Reece still managed to sound like the man in charge. "I'm so fucking close, Morgan. Just don't stop." She wasn't planning on stopping. Instead, she brought one hand around and gently cupped his swollen balls, sliding her fingers around him until the pull on her hair was no longer gentle and he was no longer saying anything.

They came at the same time, wild and uninhibited, his dark, overwhelming release, the moment he gave over to his pleasure one of uncontrolled lust, sending her into a tailspin of her pleasure and she shuddered against the orgasm, her body a riot of emotions even as she swallowed his release and sucked him clean.

Reece was wrecked. When she finally looked up to meet his eyes, they were glazed and half-lidden, potent with lust. His long hair was messy and spilling over his shoulders in a golden waterfall of smooth, curly silk, and his lips were swollen and pink, like he'd sunk his teeth into the flesh to keep from a grip on his control. Morgan's pride surged with the knowledge that she'd made a man like Reece give that control up and the notion sent another wild wave of pleasure wracking through her already spent body.

After a moment, Reece helped her to her feet and brought her in close to his body, hot to the touch, muscled and powerful, and for a moment, Morgan just let him hold her, content to simply be in this wild moment, with this wild man.

Chapter Twenty-One

Reece woke to a sense of utter serenity, and it took him a moment to realize it wasn't merely the comfortable bed below his back and the soft pillow under his head that had made the full night's sleep so incredible. It wouldn't have mattered if he'd spent another night out in the wilderness under the stars, with the cold, hard ground beneath him, as long as he had Morgan Tempest in his arms, the way he did right now, snuggled up and warm and so incredibly soft, like she was made of all the goodness and sweetness in the world.

They'd spent the whole night together, wringing pleasure from one another's bodies until they had collapsed, overwhelmed and exhausted from the intimacy and pleasure and all that they had survived in the last two days.

The memory of why they were here, of what they were hiding from, hit Reece hard in the gut. Because he had brought Morgan into danger with him, by allowing her to follow up on this lead. He had gotten her shot, had gotten them both put on who knew how many watch lists for a company that had connections as high up at the United States Congress. It wasn't a good feeling, the nausea roiling around him, and he reached for the talisman that he always turned to when his skin got too hot and his palms started to sweat.

Her.

Morgan. The girl from the marketplace, with her brilliant blue eyes and soft smile and the feeling he'd always had that she was a different path for him to take in life.

Only she was no longer the nameless stranger in the crowd, and sooner or later he was going to have to tell her that she had meant more to him over the last few years than she could possibly know, and if the thought was a terrifying one, Reece wasn't all that interested in exploring why.

There were many other things he was far more interested in exploring this morning, with this lovely, lush woman asleep in his arms like she belonged there. He could easily ignore the voice in his head saying she did, making him ache to claim her with every kiss, every touch.

Morgan shifted in his arms, and Reece forgot about his secrets, about his fear of their intimacy, about everything but the soft smile she gave him as she slowly pulled from sleep and looked up into his eyes.

"Good morning." Her voice was a little bit raw, and he took far too much masculine pleasure in the knowledge that she had screamed her pleasure all night long at his touch.

"Good morning." He stroked one curl out of her eyes and tucked it behind her ear. "Your hair is curly." It was a ridiculous thing to say, but he liked this little look into Morgan in the morning, into the touch of her hair on his skin as he held her close, into everything she was willing to share with him.

"It's wild," she said with a smile.

Reece couldn't help himself. He leaned down and kissed her. This kiss was nothing like the kisses of the night before. It wasn't a way station to bigger and bolder pleasures. Instead, it stood on its own as an act of intimacy that Reece knew he would never forget.

"I like you wild," he said. "Don't try to tame who you are."

She seemed to take his broader meaning and nodded, and God above was there anything more beautiful than a satiated woman in his arms, smiling up at him with that perfect morning joy. Yes. Morgan in his arms.

"I don't want to anymore," she said. "I have every intention of running free."

"Can I come with you?" Not a question he intended to ask, but Reece realized exactly how much he meant it after the words were there, dangling in the air between them. Unfortunately, so was the ringing of his phone.

"It's Gabriel," he said. "That can't be good."

"We should try to figure out next steps," Morgan said. "I think Rhylee said she'd be back from the lab today with the results of the water."

They should. In the normal course of things, Reece would be back at the lodge by the time the sun came up, raring to take the next lead for the story, to do whatever it took to bring Malvern's shady business practices down, so they could no longer wreak havoc on the Montana wilderness. But with Morgan beside him in bed, Reece was pretty sure he could go a week without thinking about work once.

Still, the sooner they got to the heart of this operation, the sooner he'd know that she was safe, that they were all safe, and that the mountains would be protected for another day.

The sooner she'd be gone.

"Gabe." He didn't bother with niceties. He had planned on seeing if Morgan was up for a morning romp, and Gabriel probably already knew that. Still, it meant a lot that his friend had dropped everything — and in Gabriel's case, that was likely to affect the global economy — to come help Reece on a story. So, there was no use in being an ass about it.

"We have confirmation that Malvern owns the Conlon Group," Gabriel said without precedent. "It took some serious digging. He's surprisingly good at covering his tracks, but if he was looking to cut down on the bottom line, hiding the factory would be an easy place to cut costs. And that's not all."

"Of course it isn't." There was no way that kind of corruption possibly end with illegal dumping.

"The amount of money they're moving can't possibly be accounted for from a single factory's production. So, either he's laundering money or…"

"Or he has more than one factory." Reece finished for his friend. The look on Morgan's face showed that it was clear she had heard and understood the statement.

"Want more bad news?" Gabriel asked. "Or would you prefer a cup of coffee first?"

"Give us ten minutes and we'll meet you at the lodge," Reece said, realizing he'd grouped himself with Morgan in a way Gabriel couldn't possibly miss. But his friends were observant as anything. It was part of what made them so good as dominants. There was no doubt in Reece's mind that they'd already picked up on the something very serious going on.

"Rhylee made blueberry," Gabriel said, and hung up.

"We have work to do," he said. But he couldn't quite help the instinct to push up from the comfort of the bed to loom over her, taking in the soft flush of her morning skin, the curls of her dark black hair. The blankets were wrapped loosely around her, but her shoulders were soft and lovely. He knew exactly how soft her skin was.

"Then you should probably stop looking at me like that," she whispered softly. "Sir."

Reece had always prided himself on being the adventurer. His friends were all wild in their own ways, with lifetimes of stories to tell about rock and roll or the ability to move the global economy with the flick of their wrist, but Reece was the one who jumped in with both feet, who dove into deep waters and spent more time outdoors, under the stars, than he ever did in his own apartment.

And right now, he knew with the heart and soul of that seasoned adventurer, that he was in well, well over his head.

Morgan grinned, apparently pleased that she had stunned him, and slid out from under the covers. She wore nothing at all and the sight of her, back turned to him, her silhouette framed against the mountains of wild Montana, made Reece's heart stop pounding, then pick up in double time.

She was a woman as much determined to chase the horizon as he was, and neither of them had even begun to discuss what tomorrow might hold, or the day they finished their article—for he was definitely starting to think of it as *their* article—but Reece found that his imaginary future was made a lot brighter by the sight of Morgan stretching out a night of pleasure in his bedroom at The Ranch.

And that meant a world of trouble.

"Do I have time to pop back into the room?" she asked, apparently oblivious to the effect her effortless stretching was having on his body. "I don't think I can go to breakfast in this." This being the pink leather skirt, sky-high black boots and mesh long-sleeve shirt she'd worn to the barn the night before.

"Sure," he said instead. "Toss this on and we can head down the mountain." It was one of his flannels, long and comfortable on him, built for warmth and breathability in the cold mountain air. On Morgan, it fell to the knees and as Reece watched her button up, he found a whole new series of fantasies that very much involved her buttoning down. Or him buttoning down. *Jesus fucking Christ, Prescott.* The knee-high socks she pulled on were definitely, definitely not helping the issue.

"It's a look," she said, pulling those ridiculous boots back on. "I can't be the only one here who needs a change of clothing in the morning."

"No shame in that game," he replied, feeling like an absolute dork as he pulled on his own boots. When was the last time a woman had sent him this off balance? Reece couldn't be sure, but he knew that with everything they had on the line, with the threat looming around the corner, with the way he lost his damn mind around this woman, he was definitely going to have to get his head on straight. It was the only way to keep them both safe—from physical harm, and from a pain much more lasting.

Morgan was coming to associate the employee kitchen at the lodge with a sense of home. The hardware was all soft, dark wood and the room always smelled of fresh coffee and something recently baked. In this case, the blueberry muffins Rhylee had apparently brought up to the lodge earlier that morning. The woman was more interesting with every new fact Morgan learned about her. Reece had explained that there was a larger, industrial kitchen for the guests and for their actual chefs to work, but since many of the guys lived on or visited the ranch regularly, they had wanted a communal space to be away from guests. And what better way for men to connect than around food?

A large, comfortable couch lined the one wall, and it seemed like every time they visited, there was someone sitting or leaning against one of the counters, even though she had distinctly heard Caleb mutter, *counters are for glasses, not asses*. He hadn't said it when Skylar was the one sitting at just the right height to wrap her legs around his waist, though.

Today, the employee kitchen had one addition, in the form of a bulletin board that had been pushed up against one wall. Gabriel stood beside it, pinning on what appeared to be a spreadsheet of numbers that couldn't possibly refer to money. Maybe in his world, but definitely not hers.

He had rolled up the sleeves of his button-down shirt and removed his jacket, but those were the only concessions he'd made to the early hour, and Morgan was grateful yet again that they'd stopped back at Reece's cabin to change. It wasn't as though anyone would be surprised to see her in clothes clearly intended for the club, especially not Rhylee and Skylar, but she needed to figure out this thing going on with Reece before they broadcasted it to the whole world.

"Went old-school for this." Gabriel indicated the board. "I doubt Malvern is doing the dirty work himself, but it's extremely easy to set up a trace on specific searches, and I don't want anyone to be able to follow this trail back to us, at least until we know more." Because Morgan had already been shot and the consensus seemed to be that these men would stop at nothing to protect their apparently extremely valuable assets.

Morgan accepted a cup of coffee from Rhylee, who was sitting on the counter beside the coffee pot, then a large muffin from the basket. It was only the four of them in the room right now, and Morgan was a little grateful for the fewer distractions. This required her full attention, and it was hard enough to stay on task with Reece next to her looking as beautiful and powerful as he did, and with her knowing absolutely everything he was capable of doing to her. Maybe not *everything*, but certainly enough to make her blush over her muffin.

"Alright, so what's the news you couldn't share over the phone?" Reece asked. "I'm assuming it has something to do with the fact that our resident scientist is back on campus."

Rhylee stuck her tongue out at him. "Do you want the results from the lab or not?" she asked.

"Pretty please," Reece said with a stone-solid face. "May I have the results from the lab?"

"This is why we're really in trouble," Gabriel said. "Fen-Phen."

"Come again," Morgan said.

"Fenfluramine and phentermine," Rhylee explained. "Technically, both legal to produce in the United States. In combination, a dangerous weight-loss drug popular on the black market. Especially in Canada."

It took a moment before that information fully sank in. Then Morgan's stomach went a little sour and the coffee and muffin she'd been so enjoying settled like stones in her gut. They weren't just dealing with a senator on the take who cleared the ordinances in his way to make some extra cash. They were up against international drug smugglers.

Okay, so when she thought about international drug smugglers, she typically thought about jet planes and the South American drug cartels that the politicians were always using as an excuse to close the boarders and harass people of color in the southern US. One didn't really factor Canada into international drug smuggling, unless one happened to be in a border state that could legally produce drugs without much oversight.

"That's going to change things," Reece said quietly. "I should probably let my editors know that this is a much bigger situation than we originally realized. They may want to pull back and it's better to know what our platform is before we take next steps." Which meant he still intended to follow through on his story, even if *One Leap Magazine* wasn't behind them. Which meant he could be putting himself in serious danger.

And her, too, Morgan realized belatedly. Interesting how that hadn't really seemed to factor in when her thoughts went to Reece.

He disappeared from the kitchen, presumably to get in touch with the magazine, and it was impossible to miss his gentle touch on her shoulder as he left.

Impossible for Rhylee, too, who jumped down from the counter and settled into the seat beside Morgan with a conspiratorial smile.

"So," she said, leaning in. "How was your night?"

"Not everyone is as keen to share their personal lives as you are, Rhylee."

This was from a new voice, and Morgan looked up to see Van walk through the back door of the kitchen, a scowl on his otherwise handsome face. It probably didn't matter what Rhylee said or did, he was going to find something to grumble about. Of course, Morgan could find a pretty good reason why he was always so quick to irritation around Rhylee Cash, and it had nothing to do with dislike at all.

"I don't remember asking your opinion," she said sweetly. "And not everyone is as fond of the silent treatment as you are."

Her tone was a touch icy, and it was clear to everyone in a five-state radius that things between the two of them were going to have to come to a head eventually. The outcome of that explosion was still yet to be determined.

"If the high school drama is over," Gabriel said, straightening up from where he was reading at the bulletin board, "I need to be on a call to London in the next hour that could have considerable impact on the free market and we're trying to bring down a corrupt senator and international drug smuggling ring. So focus, please."

For a flash of a moment, Morgan realized that he wasn't actually as polished as he seemed on the surface. There were thin lines around Gabriel's eyes and his hand shook ever so slightly when he pushed the pin into the board.

She navigated away from Rhylee and Van, who were glaring at each other, and came to stand next to Gabriel.

"Listen," she said, "I know we don't know each other very well. Like, at all. But you're one of Reece's best friends and I know how much he cares about you." She paused and looked at the board before them. How he'd had time to do all this, she had no idea. "You've already done so much for us. I'm sure a short nap would be fine. We can cover it until then."

"I can see why he likes you," Gabriel said quietly. "I have to head back to the city later today, but I'll make sure to catch up with you guys before I leave." He collected his jacket from the back of the chair, and she realized it was the same one he had been wearing the previous morning. Had he spent the entire day in this back kitchen, working out a mystery while she and Reece had...?

"And Morgan?" He turned, halfway to the back door. "Thank you."

She nodded and watched him go, then turned back to Rhylee and Van just as Reece stepped back into the kitchen.

"They're going to run it," he said. His face was a little tired, but there was pure relief etched into his pretty eyes. "They told me I needed to be very, very sure of what I was talking about, but they're giving me a free check to follow this story wherever it might lead. So that's good." It seemed like all the men around the Sinclair Ranch were sounding and looking beyond their years.

"Take a breath," Morgan said. "Let's have a cup of coffee, then we can start going through these tax files. I'm sure there's a smoking gun somewhere in all this mess. We can get him on illegal dumping, but I say we take him off the board for good."

Chapter Twenty-Two

It turned out Morgan Tempest was much prettier than the offshore tax accounts of a corrupt senator. Reece had been digging through files and receipts and spreadsheets for hours, and the first few had been effective. They had drawn comparisons and parallels between specifics deposits and the movement of money into Malvern's campaign account, had highlighted a dozen ghost donations for excessively large contributions that matched, had found corporations with strange connections to the Malvern name. But it was late in the afternoon now, and all Reece wanted to do was look at Morgan. Well. That wasn't *all* he wanted to do.

Morgan must have realized he was watching her, because she sat up and stretched, cracking her back and pressing her pretty, lush breasts up and forward. He wondered if she was still sore, if she would come to him tonight again, at The Barn, in his secret hideaway space where he leaned into the other persona of himself and embraced the piece he usually kept hidden. He hoped she would, but he had no intention of pushing her. Reece knew that this world, The Ranch, The Barn, it could all be incredibly overwhelming, and with everything else they'd been dealing with all day, it would be little wonder if she wanted to head to bed after a nice dinner and shower.

"Gabriel said he's heading out this afternoon," Morgan said after a moment. "Should we take a break, try to catch him before he leaves? He's been really helpful on this story." Reece knew he should feel jealous. He'd felt jealous the moment that Gabe had flirted with her the first time they'd met. But all he felt was pride, relief that she liked his brothers enough to care, comfort in the knowledge that it had been his bed where she'd spent the night, and if she were to visit anyone tonight, here at The Ranch, it would be him and him alone.

What that meant for them tomorrow, when this story was over and done with, Reece couldn't say. Maybe he could stretch the whole thing out, take years to uncover the conspiracy with Morgan at his side. They could be the Woodward and Bernstein, the Barlett and Steele of Montana drug smuggling rings and congressional conspiracies. Of course, at some point Morgan was going to have to go home, get back to her business and the life she led in California, and Reece was going to have to find a reason to get her to come back.

Strange, that he was able to just accept that he wanted her to come back, when he, himself, had such a difficult time staying in one place long enough to call it home.

"He'll find us before he leaves," Reece said. "But come on, there's something I want to show you."

Because if he looked at one more spreadsheet of tax accounting, he thought his eyeballs might just fall out. And, beyond that, Reece wanted to show her Montana, to show her the world that he returned to because it was the closest thing he had to a place to hang his hat.

"Are you hungry?" he asked, as Morgan stood and began working the kinks of out her back and shoulders. Of course, he couldn't be sure if those kinks were the result of sitting at the kitchen table pouring over documents for the last several hours, or from a night of debauchery under the starry skies. Reece knew which one he would prefer it to be.

"Starving," she admitted. "You?"

He packed them a quick lunch from the always-ready food available in the walk-in, then they were headed out into the fresh mountain air.

"I know this sounds crazy," Morgan said, when they'd been walking for a few minutes, "But I just can't imagine spending all my time indoors. I get antsy after a few hours."

"Doesn't sound crazy to me," Reece replied, looking out at the vista surrounding them. Montana was a wild place, a place still not tamed by the many industries and developers that had swung into the state through the years. Mining and agriculture and industry, they'd all made their statements, but there was still so much left untouched, trees older than the continents, valleys carved by the ice ages. It left a person feeling important in their time, but aware — and grateful — for all that had come before. Perhaps their touch would be felt in future years too, and Reece was determined to make his impact a positive one.

"Will you go back to California?" he asked, after a few moments of companionable silence had passed while they followed the makeshift trail he could navigate with his eyes closed. "Or will you move someplace new?" It was an innocent enough question, except for the fact that the answer felt more important than anything he'd every waited for in his entire life.

"I don't know," Morgan answered honestly. "I love where I live, but it's all wrapped up in these memories. And, of course, I've got the business set up there and there's a lot of logistics in moving a business out of state. Plus," she smiled at him, "I feel a little claustrophobic if I can't see the ocean."

He grinned and nodded to the wide-open valleys that stretched out before them.

"This makes you feel claustrophobic?"

Morgan shook her head. "Show me a place where I can surf in Montana, and I'll take it back."

"No surfing," he admitted. "But we do have skiing and snowboarding." He pointed out to beyond the ridge of mountains. "And you'll find amazing lake snorkeling, too." He couldn't be sure why he was so interested in selling her on this place, or rather, he certainly couldn't admit it to himself. "Come on, we're almost there."

They walked the last few moments in quiet, both of them taking in the natural sounds of the mountains and the trees, then they came to a clearing in the brush. It was Reece's favorite spot on the entire estate, and the Sinclair Ranch land stretched for hectares in every direction. But here, in this little clearing of trees, he was able to capture a touch of that quiet he so appreciated from nature, privacy and beauty, a place for reflection and calm and peace.

He turned to her. "I found this spot when I was seventeen," he explained, laying down a soft, flannel blanket on the flat space he'd discovered all those years ago. "I was a bit of a troublemaker, you know. Not anything bad, but always looking for the next great adventure."

"I have no idea what you're talking about," Morgan said grinning. "I'm shocked."

Reece couldn't help but smile back at her. All she ever made him want to do was smile. Well, not all.

"But that summer I went to work for Beau Sinclair, along with the rest of them—" He indicated down to the ranch, where most of his best friends were currently working or busy with ranch tasks. "They called us the Sinclair Seven and we ran this ranch like a well-oiled machine for the old man. Then we went into town and raised all kinds of hell, the way a group of rough-and-tumble kids always seem to do."

Morgan nodded. "I might have some experience in the art of rough-and-tumble."

He'd been rough as they tumbled last night, and apparently even reminiscing about his childhood and the man who had taken on that essential father role to him when Reece didn't really know what a real man was supposed to look like, wasn't enough to keep his libido in check. At least, not where Morgan was concerned.

"I always took on the wild jobs," he said. "I'd volunteer with the impossible horses, try to ride the bulls, climb up trees to hang wires. Whatever I could do to get my adrenaline pumping. And apparently, I haven't much learned my lesson." Finally, he sat down, remembering what it was like all those years ago with Beau Sinclair by his side.

"I got injured on the back of a bronco," he admitted to her, pulling food out of the cooler so he didn't have to look Morgan in the eye. "I got lucky, mostly just scrapes and bruises, sprained wrist and a black eye from where my face caught my fall. But it could have been a lot worse. I could have died that day in the corral, and that shook me more than I wanted to admit to anyone. So, I came up here to work out what I was feeling about life and death and all that. Beau found me."

Morgan's hand on his arm was the talisman he'd been relying for all these years, and that old familiar guilt surged in his stomach. He was going to have to tell her sooner than later, and he knew that was going to be a bitch of a conversation.

"He sounds like a great man," she said, her voice quiet and understanding.

"He really was," Reece said. "I didn't realize he knew about this spot, or that it was my favorite. But he came through the brush, nearly scared me half to death, and settled down right here." Though the memory was more than a dozen years old, it felt like just yesterday that Beau had put his hand gently onto Reece's shoulder and they'd sat there, taking strength from each other. And Reece had realized that Beau had been just as terrified of losing him as he'd been.

"He said that there was a difference between being adventurous and being stupid. And that really brave men, they knew when to pull back, when to walk away from a dangerous situation to keep themselves safe. And that really stuck with me. Because Beau knew I was going to keep doing the things I wanted to do, trying out the dangerous and exciting opportunities when they came to me, but he gave me advice I could follow, that it wasn't cowardly to step back when the going got rough. I took that with me."

The look in Morgan's eyes was so admiring and sweet that Reece actually had to look away. It was like staring too long into the sun, and he wondered what kind of protection he might need to keep himself safe from her.

"Beau was gone, by New York," he said, "I'm glad for it. I wouldn't have wanted them to worry about me." He couldn't help but smile at the memory of Beau in his Carhartt coveralls standing on his front porch. "But it was like they were with me, Beau and Mary. And I kept thinking of what he had said to me, when I told him I was scared to get back on a horse after I got thrown. He said that it was the moving forward even when you were scared, and the knowing when to step back."

Reece sighed and looked out at the great wide Montana sky. "I thought about that—about him—so many times. It kept me from giving up and staying behind a desk my whole life." Even after he was gone, Beau Sinclair had saved Reece.

Morgan was quiet for a long, long moment, but she wrapped her hand in his and threaded their fingers together.

She caught and held his gaze and goodness if that wasn't far too much honesty and intensity for him in that moment. "Our demons may look a little different," she said, "but I know the journey you went on and I know how hard it is to feel like you're truly the person you thought you were after everything. The credit I give you for continuing to live your life comes from a place of personal knowledge." She stroked his hand. "Thank you for sharing him with me."

"I think he would have liked you," Reece said, trying to focus on the things she had said that he could formulate some response to. Because the rest of it was all too overwhelming to think about. She was the strongest person he knew and here she was, praising his ability to survive in the worst of circumstances. Funny world he found himself living in.

"I'm glad," she said. "He clearly means a lot to you."

"He's not the only one," Reece said. "Morgan, if you want to walk away from this, from the story, from this lifestyle, all you have to do is say so. I want you to be safe and happy, and I'm willing to say goodbye to you if that's what it takes."

She raised an eyebrow, and her eyes went hot and demanding. Lord only knew he was all too familiar with what she looked like when she wanted something.

"Do you want me to go?" she asked.

Reece just shook his head, aware that if he opened his mouth, he might say a lot more than he intended to about how much he wanted her to stay.

"Good," she replied. "Because last night meant something to me, Reece. It was—it was healing. Important. A step I needed to take on my journey. And I'm glad I took it with you." She had said the first with such stretch and resilience in her voice, but now he heard a little of the hesitancy, and instinct took over. In the next instant, he had her pinned on her back against the blanket, her uninjured arm above her head, and her body flush and warm against his own.

"Do you know what you do to me?" he asked. "Did you see how desperate I was for you last night? Every day since we met? Did you see? Did you feel?"

She nodded, the light catch in her throat making Reece's cock harden and ache behind his jeans.

"Then don't you doubt for a second how much I want you back," he said. "How desperately I ache for you, for your pleasure, for your release." He leaned down and nipped at her neck. "I could have you in my bed every single night and it still wouldn't be enough for me." It was the closest he could come to admitting how he felt about her without overwhelming, without saying the things that he couldn't take back.

"Reece." Her voice was already desperate and keening, just from the simple press of his lips to her skin, and Reece's body went hard and hot at the sound of his name begged from her lips. Still, he had a job to do and every intention of doing it right. He pulled back and looked down at her, and recognition flickered in those beautiful blue eyes.

"Master Reece," she corrected, just a hint of danger in her gaze, like she knew that she was pushing him to the edge and she had no intention of stopping.

"Mmm, do I detect a hint of sarcasm?" he asked. "That didn't sound very respectful, pet." He did have great appreciation for women who knew how to push him back, just a little bit.

"No sarcasm, Sir," she said, the words belied by the touch of a smile at the edge of her lips. "I would never."

"Now that I don't believe," he said. He brought one hand up to her breast, covered in another light-colored workout top, and he stroked her nipple through the fabric. It puckered and tightened up his touch and it was all Reece could do to keep from leaning down and taking her tight nipple in his mouth.

Instead, he continued to tease her with one hand, while running the other hand down her waist, down the exposed curve of her skin above the line of her workout pants. She gasped when he brushed her hipbone, and so he did it again, a little more intentionally this time, likely to leave a mark, and Reece knew he shouldn't find that nearly as arousing as he did. He wanted to mark her, to claim her as his own, and he didn't even really give a damn if that made him some kind of caveman. As long as Morgan enjoyed herself—and if the expression on her pretty face was any indication, she clearly enjoyed herself.

"See, I think you enjoyed last night a little too much," he said, leaning down to whisper in her ear, to feel the plush press of her breasts against his skin. He brought his hand down lower, then began exploring the inside of her thigh, until he was gently caressing her mound through the fabric of her workout pants, just barely a touch, whisper light and designed to make her absolutely wild. Which it seemed to be doing quite well, as she bucked below him. "So we're going to try something a little different tonight."

Morgan looked up at him, realization dawning behind the pleasure that clouded her eyes.

"Sir?" No hint of the sardonic tone or bratty smile behind the title. Just Morgan, and damn if he didn't love that.

"Yes, pet?"

"You're not going to deny me..." She wasn't quite able to bring herself to finish the question, but Reece would give her the credit she deserved for trying. He stroked her again, loving the feel of her clit quivering against his palm.

"I think I am," he said. "See, I meant it when I said I own your pleasure. That it's mine to do with as I please. Last night, I wanted to make you come as hard and fast and as often as I possibly could." He caught her gaze and held it. "I do so like seeing you lose control." He stroked her clit again, loving the way her eyes grew large and her breathing got desperate when he touched her. "Today, I don't think I'm going to be quite so generous."

He pulled back and sucked his thumb into her mouth. Morgan's clothing had captured her juices, but he still smelled her arousal on his skin.

"You're not going to come until I say so," he said, the order coming from some innate part of himself that felt right and genuine and honest. "You're not going to touch yourself and you're not going to come. Do I make myself clear?"

She whimpered, and Reece, who very much valued his own sense of control and honor, very nearly lost his own resolve. Because when Morgan whimpered, whimpered because he was denying her pleasure, it was like all his darkest, most demanding fantasies had come to light.

"Please," she said. "I can't wait for tonight."

He pulled back, finding it as necessary to give himself space from her as it was to deny her what she so desperately sought from him.

"You wait," he said, "or you won't get what you want tonight, either. Not tonight or any day until I think you've earned it. Do I make myself clear?"

She pouted, but finally nodded, and Reece had to give her credit for leaning all the way into the role. She was a natural and he loved taking her down paths she might otherwise not explore. And the way that she had told him that it had been freeing, that it wasn't scary or overwhelming, but an important journey for her, that had meant the world.

"Yes, Sir," she said quietly, and he appreciated her all over again, for agreeing because she knew it made him proud, for accepting the long-term benefits, in favorite of immediate satisfaction. And all of the immediate satisfaction they had shared the night before was a small part of why he wanted to take just a little more time before they touched. Last night had been wild and intense and Reece didn't want to push her body or her heart before she was ready. He tapped his finger under her chin, just enough so she would meet his gaze.

"You're perfect," he said, maybe not the words he had intended, a little too raw and definitely too honest, but the hot flash of desire and pride in her eyes ensured that Reece couldn't possibly regret them. This woman was taking him on an adventure of a lifetime, and no matter what happened, no matter how they left things when the story was over, when the week was over, he knew he would remember it for the rest of his life.

Chapter Twenty-Three

It was funny how normal the whole thing was. Everyone knew certain intimacies about each other's lives, and yet, they were all just down at Caleb and Skylar's house for a barbecue, like any circle of friends might be. They joked and teased one another, and though the group of them couldn't be more different — Gabe in his suit and tie, Dante with his sleeves of tattoos, Reece in his hiking boots, Caleb in his cowboy hat, Van with the straight posture of a man trained for battle — it was clear they shared a special kind of love, a bond of friendship and brotherhood that could be tested and challenged and would come out stronger every time.

And the whole time, Morgan felt at ease. They didn't wait on her, the way people typically did with guests. They let her help with set-up and spoke to her as though she was an individual, not the extension of their friend, and, of course, Skylar was close by her side when Morgan needed a friend — because it seemed she had found an innate friend in the two women who were as much intrinsic parts of this Ranch as the men who had founded it.

It wasn't exactly a secret that she was here with Reece. They shared his small cabin and she had no doubt that his friends knew they had shared a night at The Barn, as well. But that was sex, and there was something so much more intimate about initiating an innocent touch in the kitchen.

Will you go back to California?

It was impossible not to think of the intimacy and honesty they had shared that afternoon. She had almost wanted him to add, "because I don't want you to. Move here. Take a chance on me." But that would have been absolutely insane, and Morgan knew somewhere deep down that Reece would never ask that of her. He understood her need for freedom and the need to make her own choices better than anyone. He would never put her in any kind of position where she felt trapped, and asking her to stay would definitely qualify.

Except, it didn't feel as scary as it might, to want to be with a man again after everything she had been through. And not just be with, though the marathon of sex had been fantastic, but be vulnerable with, open and close to.

And now she was fantasizing about a whole lot more than running her hands through his soft, sun-soaked hair and pulling tight and—

"Where's Rhylee?" Morgan asked, as the small group of them had begun clearing dinner plates and dropping beer bottles into the recycling bin.

"Contrary to what it might seem," Caleb said, his tone dry but affectionate. "She doesn't actually spend all of her waking time here."

"I assumed she lived her, to be honest," Morgan admitted. "I guess it would make sense for her to be closer to work."

"The lab is on the outskirts of town," Caleb agreed. "But I think she might be going out with some guy from work tonight. Not that she ever tells me anything." He made a face. "Loves getting all up in my business, but..."

"You should be grateful she gets all in your business," Skylar pointed out. "I am." Oh, there was a story there, but before Morgan could pry, Van cut in.

"Who is this guy?" he asked. "Maybe we should run him through the system."

"What system?" Reece patted his friend on the back good-naturedly. "None of us are cops, so not like we can do a background check on every one of Rhylee's boyfriends."

"They're not her boyfriends," Van muttered. "She doesn't keep them around long enough for that." He didn't seem pleased by the fact that she saw men at all, or that she got rid of the bad fits with apparent ease, and Morgan had to wonder how long it would be before Van and Rhylee finally saw what was in front of them.

"Good for her," she put in, trying to lighten the mood a little. "She deserves to live her life on her terms."

"Amen to that." Skylar raised her beer from where she was perched on Caleb's lap. "Finding peace with yourself is no easy feat."

It wasn't, but here at this beautiful Montana ranch, it felt a hell of a lot easier.

"What do you want to do tonight?" Reece pressed against her back before whispering in her ear. God, he was big and broad and so intense she wanted to take a dozen years to break down his walls and make him fall apart in her arms, just as he had done to her. "Do you want to rest back at the cabin or..."

"Take me to The Barn," she whispered back, aware of how easily the response had come. "Please I—I want to see more." She wanted to see just how far he was going to try to push her, and how far she could go without completely losing her mind, and she had loved the feeling of him inside of her, of their falling over that edge together. It felt like a waste to sleep when there was so much more to learn.

"So eager." He pressed up against her with a little more roughness, and no, it turned out she was not the only eager one between them. "Ask nicely. Don't be shy. Everyone here is a friend."

And even though Morgan knew he was testing her limits, testing to see if she really wanted to be on display, the way she had said she did, she turned to him, bit her lip into her mouth until she felt that sharp burst of pain against the sensitive flesh and said, loud enough for the rest of them to hear,

"Please, Sir, will you take me to The Barn tonight?"

Pride sparked in Reece's brilliant green eyes and it sent satisfaction racing through her own body, lighting her on fire from the inside out as she thought about all the other ways she might please him.

"That sounds like an excellent idea to me," Caleb said. "Sunshine, what do you think?"

Skylar smiled. "I think you have some dishes to do," she said, sliding down from his lap, "while I change into something more comfortable."

A good-natured groan from the rest of them.

"I'm catching a helicopter in the next"—Gabriel glanced down at his watch. There was no way that wasn't a genuine Rolex—"fifteen minutes. So this is where I make my getaway." This came with a series of handshakes and manly pats on the back. Reece stepped away to give Morgan and chance to say goodbye. Funny that, how he seemed to innately understand her affection for the top-of-the-world businessman who seemed so alone in his tower.

"He's good for you," Gabriel said, wrapping her in a hug that felt far too comfortable for two days of friendship. "And you're good for him. He's been more honest with us and himself because of you, and that means everything. He can heal again."

"I won't hurt him," she said, pulling back from the embrace. "I know you want to be all brotherly, but I won't hurt him."

"Nothing brotherly about it," Gabriel said, stroking her cheek and giving her one of his rare smiles. "If you two don't work out, I can always swoop in and save the day."

She laughed and shook her head. "You wouldn't."

Gabriel nodded. "You're right," he said. "I wouldn't." He turned to go, but she held him back with a touch on the arm.

"Take care of yourself," she said, glancing into those dark brown eyes and knowing it had been far too long since anyone had said that to him. "If not for yourself, do it for them. Just, take care of yourself." They glanced at his friends — *their* friends — and he nodded.

"I'll try," he said. "If you promise not to get shot again."

Then he was walking up the hill and already accepting the next call and Morgan was very, very aware that nothing was keeping her here at this cabin or away from the barn any longer.

Reece guided her away from the group with a strong, powerful hand on her waist.

"Say goodbye to the nice folks," he said, as if they didn't all know exactly what game was being played here, as if all of them hadn't played some variation in their lives, of performance and eroticism, power and control.

"Thank you for dinner," she said to Skylar and Caleb, hearing her own voice crack just a little as he guided her away from the group and up the hill. His hand was warm on her bare skin and Morgan wanted him with an intense, visceral need that belied common sense. Only, he'd been denying her all day, keeping at the edge with those promising glances and demanding touches, and she knew she was nowhere near the moment when he would give her access to her pleasure.

She had told Gabriel that she wasn't going to break Reece's heart, but Morgan couldn't be sure that the same could be said about her.

"You're awfully quiet, pet," Reece said. He had released his hold so they could carefully navigate the hillside without rolling an ankle, and she missed his touch, missing his warmth and the way he ran his fingers over her bare skin like a promise.

"Gabriel is working himself too hard," she said, rather than all the rest. They'd dived headfirst into this thing between them, and she had no intention of scaring Reece away by bringing up tomorrow. *Even if he did bring it up first.* "He looked exhausted today."

"Yeah." Reece was quiet for a long moment. "I worry about him sometimes, which makes me a hell of a hypocrite, I know, since they worry about me. But there's so much pressure on his shoulders. He never learns how to put the world down."

"Atlas supporting the earth," she replied. Certainly, he had looked it this afternoon in the kitchen.

"Something like that," Reece said. "He likes you a lot, Morgan. They all do." They came to the clearing at the back entrance to The Barn and Morgan realized his room likely had a private door that wouldn't require them to walk through the club again. Good. She wanted Reece all to herself tonight.

"I like you too," he said, and though the words were simple, the impact was intense, wild and over-whelming. This didn't answer any of her questions, about what tomorrow might bring about if they might have a second chapter to this wild story they were sharing. But even though it only brought more questions with it, it still settled something in her gut, put Morgan's mind at ease, and allowed her to breathe just a little bit easier. This was intense for both of them, an adventure of the most wild and extreme sort, and they were taking it together.

"I like you too," she said back, and stepped through the door and into Master Reece's private room of The Ranch.

Chapter Twenty-Four

Morgan shouldn't have been surprised to see the yoga mats spread out on the floor before the bed. She'd seen Reece do yoga near every day they had been in the mountains — had admired it on each occasion, the way his body flexed and gave as he moved. He was an incredibly beautiful man, and there was no denying the power of his form. And even his erotic den of iniquity was shaped to his style and vibe, all dark woods and open skies. Of course there were yoga mats on the floor of the room. But she had the distinct sense that they probably weren't going to be doing yoga.

"Have you done yoga with a partner before?" he asked her, stepping into the room and closing the door behind them. He sat down at the small stool and removed his boots, then walked over to the shower, which she hadn't even realized stood in the corner of the room. It was a rain forest shower and blended in with the dark, wooded style of the space, which was why it had disappeared when she'd had much more interesting things to focus on. The door was entirely glass, and she could see that there was a small foot shower, where he was currently cleaning, then drying his feet before stepping back out into the room. She absolutely loved these tiny glances at the luxuries and indulgences that Reece enjoyed, into the pieces of himself that he kept hidden away in his space.

"I have," she said. "I taught for a while. We did a few partner sessions." Aaron had found out that she was teaching, and what exactly it was that she was teaching, and she hadn't been permitted to return to the studio. Of course, he hadn't framed it as such, but Morgan remembered the innate sense of disappointment she had felt at not being able to expand her craft, and to learn more about the world of intimacy and closeness that had come with yoga.

"Of course you did," he said. "This is likely going to be a more intimate variation on what you taught. My special blend."

He winked at her, and she knew he hadn't been exaggerating or teasing when he had said that tonight would be the absolute opposite of everything that they had shared last night. Tonight would be slow and decadent and intense all on its own, and she had better come prepared. Ha, that was assuming that she came at all tonight.

"If you want to wash or change," he said, "the space is entirely yours."

She had been wearing her running shoes, not her heavy hiking boots, but the small shower looked inviting and cleansing and she followed Master Reece's example and washed her feet with his wide collection of soaps before drying and coming out to stand beside him.

"Do you remember your safe words?" he asked her. "From last night."

Morgan nodded, appreciating the gentle touch, even as she ached for so much more. The time would come when he would simply believe she was ready. She hoped the time would come.

"They apply for all manner of physical and emotional intimacy," he said. "This activity is all about communication and trust, so I need you to promise me that you'll tell me if I push things too far."

"I promise."

"Good," he said. "Now go sit on your mat, back straight, spine long." She sat, assuming the familiar pose and appreciating the way it tugged at tired muscles and tried to give her relief from aches and pains that had been building for days. Incredibly, her arm barely hurt, and she knew she had been lucky in dodging most of the bullet. It was ridiculous, but she was more grateful that she hadn't been seriously injured because it would have meant that this would have been truncated and even slower, than she was for the potential pain and discomfort.

Then she wasn't thinking about her bullet wound at all because Reece was setting behind her, lining up his own straight back with hers until they were pressed entirely into one another. He was hot, warming her with the simplest touch, and she knew that tonight's slow pleasure would rival anything they had tried the night before.

"Deep breath in," he said. "Match my breathing." They each adjusted until they were breathing in at the same time, raising their arms in unison and brushing skin to skin as they lowered their arms back down to their lap. Again, they breathed, raising their arms then lowering in a lovely, choreographed dance. And once last time, up then down, until they were settled again in their seats, their breathing beginning to sync and Morgan's body very, very much beginning to warm at the nearness they shared.

"Spread your arms wide," Master Reece instructed, his voice so gentle and warm it made it difficult to focus on what he was saying with his words. "And twist your body."

They twisted, so her left hand came to her right knee and her right hand fell to his knee. Reece's hand came to her, and they settled there for a moment. There was something different about touching him this way, nowhere near as intimate as some of the touches they had shared and yet, a chance to take her to time, to explore the corded, powerful muscles below her fingertips. This was the opposite of all they had shared so far in this wild whirlwind, and she appreciated that Master Reece always kept her wondering, exciting, waiting to see what was going to happen next.

"Take a deep breath in," he said again. "Match my breathing." In this position, it was almost more natural to match his breathing because it felt like they were intertwined, locked together, and they were, in a very real, very physical sense. And more.

"Back to center," he said, and she followed his instruction, bringing her hands back to her heart and feeling the pounding of her heart where her thumbs touched at the center of her chest. In the normal course of things, yoga calmed her, it put her at ease and helped Morgan to find her balance, but there was nothing calming about what was happening to her body right now.

"And onto the other side," Reece said, "slowly, breathe out." They were breathing in unison more naturally now, syncing up their breaths without having to stumble, and she twisted in the other direction, bringing her other hand down to his strong thigh. Reece matched her in so many ways, pushed her to her limits and made her want to try harder. Morgan had always been the most adventurous of her friends and family, always the one encouraging the others around her, but with Reece, she wanted to go all the way, no limits, no holding back, no trying to keep pace, she would race beside him, climb beside him, jump beside him, and she would do it with a smile on her face every time.

"Back to center," Master Reece guided, and she followed his directive, bringing her hands back to her heart.

"Begin by leaning forward as far as is comfortable," he said. "Settle into a position where you can breathe freely." Morgan did so, learning forward and wrapping her hands around her ankles, then bending her head into the diamond of her legs.

"I'm going to lean against your back," he explained, "and gently apply pressure to your stretch. Tell me if I push too far or hold for too long."

She nodded and settled into position. In the next breath, she felt Master Reece begin to lean back into her. His back was so strong and his movements were slow enough that she could feel the press of individual muscles against her own back, as if they were blending together. Then he spread his arms wide and gently leaned farther into her body, pressing her more firmly into the stretch. Her thighs and inner hip flexors burned in the best way and Morgan leaned into it, the movement of their joined bodies, until Reece finally pulled back up, releasing her from the pose.

"Now I'll lean forward," he said, "and you'll press into me."

This was so slow, so astounding slow, each movement making Morgan want to beg, to demand that he return to her much preferred form of punishment, the kind that he had shared with her the previous night, of too hard and too fast and far, far too much pleasure. But he knew exactly what he was doing, pushing her to these limits, because each intimate touch, the joining of their breath as he settled into place and she began to lean back into with her arms spread wide and her chakras open to the room, to the sky beyond those panes of glass, brought them closer together, connected them in a visceral, dangerous way, made her want for the long, powerful explosion she knew waited at the end, rather than the bursts of pleasure that would mean short-term satisfaction.

He guided her into and out of the pose, then through a series of sun salutations that brought them closer together, then farther apart, each movement of their bodies making Morgan ache with that impossible build of desire and need.

And Master Reece pushed her higher, caressing her inner thigh as they drew their legs together, lingering at the curve of her waist with those strong, powerful fingers as they came into their twists, then released. They shared poses to open the hips and the shoulder, to expand the hips and the waist and to relax the lower back, and all the while, she felt closer to him with each shared breath, each quiet touch.

This exploration of body and skin and need was painstakingly slow. There was no hiding the imperfections of scars or scrapes or stretch marks against her skin, not when he was taking his time with every inch of her being, and the soft touches, the occasional kisses that burned like the touch of the sun, were all the reassurances that she needed that he saw her, inside and out, and he liked her all the same.

And she explored him in return, learning how to take his silent commands as the spoken words faded away. She found scrapes and scars on his skin, just as he found on hers. Some, no doubt, had stories of adventure or joyful moments on the ranch or the road. Her fingers briefly skated over the shrapnel marks in his shoulder and calf, and she knew just how vulnerable he had to be to show her this side of himself.

He was careful with her injured arm, as he brought her into balancing poses, where Morgan wrapped her legs around his waist and they used their combined strength to defy gravity, then he brought her down, not to the position she had been in before, but slowly lowering her to his lap, settling her against him, groin to groin, a thread of bodies that had seen each other on the surface and would now connect to all that was below.

In their thin workout clothes, it was impossible not to feel him. She was so aware of his body's needs, of the way he responded to her touch, his muscles jumping and his skin heating, and she felt him now, thick and swollen against the soft flesh of her glute muscles, as she settled into the pose. Reece continued his steady breathing as he held her in place, only this time he leaned down and nipped very gently at the soft flesh of her thought, leaving a hot, aching sensation burning in its wake. She allowed her head to fall back, allowed him greater access to the slick skin of her collarbone and the dip of her cleavage, and he took it, maintaining their balanced position he as kissed down her skin, buried his face into the swollen flesh of her breasts, leaned down to kiss her stomach, where the muscles strained from holding the position.

He continued to kiss her, barely losing their position at all, the only indication that he wasn't nearly as unphased as he seemed the tight catch of his breath with each new touch and exploration, and the way his cock throbbed against her flesh when she moved at his soft caresses.

She very much liked the way he throbbed, the way the powerful muscles of his stomach were pressed against her swollen clit, and Morgan rocked into him slightly, slowly, moving one muscle at a time until she was able to ride the blast of pleasure that came from the added contact with slow deliberation. Her muscles surged and she lost her measured breathing, only for a moment, then she caught it again, returning to her position and allowing Reece to continue his exploration.

"Your body is magnificent," he said, the words rolling over her as if they had been shared through telepathy more than spoken in this silent oasis. "You've climbed and you've hiked, and you've explored. It's like a map to the woman below."

Her thighs quivered from holding the pose, or maybe because his soft, dark words, whispered at the edge of her ear, were enough to make her panties wet and her nipples hard. She pressed back into him so that he might see the effect he had on her, the way she ached for him, especially now that they were so close and he continued to deny her the contact she so desperately longed for.

"Slide your leg over my shoulder," he whispered to her, the sweetness in his voice belied by something a little rich and heavy, something that made her want to do exactly what he said and also the complete opposite, so he would finally give her the pleasure she was so desperately longing for. But given the mood that Master Reece was in tonight, there was a far better chance he would give her nothing, and that absolutely would not stand.

So she slid her leg onto his shoulder, easier now than it typically was, since her body had been cooled and relaxed with their shared practice, then Master Reece moved his hands below her ass, pausing to squeeze her there as if he couldn't possibly help himself, then moving higher up to toy with the elastic at the top of her pants.

"Hold your position," he murmured, and it should have been easy, except that he leaned down and slowly began kissing the inside of her extended thigh, so close and yet so fucking far from where she wanted him most. He nudged her pants down slightly, and she moved with his movements, keeping the sync that they had slowly built until he was able to slide his finger over his swollen clit.

He pressed his thumb to the seam of her lips, and she opened on instinct, allowing him to press inside, to explore her tongue and her mouth, then she was licking and sucking his thumb deep, coating him in her salvia and releasing him from her lips. He brought his slick thumb down to her swollen clit gently, almost too soft to feel. Well, it would have been if her body wasn't entirely overwhelmed by need and desire. He circled her, pressed against her, made her squirm and roil and ache.

He brought his hand to her other leg and pinned her hip into place as he circled her swollen flesh. Then, hand still holding her steady, he leaned down and sucked her clit into his mouth.

Morgan nearly lost her balance, nearly lost her grip on everything tethering her to this world was pulled away in the quest for pleasure and release. Master Reece had been teasing her, preparing her, touching her in all the ways designed to drive her to the absolute brink, and now that he had her in his grip, she was dangerously close to falling over the edge, to giving in to everything he had to offer and submitting to the pleasure of it all.

But they had come this far together and she was determined to hold on, hold off, because she knew that was what he wanted from her, what he needed from her, and she was very much beginning to realize that Master Reece somehow knew her pleasure better than she did. When she trusted him, it was always worth it in the end.

So she focused, calmed her breathing the way they had been doing throughout this entire practice, and held herself in the pose, right at the precipice of her pleasure, until the mere act of holding on became nearly too much and she found she was trembling with the need to find her release, to give over to his touch and his pleasure.

But then he pulled back, and God if the pride and satisfaction in his eyes wasn't enough to bring her right back to the edge. He liked that she hadn't given over, liked that she had held on tight, and for him to look at her like that was enough to make it worth it.

"So good," he murmured, the words low so as not to destroy the peace surrounding them. "I am so proud of you." And she felt in her bones, felt in the way he held her strong and powerful, and she smiled at the praise, felt the renewed strength that would have made it easy to follow his directions to the very end.

Master Reece moved then, slowly pulling her workout pants down farther, as far as he could without changing the position he and Morgan shared, snagging her panties with them and baring her slick, hot pussy to the world. To him.

"Hold," he said slowly, and she did without question, engaging her core so that he could reach down and pushed down his own pants, slowly, achingly slowly. His cock sprang free and God, if this man wasn't a magnificent sight in all his glory. He was large and thick and throbbing before her and the swollen tip was slick with arousal and desire that Morgan ached to lick clean. She must have licked her lips because Master Reece laughed a growl into her ear.

"You'll make a man feel ten feet tall when you look at him like that," he said. "Hold still pet, let me get covered."

"No," she said, the word come out on a breath. She heard it at the same moment he did, as if the meaning hadn't registered until it hit the air.

"No." It was almost a question.

"Please, I…" This was ridiculous. She'd made Aaron wear condoms until they were married and yet, it felt right, the final culmination of all they had been building to.

"I haven't been with anyone since my divorce," she said quietly. "And after, I had myself checked because I didn't trust him. I'm safe. And I'm on the pill."

"Are you sure?" he asked, no teasing in his voice now, just the deadly calm of a man who wanted to protect her with every fiber of his being. "I'm negative too. It's club protocol, but I want you to be absolutely sure."

"I am," she managed on a breath, feeling dizzy and overwhelmed and oh, so aroused. "I want you, Master Reece. All of you."

Reece had heard some pretty words in his life, as a man, as a dominant, but nothing would ever compare to Morgan asking him to fill her, bare and natural, to give them the most intimate possible touch. Her eyes blazed with the slow burn of desire, and he felt her body in an entirely new way as she squeezed and moved around him. It had been a special kind of torture to move through those intimate scenes and poses together, but it had clearly been worth it, if it meant she wanted him to...

"I can't deny you anything," he said, not when it mattered, not in the real moments they had been sharing these past days. "Tell me if it gets too much." And he trusted that she would. She was smart. She had to be smart to be an adventurer, a survivor, someone who knew when to pull back if the cord didn't feel right or there were dark clouds ahead. But somehow Reece knew she had no intention of pulling back, not this time, and he was thankful as all hell for it because he wasn't sure how the fuck he'd be able to convince his body of what his mind knew to be the best thing.

Except now, he wasn't thinking with his mind at all, because Morgan was looking at him, just looking, like she wanted to consume him, to become part of him, to tangle up and never look for the ends.

"Okay, pet," he said. "Go slow."

She did as he bid, leaning into the combined bodies until the slick entrance of her sweet, sweet pussy was pressing against the head of his cock and God above, he was going to come right here and right now if the way she was touching him got any better.

"Slow." He practically growled the word, and the flash of satisfaction in her eyes was something else entirely. She liked pleasing him. It wasn't an act or some big new adventure for her, the way he had wondered it might be. No, this was genuine. She was giving herself all the way over to him, and all that he had to do was accept it for the gift it was.

The agonizing slowness was an overwhelming incredible gift that had him straining and aching to move into her the way they both so desperately wanted him to do. She was so close now, her lips wrapping around the head of his cock, and Reece absolutely couldn't take one more second of denied pleasure, not for her and not for himself.

"Slide down, princess," he murmured, surprised that his voice didn't shake when he was so close to shaking himself. "Fill yourself with me. Connect us together." As far as his dirty talk went, it was tame, but it was so in line with everything they had shared up to that point. Because it had all been culminating in this, a final completion, and coming together that he was fairly certain was going to wreck them both.

And then Morgan did as he told her, sliding all the way down, consuming him, taking his cock hard and deep inside her tight, sweet heat, and Reece saw flashes of fireworks and explosions behind his closed eyes. There was no latex between them, just Morgan and Reece connecting in absolutely the most visceral way, and when she bottomed out where their bodies connected, Morgan let out the soft, sweetest *oh* that nearly had Reece losing his goddamned mind.

Then they were moving together again, just as they had done throughout their practice, meeting each other's rhythm, stealing kisses as they moved back and forth, taking and giving and moving so incredibly slowly, as if they had all the time in the world to meet and explore and know each other, and it felt as though they did, now. Just Reece and Morgan wrapped up in their own world of pleasure.

He lifted up and she slid slightly, her position causing her to release a low, soft gasp, as if he had touched something special with his desire for her, and so Reece moved again, loving the way that she clenched around him with each desperate tug of movement, loving how he could feel her inside and out, slick and hot and ready for him.

Slowly, he placed his hand below her raised leg and helped her to bring it down from the perch on his shoulder. As if on instinct, she wrapped it around him, bringing their joining closer, creating that pinpoint space where they were one with each other's bodies. She pulled back and away from him, just for a second, just to rip off her pants and bra and toss them aside, and Reece scrambled to remove his own pants, baring himself completely to the room, completely to her.

Then they were there, her legs wrapped completely around his waist as she settled back down upon him, and they shared the same intense inhale as she squeezed his swollen cock with her tight, hot pussy. Morgan was close, he knew how she looked right when she was about to come and her body was tight around him and the knowledge almost sent Reece right over the edge and they were, just there, *oh God, oh yes*, blending words, blending kisses, the ultimate release of pleasure and need and falling, falling, falling together.

Chapter Twenty-Five

"There's something I need to tell you." Reece didn't really want to shatter the calm of the room, of the soft rainfall against the skylight or the way that Morgan's body had relaxed so completely against his that it was difficult to tell where one of them started and the other stopped. But this needed to be said, especially since the real words that he wanted to say were sitting right there on the tip of his tongue, and she deserved to know all his dirty truths before he said those particular words.

Was he losing his way here? Surely this was too early, too much, and too fast to be having feelings this strong. But Reece didn't lose his way, not in the mountains and not in the cities, and he was starting to think this was very much the direction he was supposed to be going. Rather than getting lost, it felt like thawing out, like feeling the sun on his skin and the spray of sea waves for the first time after so damn long.

"Okay." Morgan's voice was suspiciously calm, like she had schooled it to sound unbothered, but had overcompensated. Or maybe he was just getting better at recognizing the tiny notes in her voice that meant she was ill at ease. Getting better at recognizing her.

Reece sat up, gently guiding her with him. Their clothes were scattered and tangled around the floor, and he had to admit that part of his mind was still preoccupied with the incredible way they had come together, how they had seen so much with the more intimate and softest of touches. Which why exactly the reason he needed to be honest.

"Remember that day we almost met?" he asked. "In the marketplace in Istanbul?" This was a conversation he could never have expected to have, could never have believed real. That Morgan, the one from the marketplace, was a million miles away. She was halfway across the world, covered in a white headscarf and ankle-length skirt. She was a stranger in a crowd.

Because now, in his arms, he held the real woman. Her eyes sparked with joy and confidence, not muted by the overreach of a man she was meant to trust. She was passionate and engaged and looking for adventure, rather than scurrying past it. And he knew that now because he knew her, not as some amorphous talisman from a lifetime ago in a saturated city, not at the touchstone that tethered him to the world. He knew her. And she knew him. And he was starting to think that wasn't nearly as terrifying as he first might have believed it to be.

"Of course," she said. "Of all the gin joints in all the world."

Reece couldn't help a chuckle. There were similarities to be acknowledged. He did hope their story had a rather different ending.

"Something like that," he said quietly. *Just jump. The water will warm after a moment.* He had learned that many adventures took going through, rather than skirting around, but it was precisely those experiences that made life worth living.

"I don't quite know how to say this," he said, and he could feel her tense under his touch. "So, I'm just going to say it." A deep breath. "You saved me that day," he said. "I was just back on the travel beat and I was still having panic attacks after New York, and I could feel one coming on right there in the square. Then I saw you."

She turned to him, and it was those same eyes looking back into his own that he had seen a million lifetimes ago. Same, and entirely different.

"I took this image of you with me," he explained. "This beautiful stranger in a market, this moment of peace, you know? And any time that I felt those shakes or the sweats or my stomach get hot, I thought of you." He paused. "It didn't work every time, but it helped. You helped. The sight of you in that market got me through the worst months of my life, Morgan."

It was the most he'd ever said about her, about the stronghold she'd had over him in the years since. It felt somehow freeing and terrifying, because God only knew what she could be thinking in response to this intense revelation—and make no mistake, it was an intense thing for him to say. Reece felt that free-fall fear in his gut like he was too far over the edge of the plane window to turn back again.

Morgan was silent for a long time, and finally Reece couldn't handle the quiet anymore. The peace of the room was starting to feel a little too cloying and close, and the irony that he was right here in the room with the woman he would typically think of at a time like this wasn't lost on him.

"Is that why I'm here?" she asked him finally. Her words were very, very quiet, and when she turned her face away from him, he could barely hear her.

"What?"

"Is that why I'm here?" she repeated, a little louder, a little more Morgan. "I'm just trying to understand, Reece, truly. Is it me you like? Me you want to bring back to all of this?" she gestured to the room at large, the room that had been sanctuary to both of them. "Or is it the fantasy version of me. The one you've created?"

Morgan was having a hard time breathing. She was in the best physical condition of her life, a multi-time marathon finisher, capable of scaling tall mountains and barely breaking a sweat, and it was this conversation here with Reece that had her chest tight and the air stuck in her throat.

She was going to tell him the truth. That she loved him, that she was falling in love with him, had been since the day they'd shared a tent at the top of a mountain in a rainstorm. His quest for the truth, the care and empathy he felt for others, the way he was willing to do so much to protect the world he loved, the way he always took care of her. She was defenseless against the gentle way he'd infiltrated her mind and heart and body and soul these past days, and she had been just about to tell him such, when he'd spilled his secret first.

It wasn't that she minded, being his rock in a storm. It lent some credence to this feeling of inevitability, like their paths had been destined to cross since light first touched grass. There was something truly humbling about being the face a wounded man thought of when he needed to find peace in his troubles, when he needed to find a bridge to the other side.

If her feelings for him weren't so strong, if she didn't want him to see her for her so badly, she would be nothing more than that. Humbled, grateful for the chance to have been able to help.

But her feelings were more, and the idea that Reece might have built her up in his mind, might have created some fantastical version of the woman from the marketplace, it terrified her. How could she possibly live up to the woman who had saved him a hundred times over, when she was just as fallible, just as wounded in her own way, as he was?

"It's not like that," he said quietly. "I don't think of you like that. Not now that I know you."

She smiled, but it felt weak. The ping-pong of intimate, incredible, beautiful sex with this strange and complex revelation had her struggling to keep up.

"You think so, at least," she said. It wasn't an accusation. How could she accuse him of using the tools at his disposal to navigate the roughness of his memories and most vulnerable moments? But how could she do anything but protect herself, either? "But you've been living with that version of me for much longer."

"Morgan," he reached for her with the arm that wasn't already tucked beneath her shoulder. "Please."

"I need some air." Her words came out a little tight, like she was swallowing around shards of something broken, and she untangled herself from his hold and began collecting her clothes from the tangle on the floor. It was hard to explain, this feeling. It wasn't anger precisely, though she felt a certain sense of anger that he couldn't see what she so clearly did. It was fresh sadness, perhaps, at the loss of something that might have been, at an ending that came before a start.

Because they didn't have anything here between them, not really. She had a life back in California and he spent his days on the go, refusing to even come home to see his closest friends. And while getting shot at went a long way to cementing a lifelong friendship, they'd only been together for a few days. A few wild and intense and deeply satisfying days, but not enough for love, surely.

Except maybe it was, and maybe she was overreacting to the feeling that Reece was being open for all the wrong reasons. He was trying to be honest, trying to clear the air, and she appreciated that for what it was. But how could he not see, how could he not know that part of him would always see her as some untouchable icon, some symbol of peace and safety that would set her apart from the real person she was, with all her humanity and flaws and quirks.

"Morgan," he tried again, standing with her and pulling on his own workout pants. "We can talk this through."

"Yes," she said, as carefully as possible. It was getting more and more difficult to tell if she was being careful to prevent the onslaught of anger or tears. "We can talk this through, and we will, but for right now, I need some air." She turned back to him. "And I need to be alone. Okay?" And there was the crack in her voice, signaling to both of them, to the night of fresh, post-rain stars, that this meant too much, that she was in way over her head when it came to the way that Reece made her feel.

"It's not safe for you to go out there alone," he said quietly. "There are wild animals." Like they hadn't just been shot at. Like she hadn't been camping a hundred, a thousand times in her life.

"Reece, I need…"

She needed a moment, to be here with this confession, to let it settle in. Because she had no doubt in her mind that Reece had the power to break her heart. It was such a shiny and newly whole heart, a heart worth having, not that she hadn't been worth having before, but a heart she felt safe sharing with someone else for the first time in so long. So was it better to walk away from this now, before it became defined and concert? "Please, just give me a moment."

He paused, his pants halfway back up those beautiful thighs. He was such a startling, beautiful man. All blond hair and green eyes and a sense of freedom and nature that shouldn't have matched the deeply demanding nature of his dominant side. Reece was all adventure, the pull of the sunset over the mountain, the glitter of the stars in the blue, open skies above.

And Morgan couldn't breathe.

She stepped outside, out of the small haven they'd made for themselves in his secret space in The Barn, and the fresh air was warm and freeing on her face. One step, two, each move she took away from The Barn made it just a little easier to get that deep breath in, to fill her lungs with the sweet summer air of the mountains, and to think, truly think, about what he had told her.

The sight of you in that market got me through the worst months of my life.

How could she meet that standard? How could anyone meet that standard? She wasn't the perfect, fantasy version of that woman in the market. She had scars and a past full of memories, and God, hadn't she been someone else's whole world already?

Not that there was any likeness between Aaron and Reece. Aaron had been manipulative, conniving and driven by ego and display. Reece was humble, more interested in the land the open spaces of the world than having his name on a magazine cover. But she had been the center of so much of Aaron's need, the core of his day, giving him everything, from her business to her sanity, and the idea of being at the center of someone else's world, even if that someone else was Reece, it scared the living hell of out of her.

That was it. Nothing else, nothing else driving her sudden need for space and fresh air.

Liar.

She had left her phone back in the room, but she wished she had with her now, so she could check her Twelve Houses App. Though Morgan was fairly sure what it would say.

Stop running away from challenges or *Your rising moon makes you afraid. Ignore the fear and embrace your Mercury to properly communicate today.*

Because she was a little bit afraid, too. Because part of her, however small it might have been, had been waiting for some excuse, some reason to pump the brakes on their sudden and intense relationship. Some reason to turn tail before he broke her heart, which felt like the ultimate inevitability.

Morgan heard a rustle behind her, and only then did she realize that she had walked quite a way away from The Barn. There hadn't been many people at The Barn tonight, which meant it was dimly lit, as if part of the night landscape of the mountains, and the surprising distance she had covered while in thought made the building's lights barely stand out from the night at all.

Montana didn't get very dark in the summer, but a thin layer of purple light filtered over everything and cast the space around her in deeper shadow than if night had truly fallen.

Large patches of brush and trees peppered the mountainside, and when Morgan looked to where the sounds had come from, she saw she had wandered in a wooded area, where the light of the moon and stars above barely cleared through the leaves.

Enough. She had been traveling on her own around the world for long enough to know when it was time to retreat, and her instincts were firing on all cylinders right now. In truth, it wasn't like her to lose her sense of reality when in a new space, and the fact that she felt safe enough here at this Ranch said a lot she wasn't necessarily interested in thinking about.

But there was definitely movement in the trees behind her, movement that could have been any number of animals, from the innocuous deer to a mountain lion. Hell, they even had bison and bears up this way, though likely someone would have noticed a fully-grown bison making his way up the mountain range. She hoped.

She turned back around, aware that the prickle at the back of her neck was seeming to increase with every step she took. This was dumb. She had dedicated her life to making travel as safe for solo women as possible, and she had walked into a dark clearing of trees without a phone and without paying any attention to the world around her.

Your mind is just playing tricks on you.

It was a difficult sell, considering she was starting to see the shifting patterns of shadows that very much indicated she wasn't about to run into a sweet doe.

"Reece." She was definitely too far away from The Barn for him to hear her, but she felt better calling to him, like maybe the sound would carry on the wind and he'd just appear, and they could walk back to The Barn together. She'd take the awkward and uncomfortable discussion about what was unfolding between them over the sudden sense of panic and fear that was gripping her now, anyway.

If it was a bear, it would be better to make as much noise as possible. Mountain lions, a person wanted to avoid at all costs. Sound might help, but she didn't want to bring any attention to herself until she knew what she was up against.

But in the pit of her stomach, and with years of experience on the road and around the world, Morgan knew it wasn't a bear and it wasn't a mountain lion. She had gotten herself knee-deep into trouble with some pretty bad folks, as it turned out, and running down the mountain to hide out at this hidden oasis had only stalled the invertible.

"Reece," she called again, but the sound got caught, tangling in the trees, trees that seemed to be moving closer toward her, that seemed to be stepping into her space and...

"He can't hear you." The voice seemed to come from the shadows themselves, and Morgan's stomach dropped heavy and cloying. This was an entirely different feeling of not being able to breathe. She'd bested these men in combat before, but she hadn't been alone. And she hadn't gotten out unscathed, either. The bullet wound in her arm was proof enough of that.

"You're all alone in these dark woods and no one can hear you."

The men seemed to step out of the shadows now, and Morgan inanely wondered how it was they had gotten onto the properly. Like it mattered. Everything that Reece and Gabriel had dug up on these men had indicated that they were powerful, with long-reaching influence that went as high as the United States Senate. And she was about to get shot in the wood.

"What do you want?" Amazingly, her voice didn't tremble. It turned out tonight was becoming a hell of a time for Morgan Tempest to stand up for herself. There was a big difference between a metaphorically broken heart and a gunshot to the chest, though.

"We just want to know what you know," said the man.

He stepped into a clearing of moonlight, and Morgan could see the same fatigues and black military boots that had been on the men back at the compound. It was difficult to tell, in the darkness, but it looked like this man was sporting a fresh black eye. That meant he wasn't only here on the order of his commanders, whoever they might have been. He had a personal score to settle as well. *Wonderful.* Exactly what she needed.

"I don't know anything," she said. "I'm just here on vacation." Here to rest after the bullet wound she had gotten when breaking into their compound, but that wasn't necessary to disclose.

The man hit her. Morgan's instincts kicked in and she moved out of the way, so that only the tips of his fingers touched her jaw, but it was enough to send a shudder of disgust rattling down her spine. It was also enough to really piss the guy off, which, considering the large gun he currently had strung over his chest, was probably not her best course of action. But she also wasn't going to just stand here and let herself get beaten by some mercenaries with a score to settle.

"Hold her." Two more men came out of the clearing, and Morgan knew that the time for action was now. Once they had her hands tied, her chances of getting out of these woods alive dropped significantly. So she moved, allowing her training and her practice and the riot of anger and frustration she'd been holding in for so long to guide her through the movements.

She punched the commander first. His strutting and demanding made her think of Aaron, an absurd comparison in the moment, but hitting him square in the nose was satisfying as she would have expected it to be. Blood spilled from his face and he covered his nose with one hand and began shouting order to the others.

Morgan did her best to circle and contain the threat, but it was difficult to know how many of them there were when they seemed to be coming out of the shadows like specters of the night. She elbowed a man behind her with a move that sent her arm rattling, then brought the arm back to catch an incoming blow.

One of the men, who looked so damned young in the light of moon, got in a solid punch to the gut that knocked the wind of out of her and sent her stumbling backward. Two of the others caught her and Morgan stomped hard on the instep of the one to her right until he released her wrist from his gloved hands. But the one on the left held her tight, dodging both her thrown elbow and the crack of her head as she tried to get free.

Then he was pushing her down to her knees in the dirt of that tree clearing and tying her wrists a little too tightly behind her back with a plastic tie.

The big man, whose face was still bloody from her initial throw, a fact that delighted Morgan despite her circumstances, came up to her and used his free hand to thrust her chin up.

"What do you know?" He was pissed now, and the blood streaming down his face was a clear an indication as any that she was going to get the brunt end of anger.

"We don't know anything," she said. Her voice hurt and her breath still wheezed out of her stomach from the rough blow. "I don't know anything. Please just let me go."

"Do you have the man?"

She realized, belatedly, that the question had come from over the radio that currently hung on the big man's belt. It crackled a little and Morgan's stomach, still sore from the last punch, fell the last few inches into the dirt under her knees. This had to be a crew of at least half a dozen men. That was bad enough. But that they weren't working alone was much, much worse news. How had they even gotten here? How had they known where to look, when she and Reece had gotten away as quickly as they had?

But Reece was a journalist and she was a businesswoman. And despite the fact that both of their offices were in the great outdoors, neither was particularly trained in the art of espionage or escape. It was more than possible that they'd been tracked here without knowing it.

"He's not here." The man towered over her, especially now that she was down on the ground, and Morgan got the very distinct feeling that she was going to die here tonight. It hadn't been the first time she had felt like her life hung in the balance. Hell, the day she'd been scaling all that limestone rock in a sudden Montana monsoon had brought with it some pretty death-defying feats. She'd been caught in a riptide once, while scuba diving. Another time, her tank had sprung a leak, and she'd had to tandem dive back to the surface.

She'd camped in her fair share of storms, come across more than one bear and more than one shark, and even stumbled into a colony of scorpions when hiking in New Mexico. But only once in her life — the events of this current week notwithstanding — had she ever believed herself in true danger at the hands of another person.

The truth about narcissists, about egomaniacs and emotionally abusive men, was that they were often charming and charismatic. They blended well into their worlds, an easy defense mechanism for when their behavior was brought to light. *Oh him, he wouldn't hurt a fly. I'm sure it's an exaggeration. He's such a good man.*

It had been that way with Aaron, a man whose soft eyes dazzled and whose nice smile set people at ease. But when he didn't get his way, those features would become frozen, icy and flint hard. If he had hit her, and he never had, that would have been the tell-tale change in behavior. It had been that expression on his face, when she had been standing up for her herself the final time that had made Morgan realize he could, if he wanted to. That he'd been intentional in not touching her. He'd been gaslighting her since the very beginning, and what pictures or evidence could a person take of emotional scarring? What mirror could she have looked at to see the imprint of him on her heart and soul?

No, he hadn't touched her in any way that anyone else would have seen. But that day, the day she had finally left, she had realized just how capable of harm he really was.

And now, nearly a year later, she was staring into the eyes of a man who was unequivocally a villain, and it was somehow less terrifying.

I don't want to die here.

She had never wanted to die, not so explicitly. She had so much more to see, so many places yet unexplored, so much to experience. She had her mother and Emily and Alisha and her business with all its wonderful people and the community that had cropped up alongside it. She had the village she had met here at the ranch these past days, Rhylee and Skylar and...

And she had Reece.

Because it was difficult not to see, in this moment, with a bear of man glowering at her through bloody fingers, what Reece had actually been trying to say to her when he'd told her about Istanbul. He could have never said a thing, could have kept the desperate worship of the marketplace stranger a secret, but he had told her because he felt he needed to be honest, because he thought she deserved to know. Because he cared for her. Because he loved her, too.

It didn't go without her notice that she had done something similar to him, in her memories. Over the years, she'd thought about the man from the market and wondered what her life would have been like if they had run away together, if she had left Aaron at the tea stand and simply walked up to the clearly American man at the cafe and asked him to take her far, far away from her travel companion.

He would have done it. Knowing Reece as she did now, she knew he would have done it. He would have recognized the panic and fear in her eyes for what it was, dulled and flattened by routine even as it had been in those days, and he would have found them a motorbike or a car and taken her as far away from that Turkish bazaar as they could go.

But it hadn't been about him, not really. It had been about escape, about taking a leap, about protecting herself, in a way she wouldn't realize she had needed until much, much later. Just as Reece had used her as a touchstone, a way to stay grounded, to find peace in a turbulent moment of time. How could she ask him to see past her escape fantasy if she couldn't see past his?

Perhaps it wasn't that they had used each other as vivid imaginings as a way of replacing the true people who they were. Perhaps their meetings had not been accidental at all, but exactly what each of them had needed at that moment. But now, both of them, unwittingly because of each other, had turned into exactly who they had each needed in that moment. And fate—or Mercury or Venus or her wonderful rising sun—had brought them back into each other's paths for a chance at real happiness. There were just a few things they needed to work out first.

"Where is he?" Bear man had been speaking quietly over his walkie-talkie but directed the question at her, now.

"Who?" she asked. Life was a lot easier when people underestimated you. Especially people with guns.

"The man you were with." He was growing impatient. "The journalist. Where is he?"

"I don't know who you're talking about," Morgan replied. She had no doubt in her mind that if the men tracked Reece down, they'd shoot on sight. She was a means to an end for them, and growing increasingly less useful by the moment. "I'm here alone."

"Well." The man leered at her, and the metal of his gun was a contrast in coolness against her temple. "That is good news."

Chapter Twenty-Six

Reece was already in Caleb's cabin by the time he realized he was panicking. This wasn't the type of panic he'd felt in the months after New York, where his hands felt clammy and his chest got tight and he lost his balance in the real world. This was driven by real facts, facts that sent his fight or flight instinct into high gear. Morgan had been gone for more than an hour and the gut feelings that had kept him safe on more than one death-defying occasion had the hairs on the back of Reece's neck standing up.

"I don't know where Morgan is," he said, in lieu of any kind of greeting. Caleb and Skylar were sitting in front of the fire, tucked blissfully into one another's arms, and Reece didn't have the mental capacity to think about what he might have caught them doing if he'd arrived five minutes earlier.

"We...got into a fight." Kind of. He wasn't entirely sure what it had been, but he had known she needed space to breathe. He knew her well enough at this point to know that going after her would mean she never got that space to work out her feelings. He had wanted her to come back to him, arms open, at peace with the confession he'd dropped on her, but the minutes had ticked by so slowly that Reece had realized something had to be wrong.

"How long has she been gone?" Caleb asked, as he and Skylar stood up from the couch. Skylar was already in mom mode, as Reece secretly thought of it sometimes, firing off text messages to Dante and Van, no doubt, and trying to solve everything. She usually did a pretty good job of it.

"They're on their way," she said, as if she had known Reece's thoughts. "Take a deep breath. We're going to find her."

The panic settling into Reece's gut had him pretty sure that they were going to find Morgan dead in the woods, but he couldn't go there. He absolutely couldn't go there. He tried to find balance, tried to steady himself in the wake of this riot of panic and fear that never, ever got the best of him, and he saw her face.

No. He saw the woman from the market. The stranger who had run away from him with a man who wouldn't treat her well. The stranger who had simply been there, in a place and time when he'd needed to see something peaceful and beautiful. Morgan had been right. He hadn't fully divorced that talisman version of her from all those years ago from the woman she truly was — the adventurous, wild, hilarious, honest woman, who truly did put him at ease, who made him laugh and pushed him to be the very best version of himself and...

That was the Morgan he was in love with. The one he saw in his mind's eye now, the wet-haired mountain climber who had asked him if he was a serial killer, the innovative businesswoman who created a community for woman chasing their dreams. He loved how she stayed so level and grounded, and how she checked her astrology app every morning to feel a sense of connection to the world around her. And he loved, absolutely fucking loved the way she fell apart in his arms.

"What's going on?" That was Van, followed by Dante and…Cade Easton, the Sheriff of Wolf Creek and Sawyer Matthews, the Fire Captain. Their long-term partner Hollie was just behind them, and she walked across the room to join Skylar, who was already on the phone with the local sheriff.

"She's been gone for more than an hour," Reece found himself saying. "And maybe she's just lost, but if those guys somehow tracked us here…" They'd been so quick to shoot at Reece and Morgan on their own compound, there was absolutely nothing stopping hired guns from killing Morgan and leaving her body in the woods for predators and scavengers to find.

"Stop thinking like that," Van said to him quietly, so quietly that no one else in the bustle of the suddenly busy room would have been able to hear, and Reece realized his face must have gone white or red or something. He definitely wasn't doing a good job holding onto his emotions right now.

"Cops are fifteen minutes out," Skylar reported back. "I'm going to stay on the call with them."

"Who are these guys?" Cade asked. He was generally a happy-go-lucky guy, certainly more open than the stalwart Viking of a fire captain standing beside him, but he was a good person to have on a team in an emergency. After all his reporting around the world, Reece had found the same couldn't be said for most cops.

"Morgan and I found a hidden pharmaceutical company while covering a story," he said quickly, trying to synthesize what had been one very complicated fucking week. "We got shot at. She got winged. And we beat them up pretty bad before getting out there. But the thing goes high. Higher than you might expect. They want to tie up loose ends by any means necessary."

"She might just be lost," Hollie pointed out. "Even the best of us can get lost out in these mountains."

Hollie was FEMA turned rescue tracker and knew better than anyone how to navigate the Montana wilderness. But Reece wasn't going out there without a plan. Luckily, he didn't need to come up with one. Van handed him a rifle then passed one over to Caleb.

"Come on," he said. "We'll keep our phones on us in case the cops show up." This was directed to Skylar and Hollie. "But we're not waiting." And there was the military training in full action because he was soon leading the way out of the cabin and into the woods, back up to the barn where Morgan had left from.

And even though Reece was pretty sure his heart was about to stop beating, pretty fucking sure that he'd go absolutely feral if anything had happened to her, he couldn't help but be grateful. These men and women, old friends and new ones, had quite literally taken up arms the moment he'd needed them. He'd avoided their scrutiny—and their support—when things got tough, when the anniversary of the New York City explosion rolled around and he couldn't sleep and he forced his body to perform at maximum capacity until all he could focus on was the soreness and the pain.

But this just showed that they would always have his back, always give him exactly what he needed to get through to the next day. This just proved something he'd been scared to acknowledge for quite some time. He did have a home. And he did have people in his life he was scared of losing.

People like Morgan Tempest, who had captured him in his heart and in his mind. People like Morgan, a flesh and blood woman who wasn't some fake lucky charm, but the adventure partner that he wanted to keep with him on every great journey to come.

Van signaled for them all to be quiet, then their small group was carefully walking through the woods and —

Reece's heart plummeted into his gut. The movement was so fast, so violent, that it was a wonder the small group of men didn't hear it. Morgan was on her knees in front of a large gun-for-hire, who had that gun pressed against her temple. There were at least five other men standing around and who knew how many more hiding in the shadows of the woods. It was a strange thought to be having, when his worst fears were being realized, but Reece took pride in the dripping blood that he saw spilling from the large man's face. Morgan's handiwork, no doubt.

Van put his finger up to his lips and slowly crept forward. Reece was the adventurer of their little makeshift family, but he was more than happy to hand over the triage of this situation to the man with actual combat training. Those looked like some pretty heavy machines these men had in their hands. Reece felt useless and frustrated and fucking terrified as he watched Van disappear into the woods. A moment later, the barrel of Van's shotgun emerged right at the temple of the large man with the bloody nose. The man who was currently holding Morgan at gunpoint.

"Drop it." Van said, his tone darker and more intense than Reece had ever heard in his entire life. "Now."

"Or what?" the man replied. "You're outnumbered."

"Not exactly." Cade stepped out of the shadows next, then Reece was moving forward, desperate to see Morgan's face, to know that she was okay. All that mattered was that she was okay. "Sherriff Cade Easton," he said, moving just enough for the moonlight to glint off the barrel of his gun. The effect was entirely intentional, Reece had no doubt. "And my deputies." Not exactly, but it sounded a hell of a lot more official.

"He's no deputy," the man said, taking his gun off Morgan and pointing it directly at Reece's chest. "He's a journalist. And a trespasser."

"No. Please. He's not a journalist. I am." She went to stand, but another man pushed her back into the dirt and Reece nearly saw red. "I'll tell you everything you want to know. Just please don't hurt him."

Her words tore through him, made him wild and untamed and when the man turned his back, just for a second, Reece dove, punching him hard in the lower right side, a blow to the kidney that had the man reeling.

Then all hell broke loose. His gun fell and discharged, striking another one of the men dressed in black. Van and Cade both fired non-fatal shots that sent two more men down to the ground, each howling in pain. Morgan dropped, right in the middle of the gunfire, and Reece ducked a nearby blow from the combat Caleb was currently engaged in to get to her.

"I'm so sorry," she said, as they half-crawled, half-dragged themselves through the melee. The large man was still down, but the blow had only been painful, and they didn't have much time. "I realize I did the same thing to you that you did to me. Made you into this fantasy escape. I dreamed about running off with you that day more times than I can count."

"Shh." He had her by the hand now, and it might have been hindering their progress, it was kind of difficult to tell, but Reece had no plans to let her go. Not now and not ever. "You don't need to say anything, Morgan. It's okay. You were right. I haven't been seeing all of you. But I see all of you now."

"God, Reece. I see all of you too and..." He didn't know how he heard her soft intake of breath over the din of men groaning and bullets flying but he did, and he pulled her tight and shielded her from the fray and heard, in a soft, but steady tone, "I love you."

Around him, the world fell quiet. No fighting, no guns, no violence. They didn't have their dangerous, damaging pasts and all the baggage that came with them. They didn't have their explosions or ex-husbands or fears of getting too close or all the what-ifs that came with meeting each other in that marketplace all those years ago.

They only had each other.

"Me too." His words felt wrenched from him, relief that she was alive, here in his arms, overwhelm with the love and support he got from those around him. Joy that tomorrow would be written together. "Morgan, I love you, too."

It turned out that the silence he heard wasn't actually in his mind at all. Because Morgan looked up, then Reece look up and he realized that the entire

Duchess police force had their guns trained on the half-dozen mercenaries in the clearing, and that all the fray and chaos of the moment before was frozen in time. He also realized, based on the expression on Dante's face, which Reece could see clearly into the light from the police officer's flashlights, that their private confession hadn't been all that private.

And Reece didn't care. He was tired of holding his emotions in check, tired of hiding everything he felt from the people who knew him best. These men were his brothers, surely in life, if not in blood. And Morgan was his life. He would shout it from the top of this mountain for the whole word to know, because the truth of that joy, of that freedom, it howled inside him like something wild and suddenly set free.

Morgan gripped his hand, tight. The same hand that he had pulled up the mountain just a few days ago in a storm, the same hand he knew would always pull him up the tough mountain peaks. The hand that would hold him gently, caresses him sweetly, bring him pleasure, and bring him joy.

"I love you," she repeated, as she held him close. "The real you. The you right here in my arms tonight and for many nights to come."

"You're my adventure," Reece said.

And right there, in front of an armed militia, the Duchess police team, Cade Easton, Sawyer Matthews, Hollie Callihan, and in front of Reece's family, Skylar and his brothers, Reece kissed the love of his life.

Chapter Twenty-Seven

"I think it might be time for bed." Reece carried her through the door to his room at the barn as if she weighed nothing. It had been a long night, dealing with the cops and EMTs, and she had ached to be with him and just him for what felt like hours now.

"Put me down," Morgan said, squirming to get out of his grasp. "I'm fine. The medics cleared me."

"Maybe I should clear you, too," he said on a low growl, one she knew was designed to tease, but only tease. But enough was enough. She loved this man and she wanted to give everything she had over to him. Her full, unadulterated self. She was ready. Submission was a gift, as much for herself as for him. Because she was completely and entirely in control of her own life now, and that meant sharing it with the people that mattered to her. Sharing it with Reece.

"Maybe you should," she said in his ear. "A full-body examination."

She went to walk away from him, but he grabbed her by the wrist and pulled her close, and God, if the feeling of his body against hers wasn't something she would cherish for the rest of her life.

"Do you want to submit to me tonight?" he asked. "Because we can wait. I can wait, Morgan."

"I want to," she said, feeling the truth of that down to her very bones. "Master."

He slammed his mouth over hers and in the next second, Morgan was pushed back against the wall and pressing into him, desperate for so much more than kisses and gentle strokes. She wanted it all, the fire, the desperation, the possession.

"I can't tell you what it does to me to hear you say that," he growled. "Say it again."

"Yes, Master." God, the word alone made her pussy ache and her nipples go tight. Master. *Her* master.

"Good girl," he half-growled into her ear. "Now I don't have to mete outpunishment before the fun can begin." He stroked her again, more rough touches that she leaned into. "Tonight is all about what you want. Tell me, did you see anything you liked in our little guidebook?"

She was very, very quiet for a moment, then finally nodded. "Yes, Sir. Some things."

"What things?"

"Restraints," she whispered. "And forced orgasms." It felt dirty to say, in the most delicious of ways. "And…toys."

"Where would you want these toys?" he asked. Like he didn't know.

"Sir." She struggled against his stroking fingers, fingers that were playing with the waistband of her workout gear and making her buck against him. "Please touch me."

"Tell me where you want your toys," he said, pushing her pants down her hips and sliding his rough finger across her soaked panties. "And I'll consider it."

"My cunt," she whimpered and tried to rock against him, but he stopped moving his fingers. "No, please. I'll be good. I'll be good."

"Yes. You will."

"I want one toy in my cunt," she managed, arousal coating her every word. "And…one in my mouth." She could picture a thick toy moving between her lips, the sight it would make. The way he would look at her. Reece pressed her panties to the side and slid one thick finger into her waiting hole, and Morgan almost came all over him right then and there. But they had time. They had a lifetime.

"And?"

"And my…my asshole."

Reece slid his finger free of her pussy and slowly moved to the tight entrance to her ass. His finger was slick with her arousal, and he gently pressed against her opening and Morgan gasped.

"Here?" he said, circling the ring of muscle to help relax her. "You want to be filled here? With a pretty little jeweled plug?"

"Yes, Sir," she said quietly. "I know it's dirty. But it makes me so wet."

He pressed ever so gently against her hole, and it eased slightly. And God, wasn't that a headrush, the way she relaxed for him, for his touch?

"Shh, let me in," he murmured. "I promise, you're safe with me."

"I know," she murmured. "I know, Sir."

He edged his finger deeper inside her.

"What else do you want?" he asked. "Tell me, Morgan."

"I want." She moaned and bucked into his touch. "I want you to find me, wearing a skirt, with the plug in and to take it out and…" She was fully writhing against his touch now. Who would have ever thought that such sweet pleasure could be derived from such an uninhibited touch?

"You want me to fuck your asshole?" His words were more of a scrape, desperation torn from the back of his throat, and, God, she loved it.

She nodded, the sound escaping her parted lips an answer all its own.

He slowly slid his finger out and pressed back in, gently rocking in and out as he circled her clit with his thumb and Morgan bit her lip, a clear attempt to keep from crying out her pleasure.

"Don't hide it from me," he murmured into her ear. "I want to hear every moan and whisper you have to share. I want the whole club to know that I'm fucking you and making you come with my fingers."

She nodded and moaned in the same moment as he stroked back in, and this time when she pressed into his touch, Reece didn't pull back. Instead, he let her set the pace, rocking into his thumb against her clit and the finger sliding in and out of her tight hole.

"Can I?" She forgot the question halfway through. "Can I come, please, I need… I need…" She was babbling and desperate, but the pleasure was overwhelming and intense and she needed more.

"Give me a number, Morgan," he said, his voice strict and demanding and enough to make her wild. "Give me a number and you can come."

"What?"

He stopped his movement and pinned her uninjured arm tighter to the wall above her head.

"Give me a number," he said. "Then you can come."

She bucked into his touch, but he pulled back, and she let out a low, keening whimper.

Reece pinched her clit then, the tiniest motion, but it sent her spiraling over that inexplicable peak of pleasure and she went totally rigid in his embrace, rocking hard and fast and without ceremony against his fingers, then she was spilling her hot, wet juices all over his hand and whimpering his name as she came.

"Oh pet," he said, and had he ever sounded so disappointed? It made her ache to make things right. "Give me a number."

A number? Whatever for? "Um…eight, Master."

"Very good. We'll count that as one."

"One?"

How was she expected to think about numbers when he had thoroughly fried her entire brain with an absolutely mind-wrecking orgasm up against the wall? And he wanted her to *count*.

Reece's grin was nothing short of devilish, a riot of heat and promise.

"One," he replied. "Of eight."

Morgan must have gaped at him, but the heat pooled in his eyes and made her nipples tighten against the soft lace of her bra.

"But, Sir, it's too much."

"I told you, pet," he said, leaning down to whisper into the curve of her neck. He paused to bite the heated flesh where her throat met her collarbone, and Morgan bucked at the touch. Everything about this man drove her wild, and all he had to do was direct that wild grin toward her. "Tonight, your pleasure is mine."

She understood now, in a way she hadn't when first arriving at the club, that the domination, the desire to care for and control was nothing short of Reece, himself. Master, she corrected in her own thoughts, because Master wasn't the man she had traveled and camped with in the mountains. He was joyful and excited about whatever might be around the next turn of the trail. He radiated the energy of a young explorer, powerful and capable and intelligent, but open and honest and without artifice.

But this Reece, the Master who stood before her now, sucking the juices of her release off the tip of his thumb, was the other side of that man, no less genuine, no less true, a darker, more demanding, more powerful side. And it was the two together that completed a man she was coming to know and care about more than she ever could have expected. This wasn't a game to him at all. He was absolutely dedicated to providing her a night of pleasure she would never forget, and Morgan knew she wouldn't be able to say no to him if a million dollars was on the line. And they had so much more to see and feel. Together.

"Can you walk?" he asked, and she would have laughed at the implication, at his cocksureness, but she wasn't entirely certain her legs would hold her up after the last round of powerful, potent pleasure, and she gently pressed away from the wall to test her muscles. They wobbled, as if she had just gone for a ten-mile run without warming up, but they stood firm, and when she nodded, Master Reece finally released her from the wall.

"Go stand at the desk," he said, his voice strong and demanding and she scrambled up.

"I'm sorry, Sir," she said, when he finally walked over to her where she stood, hands on the desk, legs splayed wide. "I'm so sorry."

"Sorry doesn't cut it, I'm afraid," he said. "What you need is a lesson in taking what isn't yours. Your pleasure belongs to me." He gripped her chin, tightly enough that she felt it, but certainly not so tightly that Morgan couldn't get away if she wanted to. And despite the flutter of nerves in her belly, she absolutely didn't want to. Because this part had intrigued her too, the part where they walked the fine line of pleasure and pain, and she had been worried that Reece would want to tread too carefully to give her everything. Thankfully, it seemed she had been wrong on that score.

"Yes, Sir," she said. "I deserve to be punished for disobeying you."

"And what exactly is it that you did wrong, pet?" he asked. "So I know you won't do it again."

"I came without permission," she said. "I didn't wait, like you wanted me to."

"Good girl." He slid his hand lower, until he was gripping her around the neck, and the thrill sent shards of potent pleasure directly to her pussy. How could she possibly be aroused again, when she had only just come? And yet, it seemed anything was possible where Reece was concerned. Where Reece and pleasure were concerned.

"Thank you, Sir," she said. "Please, let me atone."

Master Reece stepped back. His eyes sparked hot. "As much as I appreciate the look of you down on your knees before me, I have another method in mind."

"Whatever would please you."

She wanted to watch him as he moved around the beautiful room, but instinct had her keeping her hands firmly on the desk and her head bent low. If he already had plans to punish her, there was no reason to disobey him further, not until she saw what he actually had to offer.

"Oh, so many things, my little adventurer," he murmured from just behind her, "so many things would please me." He pulled her roughly back, bringing her body in a nearly flat line with the surface of the desk, and no doubt exposing her soaked pussy to the room at large. Then she felt his eyes on her, burning hot and making her want to beg and demand and buck into his touch, but she held firm to her restraint. She was going to be good for him, and she had no doubt she'd be rewarded for it.

"Your ass is a thing of beauty," he said darkly. "It's such a shame that we have to mark up all that sweet skin."

As he spoke, Master Reece roughly massaged the globes of her ass, kneading and pinching, and each movement sent Morgan higher, made her ache in ways she couldn't even begin to imagine. It felt so wrong to want it this way. But even in her haze of lust, she could easily find the difference between the way she'd been treated in the past, and the demanding, powerful way she was being treated now. Reece was intense, passionate and wild, but he was safe, would always be safe. And while her stomach fluttered with nerves about what he might do to her next, she knew she didn't have to worry about her soul, not with him.

This was something entirely different from anything she had ever experienced before, and she had no intention of letting her past tarnish what was already proving to be an incredibly pleasurable present.

"I like the thought of you marking me," she managed. "It arouses me. Sir."

He pinched the soft flesh of her ass and Morgan gasped.

"How would you like me to mark you?" he asked. "Tell me all the little fantasies flying around that pretty head of yours."

"Spank me." It came out on a breath and she wasn't entirely sure that he had heard her until she felt the slight sting of his hand landing against her ass.

"Like that?" he asked.

"More." She wasn't above begging, not when it came to pleasure like this. "Harder, please. I deserve it." And she wanted it, wanted to know what it felt like to be entirely owned by this man, to be marked and claimed by him in the most intimate ways. And God above, was she ever ready.

"Like this?" He slapped her just a little harder, and the sensation had her whimpering and bucking and aching in all the right places, but it still wasn't enough. "Oh, you want more, don't you?"

He walked up behind and grabbed the root of her ponytail with one strong hand. Then he roughly pulled her back, so she was forced to look up at him. Her scalp prickled and ached, but she had never been so aware of her sensitive skin, of the heat pooling between her thighs. The hurt came with so much pleasure, with the perfect balance that sent her throttling to the edge of her desire with unbridled passion and need.

"Yes, Sir," she managed. "I want. I want more."

Hand still in her hair, he spanked her for real this time, his open palm landing a hard blow against her ass cheek, and it lit a fire in Morgan's belly that raced down her spine and made her pussy wet, slicking her thighs with hot juice.

"Look at you." He pulled her hair tighter. "You're going to come from my punishment, aren't you?"

She shook her head. She wouldn't, not if he told her not to.

"No, Sir. Please. I deserve to be spanked."

"You deserve to be denied release," he said, "but since I find myself addicted to the expression you make when you come, I'm not going to do that. Instead."

He released her hair and walked around the desk, where he opened a drawer and retrieved a large, dark wand. It was similar to the one she had seen used on the woman in the hidden room, and when he turned on the gentle vibrating setting, she felt like her skin was moving right along with it.

"I told you I owned your pleasure," he said. "I meant it." Then he placed the wand against her throbbing clit. Morgan screamed and clenched the desk, the sensation so utterly overwhelming it made her vision blur and her body go weak. There was no way she wasn't going to cum with that wand pressed up against her and —

"Come for me, pet," he said, and he brought his hand down on her ass. Morgan shot off like a rocket, coming so hard and fast that her fingers burned from clenching the edge of the desk, and slickness stained her thighs and dripped over Master Reece's fingers.

"Again," he said, pressing the wand against her swollen clit just a little bit harder this time. "Come for me again."

Morgan shook her head, her body still rioting from the pleasure he had given her, but he gripped her waist with one strong hand, running those thick fingers over the curve of her hipbone like he owned her. God help her, he fucking did.

"Where are you right now?" he asked.

"Green," she said, her voice sounding languid and all too pleasured to her own ears. This part, where he took from her what she didn't think was possible to give, this was the part she had wanted. She wanted to be pushed past her own limits, pressed into the things that scared her, supported by his strength and power.

"Do you trust me?" he half-growled the question into her ear, and that was an answer all too close to Morgan's reach.

"Yes, Sir," she breathed. "Absolutely."

"Then you'll come for me again," he said. "Because good girls take their punishments when they deserve them."

"Yes, Sir," she managed. "Thank you, Sir."

This time, she was ready for the smack against her ass, but the sensation was still overwhelming, the perfect balance of desire and lust mixed with the bite of pain as his powerful hand connected with her hot flesh, then she was coming, hard and fast and all over again. It felt impossible, and yet her body rippled with her release, bucking and straining into the abundance of pleasure, turning her into a bright light that radiated warmth and pleasure and need from the inside out.

"Look at how good you take it," he said. "Your body was meant for my touch. You wanted to be pushed to your limit, I'll take you there, and so much further. I promise you that."

Then he was down on his knees again, burying himself in her dripping cunt as he pressed the wand to her pussy. Morgan couldn't even scream anymore, the pleasure came with a torrent of need that stoked hot, almost burning her skin. Master Reece changed the setting on the wand as he ate her so hard and so fast that all she could think about was the press of his tongue in and out of her pussy, until the wand was vibrating harder and lower, a rough rumble against her already swollen clit.

He pulled back and she almost sagged in relief from the mercy, but all he said was.

"Don't hold back, pet. Give me your pleasure. Come for me. One more time. You can do it."

And this time, he spread her ass cheeks and buried his face in the tight flesh, licking the ring of muscle there, all the while tormenting Morgan with the rough movements of the wand.

It was too much. Her body still trembled and bucked with the effects of her last release, but he was pushing her all the way over again, as he teased her most intimate hole and stroked her clit. Then he was sliding his fingers into her slick pussy and there was no way she could hold on now, not with the overwhelming sensations of pleasure and debauchery. She was so close, riding all the orgasms she'd had that day, leaning into the almost-pain of too much pleasure and welcoming Master Reece's second finger and his third and...

He changed the setting again, the wand going higher and faster and stronger. Then it was too much, far, far too much, and she couldn't hold on a second longer. Morgan threw herself over the edge of pleasure and into the welcoming abyss of her final release.

Chapter Twenty-Eight

"Shh, I've got you, princess. I've got you."

Her sensations came back slowly, softness at first, the sweet, earthy smell of cypress, bergamot and teakwood. The smells of the great outdoors. She shifted slightly, trying to follow those lovely scents, and found she was being cradled, held in that sweet softness.

Finally, she cracked open her eyes. And there was Master Reece, looking down upon her face with such an incredible fondness it made her heart go a little warm.

Or maybe that was just the bath he was currently drawing for them. They were sitting in a pile of pillows beside the edge of the bathtub, and Reece had wrapped her in some kind of fleece or Sherpa because she felt warm and protected and entranced by the delicious soaps or oils he had put into the steamy water.

"How are you feeling?" he asked.

"Good," she said, testing out her limbs slowly. She was slightly sore, like she'd been trying a new workout routine, but it felt good, the way a long session of yoga felt good. And the pleasure that still radiated through her body made her feel like she was glowing from the inside out. "Green. Sleepy, though."

He grinned at that. "Way to inflate a man's ego," he murmured. "You do tend to pass out after pleasure, so far as I can tell." *Nope. Only with him.* "Can you stand, pet?"

She tried it, coming to her feet slowly, and he helped her up the rest of the way. It felt a shame to leave the warm cocoon of his arms, but that bath called to her. He took the blanket and set it aside, then slowly began unzipping her skirt. The touch was gentle and caring, not the rush of erotic pleasure that they had shared before, but something more intimate, more special, because she knew they weren't hurtling toward release, not in this moment. Slowly, he helped her remove the mesh top and the cotton bra, then she was taking his hand and stepping into the bath.

"Do you need a clip for your hair?" he asked, because it seemed he knew what she needed before she did, in all things. And that made Morgan bold.

"Will you wash it for me?" she asked. "Please?"

His eyes burned hot with pleasure, and he nodded, stepping away from the bath for a moment to return with a few more bottles and towels. He placed them down at the water's edge, and it was only then that she realized there was a large tray of finger foods beside the bottles of soap, cheeses and fruits, nuts and sweets. It was the decadent version of what they had eaten that first night they shared a tent together, and it felt fitting that it had somehow come back around in this way.

"Are you hungry?" he asked, maneuvering behind her so he could free her hair from the heavy ponytail and begin brushing it out. She supposed it helped to be with a man whose hair was nearly as long as her own. "It's a good idea to eat."

She realized it had been some time since she'd shared dinner with Rhylee and Skylar in the mess hall, and she reached for the plate. It was a beautiful assortment of treats, each more decadent than the last, and Morgan reached for a small sandwich filled with chicken salad. Every bite was delicious, as she knew it would be, but she could have eaten old shoe leather right now and it would have been perfect. Because of Reece. And this place.

"Will you bathe with me?" she asked, aware she was likely overstepping, but feeling the instinct to ask him with every fiber of her being. She wanted to feel him, even if they did nothing more tonight, she wanted to feel the heat of his skin and the stroke of strong, calloused fingers, and she wanted Reece here with her every step of the way.

"Is that what you would like?" he asked, gently brushing her hair free. The sensation was so welcome, soft and careful, and he massaged her scalp where the ponytail had pulled, a touch that nearly had Morgan falling back asleep.

"Yes," she said, her tone definitive. "I want to be with you." She said it in reference to the bath, but they both knew that she was asking for more. The question was, would he give it to her tonight, or would he make her wait another day?

"Slide over," he said. Maybe it was the skill of an adventurer, but Reece was undressed in a flash, moving into the tub beside her before she could get a full look at him in the nude, as she had been aching to do for days.

Still, there was nothing wrong with enjoying the way he felt pressed against her, all strong, lean muscle that made her feel feminine, somehow, despite her own toned and powerful arms. Reece put her at ease and pushed her to explore further, faster, and harder, all at the same time, and she knew she was deep, deep in danger of falling off this edge of this particular cliff without her climbing gear or a parachute.

"Eat," he encouraged, using a wooden ladle to begin wetting her hair. "Tonight was intense."

"That's an understatement," she managed, but she reached for the crackers and brie and made short work of the closest stack.

"You are an incredible woman," Reece said quietly, rinsing out the shampoo and lathering her hair with conditioner that made it feel smooth and slick against her shoulders.

Of course, after the night they had shared, all her sensations were incredibly heightened. She loved that he could do that, that he could take such intimacy and vulnerability and make it appealing and freeing and not nearly the act of control that it had been in her marriage. Ironic, that.

"You're pretty incredible too," she said, leaning back into his touch. "Did you talk to your friends today?" She had assumed that once they were safe, he would finally connect with his friends, tell them all that he had told her in the safety of the mountain top.

"I did," he said. "I told them about Abby, and the anniversary, how hard it is. For some reason, it was a lot easier to talk to the guys after I had talked to you."

She turned to him again, and it was impossible to ignore the press of his hardening cock against her belly as she moved in the water. He wanted her, she knew he did, and she wanted him too, in the purest sense of the word. No games, no toys. Just him.

"Do you feel it?" she asked. "This thing happening between us? It's real, right?"

Reece's eyes darkened and she knew they were diving into the deep end in a matter of seconds. She was very much coming to recognize that particular expression on his handsome face.

"It's so real, Morgan," he murmured. "It's one of the realest, strongest things I've felt in a long fucking time."

And that was saying something, considering Morgan knew all too well what it was like to lose count of the days in the darkness, to keep the world out, and to hide in the safety of the space she had created for herself so she couldn't get hurt again. But in protecting the heart and soul and body, one often lost the chance to make a life worth living. Yes, she understood exactly what it was to value true connection.

She stood slowly and allowed him to look at her, really look at her, at the way the water sluiced down her curves in the light of the moon, at the way her breasts were already peaked and hard at just the thought of being with him.

"Then believe me when I say, I want you, Master. All of you. Forever."

He pushed up, but he didn't take her hand. Instead, he reached for a towel, then, in a single motion, wrapped her up in his arms and carried her over to the bed. Her hair was getting the pillows wet, but Morgan didn't give a damn, not when Reece was looking at her like that and they were about to finally come together under the light of the Montana stars.

"I didn't want to scare you," he said, "with all of this. With the intensity of what I feel for you."

She leaned up and captured those lush, beautiful lips in a kiss and lost herself to his touch, to the way he set her body aflame, to the press of soft skin to soft skin. He'd kissed her in the most intimate ways, made her come across his tongue, but this felt more private, more intense, a prelude to something she would never forget.

"I still owe you three," he murmured into her ear. "If you're feeling up for it."

She knew he would stop if she asked, would stop in an instant, but she was tired of the kid gloves, of the training wheels. She wanted Reece, raw and unadulterated, and she wanted him now. So, while he was distracted kissing her neck, she wrapped her legs around his waist and flipped Reece and herself, so he was the one on his back and she was just there, so close to his cock she could slide him inside in a single swift motion if she wanted to.

"Go slow," he said. "I want to feel every inch of my cock sliding into your tight, sweet body."

She knew what he was doing, teasing her, taking this gently and slowly again, so she wouldn't feel rushed or overwhelmed, even though she'd been overwhelmed from the very first moment they had met on that mountain top. But the truth was, she wanted to take it slow too, if only to remember every single second of his touch, every important detail of this moment, so she could look back on it for a long time to come.

Morgan moved forward, brushing the swollen head of his cock with her slick entrance, and reveling in the deep groan she pulled from the back of his throat.

She had the power here, to move forward, to step back, to try new things and to call an end to the scene. She was submitting to a strong and powerful man, just as she had found herself doing in her marriage, but the submission was a gift, a choice, and one taken back with ease and respect. This was nothing at all like it had been with Aaron and more than that, it felt like a great moment of freedom to be able to submit to Reece's directives, to be able to take orders after all this time and not worry for her soul. This was nirvana. This was healing.

"Please, princess," he said. "I need you."

He needed her. After all this time of aching for him, and Reece was begging for *her*. Slowly, Morgan began to lower herself down the swollen shaft of his cock, and she was incredibly grateful for his order. He was big, bigger even than he had seemed in the starlight, and though she was more aroused and ready than she had ever been in her life, she felt stretched and full as she accepted him into her body and…oh *God*.

She fell forward slightly, catching herself on Reece's toned, strong chest, and his cock hit some secret place inside her and she almost lost her mind right then and there.

"Your pace," he said. Catching her. Holding her. "We go at your pace."

Except she wanted him beside her, with her, taking and giving control in equal measure.

"Together," she murmured. "Please, Sir. Take me."

Reece's movements were slow at first, even and calmly paced, and she knew he had to be holding himself back so strongly, like the tightest leash. So, she reached back and gently took one of his tight balls in her hand, massaging it around her palm until Reece was swearing under his breath.

"Don't tempt me, pet," he said. But Morgan had every plan to. She leaned back, appreciating all those extra hours of yoga more than ever, and captured his thighs in her hands, then she began to rock. She took him in and out, in and out, each movement pressing against her clit and making her moan, ache, burn for more.

Reece brought one hand to her waist and held her in place, and the strong, powerful sensation of his hands on her was enough to spur her higher, even as he paused her motions.

"You feel so fucking good, baby," he growled through gritted teeth. She wanted to make him fall over that edge of pleasure more than she wanted her next breath. "Please, I want this to last."

Morgan ignored him, rocked hard, took him all the way in, then pulled nearly free before dropping down again. So he brought his hand to her clit and circled the tight nub there, which nearly had her spiraling out of control all over again.

"Look at how good we fit together," he said. "Look at the way your tight little pussy accepts my cock. How does it feel? Tell me."

Morgan had both hands on her breasts, kneading and massing the sensitive flesh there as she rode him, and losing her mind with every thrust.

"It feels so fucking good," she moaned. "Please, I need…"

"You need to come for me." he said. "Now." He pinched her clit, hard, and the sensation of rioting pain sent her hurtling over the edge of her pleasure until she knew she was coming hard and fast all over his cock.

"Again," he said, thrusting up hard and fast, so he hit her spot hard again. "Come for me again."

Morgan shook her head. "It's too much," she managed. "I want you to come with me."

"I will," he said. "After you finish for me one more time. Be good for me. I know you can."

She wanted to argue, but there was such faith in his voice, and more than argue, she wanted to please him, wanted to make him proud, and so she pinched her nipples and picked up speed and leaned into Reece's touch on her clit and, amazingly, she was coming again, this one catching her off-guard and sending her floating through pleasure and intensity. It was all so much, so much sensation, but delicious and soft and full of incredible joy.

Then Reece was flipping them, pinning her hands down to the pillow, somehow still managing to care for her wounded arm in the process, and sliding out of her pussy with incredible precision.

"Who do you belong to?" he asked, each inch out driving her nearly as mad as each inch in. "Who does this pussy belong to?"

"You," she breathed, aroused even more by the desperation in Fhis voice. "It's all yours." *I'm yours.*

"Fuck yeah, it is." He slid home, taking her once, twice, once more then, "come with me, Morgan, come all over my cock while I mark you." And he did, pulling out at the last minute and to send thick ropes of cum across her stomach and chest. And the feeling of being marked, the intensity of knowing her owned her and she still owned herself, sent Morgan right over the edge all over again. This time, she had taken Reece with her.

Epilogue

"Are you nervous?" He felt her presence behind him in the office before she spoke. Even after nearly six months together, six months of adventures, of travel and business building, and chasing down new stories, Reece still felt a sense of need and joy that just accompanied their sharing the same space.

"Not in the slightest," he said, pulling her into his arms and wrapping them together on the chair. The chair where they'd made hot, loud love just last night. "We've checked every source and verified every claim. It's time."

Time to release their feature exposé on Dick Malvern and the ongoing police investigation. Time to expose the illegal dumping, drug trade and bribery going on at the highest level. And Morgan's name was going to be right next to his.

"Are you?" he asked, nuzzling into her neck and inhaling the sweet smell of the fresh outdoors. She'd been outside with the dog, then, a little mutt they'd picked up on the side of the road during a sojourn across North Carolina. Reece made his home in Montana now, and it hadn't taken long for Morgan to say goodbye to the world she had lived in with her ex-husband. She'd moved the business out and now they shared a large cabin on the estate, with room for his office and her business, and plenty of weekend adventures and morning hikes to be had.

And right now, she smelled like cold mountain air and all Morgan. He would never, ever get tired of this woman and the world they'd made for each other.

"Yes," she said quietly. "But not because of the article." She stepped free of his lap and walked through the double doors of their bedroom to the enormous balcony beyond. It overlooked the snowcapped mountains and had proven to be quite a wonderful place for making love under the stars.

Reece followed her. "Why then?" he asked, watching the way the light brushed across her face, setting her dark curls to gold and pink. "My Little Storm, what could possibly make you nervous?"

She smiled and wordlessly handed him a small box from the pocket of her robe.

The tag said, *the biggest adventure is yet to come*. Reece gently opened it, his heart pounding hard and intense, an awareness of change and need rioting through him.

It was a pregnancy test. A positive pregnancy test.

Morgan. Is pregnant.

"I'm going to be a dad." The words caught in his throat and Reece realized he was crying, the joy of being a father to this woman's baby overwhelming him. The need to protect her and love her making him wild.

"You're going to be a dad."

She was crying too, and he swept her up in his arms and held her tight, but not too tight, sharing every single thing he felt in those embraces. An adventure, indeed.

As it turned out, the bedroom balcony was a wonderful place for making love in the morning winter sunshine, as well. And a wonderful place for playing with the twins, when they came, then their little girl when she entered the world, too. That balcony, their Montana home, their Ranch made up of found family, and the whole wide world, it all belonged to them. A family of wild explorers and adventurers, embracing joy, finding color, learning something new every time they left home.

And always, always, always, wherever the next trip led, holding love close every step of the way.

Want to see more from this author? Here's a taster for you to enjoy!

Triple Diamond: Wild Flowers
Gemma Snow

Excerpt

"We've got a scent!"

Axel was trying hard not to get too far ahead of Micah to see, and Micah did his best to keep pace, following the large and very determined golden retriever down a steep incline, clenching his thighs and lowering his center of gravity to avoid sliding on the wet, fallen leaves that coated the Clark Mountain Range of Glacier National Park, at the edge of the Montana–Canada border. Axel, on his four legs, was doing a much better job holding his grip on the ground, but Micah had no desire to go sliding off the edge of the mountain and into the depths of the canyons below, so he whistled a command and the dog slowed enough for Micah to catch up.

Still, they kept an admirable pace and quickly came to a plateau of flat ground. High above, at the top of the ridge, Micah heard his partner Dec — Deckard McCormick — approaching with Rosie, Axel's sister. Rosie kicked up a pile of leaves on the approach, clearly picking up on the same scent Axel had.

"Anything down there?" Dec shouted, the sound catching and echoing off the many flat walls of the mountain range.

"I think I saw a cave," Micah called back, straining to look around the corner of a large boulder that jutted forth from the ground and mountainside. "Give me a second. I'll let you know whether or not to come down."

Dec gave the affirmative then Micah crouched low to peer around the edge of the boulder.

Oh, shit.

That wasn't just a boulder. That was the edge of the fucking mountain, looking down over a sheer two hundred foot drop to the canyon below. For a fleeting, horrible second, vertigo caught his senses and nearly dragged him to his knees, making the sky and the high trees waver and tilt.

But Micah put a steadying hand on the rock wall and took a deep breath, settling the sky firmly above him and the ground firmly below. He commanded Axel to stay put—not that he needed to. Axel was a damn smart dog and knew better than to go canyon jumping. Then Micah lay flat on his stomach, damn near hanging over the edge of the mountain, to look around the boulder's protruding side.

There was definitely a cave on the other side, a yawning, darkened mouth, gaping right over the valley. The question was—was there anyone in it?

"Hello," he called, his breath labored and caught, what with his stomach pressed against the ground. And he was still pressed against the ground. He had to keep reminding himself of that. The stones and wet leaves that rasped against his forearms, giving a slight fall chill in the mountains, were all real. For this moment, at least, he wasn't plummeting toward certain death below.

"Is there anyone in the cave?" *A pause.* The silence was weighty, colored by the sounds of raptors flying overhead and wind rippling through the trees that towered high above the ground, giving Micah a very odd sense of perspective as to exactly how far up in the sky he was.

Oh, about ten thousand feet...

But now was just about the worst time to calculate the distance it would take to kill a grown man, so he focused his attention on the solid ground and his mission and called out again. "This is Lewis and Clark County Search and Rescue Agent Micah Ellison, I repeat, is there anyone in the cave?"

A sound. It was barely even a real sound and if he hadn't been trained by the very best to determine the difference between human and nature, he might not have heard it. But there it was, a whimper catching on the wind, the softest, shuddering inhalation of a very terrified child.

Chloe Robinson. Female. African American. Six years old and approximately thirty-nine inches tall. Last seen Tuesday, October Eight. Amber alert issued Wednesday, October Nine.

She'd been gone a week. In the world of search and rescue, a week was no better than a month was no better than a year. It was true what they said about forty-eight hours. Truer still when the Montana mountain ranges, of which there were many, were known for being unforgiving and merciless. Micah knew all about that first-hand.

But there was no denying the signs of life coming from the other side of the boulder. After nearly a decade of doing this job, Micah knew the sound of a frightened child all too well and unless the universe played some pretty hairy tricks, the girl on the other side of that sheer drop down to the valley was Chloe Robinson.

"Chloe," he called out, hoping the sound would carry and not get lost on the wind, as any calls he made toward Dec and the team undoubtedly would. "Chloe Robinson."

The sound of her fearful whimpering increased and when he called her name again, this time she answered him. *Thank fuck for small victories.*

"How do you know my name?"

But that was the way of kids, wasn't it? Find them hidden in a darkened cave in the middle of a mountain range and they want to know how you know their name.

"Your mom and dad told me," Micah replied. "See, they've been missing you and they sent me and my partner Dec out to see if we could find you with our dogs, Axel and Rosie. Do you like dogs, Chloe?"

A small sniff echoed across the gap, then, "I have a dog…at home. Her name is Daisy."

Micah sighed in relief. Good, she was talking, which meant she wasn't too dehydrated to function or too badly injured. He hoped.

"Well, Chloe, I'd really like to get you back home to Daisy, okay?" he said. "Now, I'm going to talk to my partner, but I'll be right back…"

"No!" she shouted the word before he even finished his sentence. "Stay. Don't leave. I don't want to be alone anymore."

Micah nodded and as carefully as he could, reached for the radio on his utility belt.

"Okay, I'm not leaving," he said. "But I'm going to talk to him over the radio, okay? I just want to let him know that I found you, all right?"

She sniffled but agreed and Micah brought the radio to his mouth, doing his damnedest to think about Chloe, the brave as all hell six-year-old in the cave, and not the freaking mountainous drop right below his face.

"Dec," he radioed over. "She's here." The radio crackled in and out, then cut out completely, plunging the mountain's edge into silence that suddenly felt a whole hell of a lot colder and lonelier than it had a minute ago.

Or maybe that was just the clouds rolling in overhead. *For fuck's sake.*

Okay, okay. He'd dealt with hairier situations than this and he was damn well going to get that girl out of the cave if it was his last act on earth and all that. He sent up a prayer to as many of his gods as he could remember in the moment then called back to the little girl.

"Just you and me now, Chloe, okay?" he said. "Now, I'm going to hook my belaying chord to a tree on this side of the gap then I'm coming over to you. You can talk to me. I can hear you."

He stood and stepped a foot in from the edge of the cliff, allowing himself one deep breath before walking over to the thick oak tree growing sideways out of the mountain. He tested a branch with his weight, finding it thick and sturdy, before tossing the end of the rope around it and securing the knot that he had been tying since he was about Chloe's age. He tugged on the end attached to his security belt and, satisfied, returned to the edge of the mountain.

"How did you end up here, Chloe?" *Don't look down, Micah.*

"I got lost," Chloe said, only a slight sniffle to her voice. *Christ, this six-year-old little girl has bigger balls than I do.* "I hid in the cave and fell asleep then there was a huge lightning storm. I woke up when all the rocks crashed."

On closer inspection, Micah could tell that a big section of the mountain had broken free, creating the gap between him and the cave where Chloe was hidden. She'd walked into the cave and hadn't been able to walk out, unless she was some sort of New Age Jesus.

"Well, you're very brave, Chloe," he said, testing the rope one more time. "I'm coming over now, okay?" And before she could answer him, he began the slow, one-foot-in-front-of-the-other walk across the large yawning mouth of the valley. He didn't dare lift his feet, but rather scraped them along the mountain's edge, making rock and dust crumble, and he gritted his teeth to keep from following their path with his eyes.

He'd been working for Lewis and Clark County Search and Rescue Team for nearly six years and he never got over that feeling of being suspended over the incredibly far valley below. Even two decades later, memories still plagued him, very nearly paralyzing a man who was otherwise incredibly good at his job.

But before Micah could give in to any of those fears or panics, his feet touched down on the other side, grounding him against the dirt and mossy leaves, and there he was, at the entrance to the cave.

"Chloe," he called, his voice soft and gentle. "It's me, Micah. Do you want to come out of there now?"

She emerged, her movements slow and wary. Her clothes were dirty and her hair had all manner of sticks and leaves tangled in the curls, but she appeared otherwise unharmed, and Micah let out a low breath of relief. "You did a good job hiding here, honey," he said. "Now, I'd like to bring you home to your mom and dad, okay?"

She nodded and sniffled. "Okay." It seemed that the bravery that had gotten her so far was just about tapped out. Well, fine, she was allowed to be a kid again. It was no longer her responsibility to get home safely.

"Okay," he repeated. "Now, I'm going to hook you into this harness, then we're going to slowly walk across that gap. My dog, Axel, he's on the other side, waiting to meet you."

She nodded and, before either of them got the chance to freak the fuck out about trekking across that massive drop again, Micah had her hooked into the front section of the harness built for rescue missions just like this one, and he was scooting them alongside the mountain's sheer face, shuffling his feet and trying to keep breathing.

Then, mercifully, they were back on solid freaking ground, both inhaling more breath than necessary. Micah slowly, carefully, stood and picked Chloe up, hoisting her onto his hip. He unhooked the harness from the tree and whistled for Axel to follow before beginning the trek back up the hill to where their point camp was located.

It only took a few minutes. Axel kept a good pace and Chloe weighed about as much as a couch cushion, and before he knew it, the blue tent from their rescue rendezvous camp loomed into sight. A brief, weighty silence stretched across the mountain. Then all hell broke loose.

Her mother screamed then both of Chloe's parents were sprinting toward them, Police Chief Cade Easton and two of his deputies hot on their heels. Mr. Robinson took Chloe from Micah's arms and both of her parents were hugging her and touching her and making sure she was still in one piece. Micah tried to fade back, but Chloe grabbed the arm of his windbreaker.

"Thank you, Mr. Micah," she whispered, her bright eyes shining. Her parents both looked up at him with the same glowing adoration.

"Thank you, Micah," Mrs. Robinson said, as Mr. Robinson stuck out his hand and shook it hard, before bringing Micah in for a bear hug. Then they were gone, carrying Chloe over to the medic tent, and Micah stepped back to watch them walk off into the distance. He should have been relieved. They hadn't expected such a happy ending for Chloe and they'd been lucky, more than lucky.

But still, the ache in his chest didn't dissipate and he knew it was no longer fear that made him feel so heavy and forlorn. Axel whimpered at his side, and Micah dug into one of his pockets to give the dog a treat. He loved Axel and Rosie and the other search dogs they kept at the Black Reef Survival Camp, but dogs were a poor substitute for family, for parents, for children, for *people* who loved a person unconditionally. Well, dogs were what he was going to get, a truth he'd come to terms with a long time ago. Family wasn't in the cards for him, not the kind of family Chloe Robinson had. No, Axel and Rosie, they were what he got, so he'd damn well better be happy about it.

"Hey there, Superman," Dec said, coming up behind him, Rosie hot on his heels. "Or should I say Spider-Man? That was some gravity-defying shit you did down there."

And Dec McCormick. Of course. He counted as Micah's business partner, search partner, family and best friend, all rolled into one not-giving-a-damn package of good-old-boy humor and charm. Dec was one of the few people in the world who knew just how much Micah hated heights, but, as with most things, he played to the lighter side of the situation.

"I can't be out-balled by a six-year-old," Micah said, suddenly feeling very weary. He followed Dec away from the camp and toward their cabin a little way down the mountain. If Cade needed them to give statements, he knew where to find them.

"Ain't that the truth," Dec said. "Come on, let's get a beer."

Micah nodded, but glanced back up at the Robinson family one more time. Growing older with a houseful of dogs and their business and Dec McCormick by his side definitely wasn't the worst life a guy could have.

About the Author

Gemma Snow loves high heat, high adventures and high expectations for her heroes! Her stories are set in the past and present, from the glittering streets of Paris to cowboy-rich Triple Diamond Ranch in Wolf Creek, Montana.

In her free time, she loves to travel, and spent several months living in a fourteenth-century castle in the Netherlands. When not exploring the world, she likes dreaming up stories, eating spicy food, driving fast cars and talking to strangers. She recently moved to Nashville with a cute redheaded cat and a cute redheaded boy.

Gemma loves to hear from readers. You can find her contact information, website details and author profile page at https://www.totallybound.com

Home of Erotic Romance

Sign up for our newsletter and find out about all our romance book releases, eBook sales and promotions, sneak peeks and FREE romance books!